W9-AVT-422

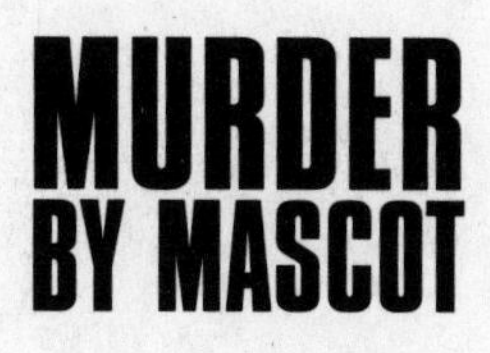
MURDER
BY MASCOT

Also available by Mary Vermillion
from Alyson Books
Death by Discount

MURDER BY MASCOT

A MARA GILGANNON MYSTERY

MARY VERMILLION

All characters in this book are fictitious. Any resemblance to real individuals—either living or dead—is strictly coincidental.

Manufactured in the United States of America.

published by Alyson Books,
P.O. Box 1253, Old Chelsea Station, New York, New York 10113-1251.
Distribution in the United Kingdom by Turnaround Publisher Services Ltd.,
Unit 3, Olympia Trading Estate, Coburg Road, Wood Green,
London N22 6TZ England.

ISBN 0-7394-6873-1
ISBN-13 978-0-7394-6873-9

Credits
Cover photography by Ken Reid/Getty Images.
Author Photograph by David Van Allen
Cover design by Matt Sams.

in loving memory of my father
Forrest Dean Vermillion

ONE

My face hurt from fake-smiling through the game's first half. The source of this pain came from the seating arrangement in section A, row 5, of Carver-Hawkeye Arena. My ex, Anne, had the aisle seat—which I didn't mind, given her legginess. What I did mind was her new partner, Orchid, who wedged herself in between us and made it nearly impossible for Anne and me to talk. She bumped my right side every time she turned to whisper in Anne's ear or to grab a handful of their organic popcorn. Things were no better on my left, where I was saving an empty seat for Neale, my long-distance girlfriend. She was supposed to meet us for dinner before the game but still hadn't shown.

Our mascot, Herky, paced the court's perimeter, his huge plastic hawk's head bobbing atop a tall, spindly body. His beaky grin looked every bit as stiff as mine felt, but that didn't stop the hoards of children who wanted to high-five him or hug him. He flapped his arms—or wings—as we scored, and Orchid clapped along.

Narrowly dodging her elbow, I adjusted my glasses and checked the scoreboard: Iowa Hawkeyes 45, Missouri Tigers 41.

"We should be way ahead by now," Orchid grumbled.

"It's the first game," Anne said. "We're just rusty."

At least that's what I thought she said.

"We don't have much depth." Orchid nodded toward the bench, which was directly in front of us. Orchid's season tickets are much better than mine, as are her luck and her job. She is the program director at the alternative radio station where I work—in other words, my boss and my constant reminder that life isn't fair.

She jabbed me in the arm—on purpose this time. "I wonder what's keeping your girlfriend," she said. Her eyes were the same color as her steely buzz cut and vulva-shaped pewter earrings.

I shrugged and summoned another fake grin before grabbing my cell phone and punching in my own number. If my housemate, Vince, answered, I'd inquire about his Persian, Norma Desmond. That was our code for *get me outta here.* Alas, Vince did not answer, so I left a message for Norma and turned my attention to the game.

Coach Bridget Stokes waved a clipboard in the air and yelled at her team to play defense. Technically speaking, Bridget was not *the* coach. She was Carol Oliver's most experienced assistant and therefore in charge while Coach Carol visited her dying brother in Pennsylvania.

Our standout point guard, Win Ramsey, dribbled the ball downcourt and heaved it to our only freshman starter. She squared her feet to the basket and nailed the three.

"Jessie March," Orchid said. "She's gonna be good. Check

out that jump shot."

What I noticed about the freshman was that she was the only player with auburn hair. For the most part, that's how I keep track of the players—their 'dos. Granted, it's not foolproof given all the faux-blond ponytails.

"The rookie is family," Orchid said. "Elaine saw her at the Alley Cat with our shortstop."

For Orchid, no women's sporting event is complete unless she determines which players are lesbians. Me, I have better things to do than ponder the sexual orientations of nineteen-year-olds.

After the Tigers scored an easy two, our center, Kate Timmens, set a nice pick for Varenka White, who drove to the hoop and got hacked by the Tiger center. It was the fourth foul on their top scorer, so the crowd erupted, hushing only when Varenka stepped to the free-throw line.

After she sank the front end of her one-and-one, there was no triumphant riff from the pep band. Except for some scattered applause, the arena was freakishly quiet.

Anne gasped, her eyes fixed on the other side of the arena. I followed her gaze past the players lined up at the key for Varenka's second shot. There, sprawled in the front row—right across the court from our women's bench—was the infamous hoopster, Dave DeVoster. With his disconcertingly blond hair, the star forward looked like a Nordic model for Abercrombie & Fitch. His outstretched legs grazed the out-of-bounds line as he laughed with two guys who looked like linebackers.

Why shouldn't he laugh? Not only had the senior forward just avoided jail, but he had also gained an extra year of eligibility when the university granted him a redshirt season and the remainder of his scholarship. This, after being charged with raping one of its female athletes.

A basketball player, if you believed the lesbian rumor mill.

Some fans glared at DeVoster, some averted their eyes, and some grinned—God knows why. As the arena began murmuring, Anne fingered her necklace. The familiar gesture made me want to reach out and stroke her hair. I studied her necklace, her largest crystal. It would take more than that to dissolve the negative energy in Carver-Hawkeye.

"He's just here to gloat," Orchid said.

I couldn't argue. I'd never seen DeVoster at a women's game before.

"Meandering in after halftime," she grumbled, "like he's the main event."

At the line, Varenka waited for the ball, arms dangling at her sides. A starting forward, she was our leading rebounder and the only player who always wore kneepads, one black, one gold.

The ref with the ball glanced at his comrades before bouncing it to her.

She spun it in her hands and dribbled three times. Then she hesitated and looked to her right. You could tell when she saw DeVoster. She clutched the ball to her chest and stepped back from the line. The Hawks who were crouching at the key stood and eyed her nervously. The Tiger rebounders shot each other puzzled looks, and our guards whispered to each other.

Finally, a whistle blew.

Bridget was still signaling time-out as our players dragged themselves to the bench. She gathered them around her and patted Varenka on the back.

"Get out, DeVoster!" Orchid shouted. She stood, her pudgy fingers cupped around her mouth.

In a rare moment of solidarity, I followed suit. Soon, half our section was chanting, "Get out! Get out!"

Underneath the basket, Herky gazed at us, his arms hanging

limply at his sides. He was, no doubt, stymied about his role. Cute antics don't cut it when there's a rapist in the house.

The announcer trotted out the sportsmanship spiel he made at the beginning of every game. "Hawk fans are some of the best fans in the Big Ten." As his hyperenergetic voice boomed over the PA system, the chanting grew louder. "Please show respect to *all* fans."

"He's no fan!" Anne stood and yelled. "He's a rapist!"

"Innocent until proven guilty," a voice called back.

I fell silent. Anne never yelled negative stuff at games.

"We have a special guest tonight," the announcer boomed. "The man who led the Hawkeyes to three Big Ten Championships and an Elite Eight." A dramatic pause. Then he stretched his vowels to the limit as he intoned, "Da-a-ave De-e-e Vos-s-ster-r-r!"

As DeVoster held his hands aloft like a champion prize-fighter, half the crowd actually stood and cheered.

"I can't believe this," I said. "A standing ovation for a slime who raped one of our players."

"That's a rumor," Anne said, "the part about our player." She scanned the section to our right.

A handful of Tiger fans started chanting, "No means no! No means no!"

"How do you like that?" she asked. "The opposing fans are doing what we should."

"R-A-P," I shouted, "I-S-T." It rhymed, and it was true. My voice quickly attracted others, and the pep band's drummer matched our cadence. Trumpets squawked and trombones farted, despite the director's desperate cutoff signals.

A few grandfatherly men in muted gold polyester jackets surrounded the court, their faces stern. Usually these guys took tickets and watched the game from the top of the arena. On a wild and crazy night, they might escort interlopers out of the season-ticket section. They weren't exactly equipped to hold the forces of chaos at bay.

Bridget left her team and strode toward the announcer. A star point guard back when I was a student, she was short for a basketball player, but her compact frame brimmed with energy and authority. She rested both hands on the announcer's table and leaned toward him, her blazer falling open. After he nodded eagerly and asked the crowd for quiet, she marched back to the bench, never once glancing at DeVoster.

I'd encountered this same stalwart refusal to acknowledge conflict or controversy every time I'd interviewed her on my radio show, *Issues in Iowa.* I'd ask about Title IX, and she'd tout the university's support of women's athletics. I'd ask about the difficulties facing female coaches, and she'd detail Coach Carol's accomplishments. Homophobia in women's sports? She'd sing her team's praises. No matter that we're both lesbians, I got the same PR-perfect answers the one time we had coffee together too.

Now she squatted in front of her team and pounded her fist into her hand. The Hawks would need her drive if they were going to keep their lead, but they seemed sluggish, trailing behind Varenka as she headed back to the line. Ball in her hands, she stared at the hoop and took a deep breath. The fans fell silent, and the cheerleaders wiggled their fingers in the air, arms raised high, anticipating the shot.

It bounced off the back of the rim and arced toward center court.

"She's a 93-percent free-throw shooter." Orchid frowned and marked her stat sheet.

Bridget replaced Varenka with a much shorter player.

"Varenka's regular backup is out with an ACL," Orchid said.

She could also tell you the exact date of the girl's injury, the ins and outs of her rehab, and her shooting percentage. Probably her astrological sign and the date of her last cold too.

As Varenka buried her face in a towel, a fiftyish woman behind me said, "I bet she's the one."

"Looks that way," her husband mumbled.

Anne wrenched around, her face flushed pink like her sweater. "How about minding your own business?"

The hapless couple had pushed her buttons. Maybe they'd hit upon the truth—or close to it. Anne directs the UI Women's Center, which sometimes assists rape victims. Of course, even if the center weren't helping DeVoster's victim, Anne would want to protect the young woman's identity—to protect the woman herself—from the many idiots who worshipped DeVoster and staked their personal well-being on his jump shot.

The crowd groaned as Varenka's sub lost the ball to a Tiger who zipped down the court and took it to the hole. The woman who'd inspired Anne's wrath slurped at her souvenir cup and asked her hubby to scoot down a few seats so they could enjoy the game in peace.

Anne didn't seem to notice. Instead, she stared at Varenka's parents, a tall blond couple sitting two rows down in the section to our right. Mrs. White seemed more focused on her husband than on the game. She patted his shoulder as he pointed at the scoreboard and shook his head.

The Tigers stole the ball and cut our lead to two. Jessie March got called for her third foul and slammed the ball against the floor.

"She better watch it," Orchid said. She got four technical fouls in high school."

After the Tigers missed the T and two chippies, Win rebounded the ball and pitched it to Varenka's sub, who got trapped at mid-court. Bridget called another time-out and sent

Varenka to the scorer's table to check back in. The pep band started playing "Thriller." Tubas twisted side to side, and the director's arms jerked like a puppet's.

Next to the seat where we'd piled our coats—Neale's seat—a young boy attacked an ice cream cone. His third snack of the evening, it melted down his forearm, a long and winding chocolate road. I didn't bother to protect the coats since Orchid's was on top.

"Maybe Neale isn't going to make it tonight," Orchid said, resting her hand on Anne's thigh.

Across the court, DeVoster signed autographs for a group of Cub Scouts.

I really needed to go home.

"Help her, help her," Orchid barked.

Varenka's elbows and braid swung through the air as three Tigers swarmed her in the key. Jump ball. Alternating possession—Tigers.

"She was fouled," Orchid yelled.

Varenka herself showed no reaction to the call.

Herky clambered into the stands and knelt next to a toddler who burst into tears and buried himself in his mother's arms.

A Tiger slipped past Varenka to the basket.

"Let's go, Hawks!" I called.

The entire crowd tried to rally the team. The pep band stomped its feet, and the cheerleaders bounced around like popping corn.

Varenka took a quick shot and missed everything. Fortunately, there was an official's time-out. She collapsed on the bench, oblivious to her teammates' hugs and pats.

Orchid marked the miss on her stat sheet, and Anne continued to watch Varenka's parents.

Mr. White gazed at the bench, at his daughter's slumped

shoulders and sweat-soaked jersey. He scowled at DeVoster and worked his jaw as his wife glanced at the media section behind them. When she leaned toward him, cupping her hand to his ear, he jerked away and leaped to his feet. Before I knew it, Anne was right next to him. He would have towered over most women, but Anne, without her Birkenstocks, stands at six feet two inches. She seemed to be pleading with him. The band started the fight song and everyone stood, so I missed the rest of the interaction.

But I'd seen enough to guess that Varenka was DeVoster's victim and that Anne knew it.

When the song ended, Mr. White was back in his seat—his wife eyeing him warily—and Anne was back in hers. "I'm fine," she said before Orchid or I could ask. "I just need to center myself." Even though the players were back on the floor, she closed her eyes.

The Tigers brought the ball downcourt, tied the game with a pick and roll, and launched their full-court press. Varenka inbounded the ball to our lone African-American starter, Hennah Jennings. She tossed it to Kate, who tried to get it to Win. But a Tiger got a piece of the ball, and it veered right in between Win and Jessie. They both hurled themselves after it. Win crashed into the front row, and Jessie landed on her ass at DeVoster's feet.

The official's whistle pierced the quiet, and the players froze, all eyes on Jessie and DeVoster. Smirking, he stood and extended his hand to her. She looked like she wanted to spit on it, her face a knot of fury. As the refs rushed over, she sprang at him, but Win grabbed her and pulled her back. DeVoster kept standing there, his arms folded over his chest, just asking for it.

TWO

The next night—still without Neale and still with Anne and Orchid—I found myself returning to Carver-Hawkeye, freezing in the backseat of Orchid's new Prius as she held forth at the steering wheel. "Guess what I just heard at the Co-op this morning? Sue and Evette are pregnant."

I had to admit that this was a scoop. Along with Bridget, Sue and Evette were assistant coaches of the women's team. Everyone knew that the two African-American women were a couple, but nobody straight ever mentioned it. I wanted to ask which one was expecting, but I didn't want to give Orchid the satisfaction.

"They probably think it'll improve the team's het credentials," she said.

"Or they want a child," Anne snapped.

"Sue got pregnant on her first try," Orchid said. "And—get this—she's expecting triplets."

Poor Sue. By the end of the evening, she'd be carrying septuplets and booked for *The Ellen DeGeneres Show.* I'd be grist for Orchid's rumor mill too, if Neale didn't show up soon. She said she'd arrive in time for lunch, but I'd lost track of her excuses sometime around five when she called to say that she was "near" the state line.

As Orchid parked and we stepped into the cold November air, Anne spotted a small group of people with signs near the south entrance of the arena. "I don't recognize them," she said. "What if they're pro-DeVoster?" Her voice was tinged with panic. She'd organized lots of protests, but they always made her edgy.

"We'll take the other side of the walk," I said, "or go to another entrance."

A Cambus zoomed past while we waited to cross the street. Anne's own signs whipped around in the wind as she tried to control them with her mittened hands.

"Let me take those for you, sweetie." Orchid stepped in between Anne and me and took the signs.

Anne tugged at her stocking cap, smashing her bangs over the top half of her glasses. "Hawkeye colors obstruct positive energy, and the town is always filled with them when the men play," she said.

"I never wear gold," I declared. "It doesn't flatter me." It was true. With my garishly red hair and pale complexion, Hawkeye gear made me look positively anemic.

Anne ignored me and turned to Orchid. "This black and gold is very unbalancing. I'm worried that it will create too much tension."

Color therapy is one of the many things I don't take as seriously as Anne and Orchid. "A protest always creates tension," I said.

A car with a broken muffler roared past, belching exhaust. We finally crossed the street and headed toward a woman who was as tall as Anne. She stood in front of a row of megaphones, ready to test one. Dark spirals of hair fell to her waist. "Once a rapist, always a rapist," her megaphone squawked, and I realized who she was: Lexie Roth, an infamous muckraking reporter for *The Daily Iowan*. Lexie was a young rebel with too many causes—and a constant source of anxiety for Anne.

"I can't believe this." She strode toward Lexie, who stood calmly, tucking her hair into the back of her parka. "What do you think you're doing?" Anne got right in Lexie's face, her hands on her hips. I knew that stance. During my five years with Anne, I'd often unleashed the fighter that lay beneath her graham cracker–colored tresses and ethereal smile.

"Take it easy," Lexie said. "We're on the same side."

"Haven't you done enough already?"

"Obviously not," Lexie said, "or Dave DeVoster would be in jail."

"You've made people feel sorry for him."

Lexie wrapped her arms around her megaphone. A gust nearly wrenched the signs out of Orchid's hands, and a siren wailed in the distance.

"You're destroying our credibility." Anne raised her voice.

Lexie's crew stopped chatting amongst themselves. A large man headed toward Lexie, and Orchid edged closer to Anne.

"You may have kicked me out of the Women's Center," Lexie said, "but I have a right to be here. Remember freedom of speech? The First Amendment?" Lexie enunciated her last words as if she were addressing an imbecile.

Anne turned on her heel. Orchid reached for her arm, but Anne jerked away.

"She has no idea what she's doing." Anne spoke loud enough for Lexie and her gang to hear. Three strides and Anne was on the other side of the walk.

Orchid and I turned to follow, but someone grabbed me.

It was Neale. She pulled me to her, and I buried my face in her long ashy curls. I breathed in the faint scent of her musk shampoo, her leather jacket. This was not okay. I needed to maintain my anger and righteous indignation. We needed to have a serious talk.

"Mar-Bar! Neale!" Vince threw his arms around us. "Let the protest begin." My housemate—he of the bad timing—twirled around, sporting a black-and-gold feather boa and rainbow-striped woolen gloves. "What do you think?" He placed his rainbow hands underneath his goatee and struck a pose.

"It looks like you had a bad accident with Herky," I said.

Vince flipped the boa over his shoulder and surveyed the crowd. "Anne will want to thank me for bringing the entire cast of *Hairspray* to swell the numbers of her protest."

Vince and I met when we were both theater majors at Iowa. He has gone on to star at the community theater, and I have found fame and fortune at the light board.

"Anne's not in a very good mood right now." I nodded toward Lexie, who was testing her megaphone again.

"Ah, young Mistress Misquote." Vince waved one end of his boa through the air. "Was there a catfight?" he asked. "Do give me the gory details."

"I'm the one who needs details," Neale said.

"I'll fill you in at home." I didn't want to waste our time together at a protest—not even for Anne.

"Wasn't Anne counting on us to be here?" Neale asked.

"I was counting on you to show up yesterday."

"Girls, girls." Vince waved his finger in my face. "No public displays of anger." He swept toward Anne.

"Come on," Neale said. "I want to say hi."

What she really wanted was to stall.

We made our way past a smattering of signs: EXPEL DEVOSTER, STOP VIOLENCE AGAINST WOMEN, PLEA BARGAIN= SELLOUT. This last sign was held by a young woman who was leaning into her girlfriend. Their faces sported more metal than my silverware drawer. You feel your age in a university town.

Anne and Orchid were underneath a streetlight, distributing signs. "I should have gotten her out of the Women's Center the first time she misrepresented us." Anne glared across the sidewalk at Lexie, who held one end of a banner that said CASTRATE DEVOSTER.

Neale said hello and got tense nods in return. Anne usually greets people with a squeal and a hug, but she could barely take her eyes off Lexie.

"What's going on?" Neale asked. "What's the story on the woman with the megaphone?"

"She was a volunteer at the Women's Center," Anne said.

"She caused lots of problems," Orchid added.

"Let's not air the center's dirty laundry." Anne handed a sign to a young man with puffy sideburns.

"You're among friends," Vince said. "Air away."

"She almost made the center lose its funding." Orchid put her arm around Anne's waist. "She organized hundreds of people to stalk DeVoster."

"Not hundreds," Anne said.

"They dogged him 24/7," Vince said. "It was all over the news."

"If you lived here," I said to Neale, "you'd know about it."

That created an awkward silence. They all knew that I'd been furious when she'd decided to join the St. Louis police force.

"Anyhoo," Vince said. "They pitched tents outside his apartment until they had to stop because of a restraining order."

I made fists inside my mittens. My fingers were turning numb.

"DeVoster complained to his coach who complained to the cops ..." Orchid trailed off.

"Eldon Bly rules this town," Vince said.

For once, he wasn't exaggerating. I turned to Neale. "Bly has been the Iowa men's basketball coach longer than his players have walked the earth."

"He has only to say the word," Vince continued, "and a sea of worshipping fans sweep away anyone or anything that threatens his team's journey to the promised land."

"Since when do you use biblical metaphors?" I asked.

Vince shrugged.

"The point," Orchid said, "is that Lexie's articles made it seem like the Women's Center had organized the stalking when they had nothing to do with it."

"I tried to tell her that I admired what she was doing, but that she was putting the center at risk," Anne said. "Then she wrote a story, quoting only the admiration part."

Orchid pulled Anne closer.

"I wrote a letter to the editor, explaining the center's stance, but it was too late. I had to ban her from the center. It was that or lose all our funding." Anne's voice caught, and Orchid rubbed her shoulder. "If only she had listened to me. She was one of our best volunteers. The day after I kicked her out, she had to stop her stalking anyway because of the restraining order." Anne edged away from Orchid, her face grim. "Now the administration is going to think she's part of the center's protest."

Vince put his hand to his mouth and stage whispered. "The banished damsel is heading this way."

Sure enough, Lexie ambled toward us, a megaphone in each hand. She extended them to Anne and Orchid. "You can borrow these tonight if you want," she said. "We've got plenty."

Orchid folded her arms over her chest as Anne scowled at the megaphones.

"No hard feelings?" Lexie grinned, tilting her head and waiting until Anne returned her smile.

I knew that smile. It meant there were hard feelings aplenty.

The hapless Lexie was not as well versed in my ex's body language. "After all," she said, "we're all in this together."

"Ooh," Vince whispered to me, "making it worse."

Anne's smile tightened. "Don't you think that the castration banner is needlessly incendiary?" When she waxed multisyllabic, you really had to watch out.

"I'm just trying to get people's attention," Lexie said.

"That's clear," Anne snapped. "You can take your megaphones and—"

Orchid stepped forward. "We need to keep getting organized, don't we, Anne?"

Lexie smiled weakly and dashed back to her troops.

I braced myself for Orchid's stock tirade about "Young Women These Days."

"She's just a baby," Vince said. "She means well."

"You know her?" Anne asked.

"From work." When Vince isn't treading the theatrical boards, he directs the animal shelter. "She adopted two cats that had only three eyes and half a tail between them."

Anne and Orchid relaxed a little. They too have a soft spot for shelter animals. We all do—except Neale, who is too type-A for a pet. Her breath swirled white as she studied the crowd. I thought about how nice it would be to kiss her—after our talk, of course.

"What's with the big bird dressed like Elvis?" she asked.

"Mar-Bar," Vince exclaimed. "Shame on you. Haven't you told Neale about Herky on Parade?" He took some signs from Anne and handed them to me and Neale. "Come," he said, glancing at a group of frat boys in black-and-gold-striped pants. "There's time yet before the full descent of the Bumblebee Brigade."

"There are ninety Herkys throughout our fair city—all decorated or dressed by different artists," Vince said.

Neale gazed at him blankly. "They're the height of camp. I'm getting my picture taken with all of them before they're auctioned off to raise money for the football team." Vince tapped one of Herky's elbows. "My fave is the Incredible Herk—all green with very skimpy pants. You can really see how ripped that Herky is, but Elvis here has a nice ass." He patted it. "They all do."

A woman with two small children hurried them along the sidewalk.

"Don't say anything about them to Orchid," he told Neale. "She wrote a letter to the editor about how mascots valorize violence."

"The only time I feel violent is when people use words like 'valorize,' " I said.

Vince raised a sign in the air (NO SPECIAL TREATMENT) and struck a Herky pose. "Look," he said, "Protest Herky."

I grabbed Vince's feather boa and put it around Herky's neck. "Tacky Herky," I pronounced.

Neale chuckled as Vince feigned a wounded look.

"The rest of us are ready to protest." Orchid's round face was swollen with indignation, and her voice was as cold as my extremities. "We're not here to have fun."

Her personal mantra. Alas, she was prescient if nothing else.

We made our throats raw chanting, "UI, shame, shame. Raping women's not a game." My frozen arm ached from holding my sign aloft (NO ONE ABOVE THE LAW), and I could no longer feel my toes.

"Innocent until proven guilty," a prepubescent boy shouted in my face.

"There are children at these games." A woman in knee-high boots poked the word RAPE on Vince's sign.

"Tell that to DeVoster," Vince said.

An elderly man with Hawkeye earmuffs shook his head at Neale. "Don't you have anything better to do than ruin a young man's name?"

Across the sidewalk, KCRG Channel 9 interviewed Lexie. She gestured toward her banner, and I imagined the cameraman zooming in on the word CASTRATE. I wondered if Anne would get her say, but I couldn't spot her in the black-and-gold swarm.

"What time is it?" Neale's sign hung at her side, and her teeth chattered like castanets. Served her right for being so spineless about our talk.

THREE

For better or worse, lesbians spend more time with their exes than most straight women spend with their husbands, children, best friend, and parents—combined. The hardest part is when you're left alone to make small talk with your ex's partner. The social awkwardness soars exponentially when the aforementioned party is also your boss and you're arguing about work while she shows you flooring samples for their add-on.

"Mmm," I said as Orchid ushered me into the recently drywalled room. *Mmm* is such a useful sound. Noncommittal. All-purpose. It frees your mind to stew about other things, like why your girlfriend is still in the car talking on her cell with her cop partner on a Saturday morning when she should be spending time with you, her actual partner. Like how your housemate is late as usual—thus extending an already torturous social occasion. Like how you have to stare at bits of tile and carpet with your ex's partner instead of helping your ex with the vegan muffins in the kitchen.

"Of course, we both want something green." Orchid didn't mean the color. She waddled back to the living room, her moon-shaped earrings swaying above an earth-toned ensemble that hovered between pajamas and Buddhist chic.

The living room was earth-toned as well, dominated by all-natural organic-cotton furniture. "What about Roshaun?" she asked as we sat down, changing the conversation from "pleasure" to business.

Roshaun was our top intern and the head manager of the men's basketball team. I'd been in charge of him and the other interns for a year, ever since Anne decided she wanted to work on our friendship. Orchid was using her power as my boss to be sure I didn't have time to "work on" anything but work. Right now that involved Roshaun's burning desire to interview Waddell Jones, author of *Kobe Bryant and the Press,* on one of my weekly shows. "Roshaun is the last person who should handle the Kobe Bryant piece," I said.

"He's got the talent." Orchid tapped her thumbs together.

"He doesn't know what he's getting himself into," I said, "especially with the parallels between Bryant and DeVoster. There's too much of a conflict of interest for him. He could piss off the entire men's basketball team—not to mention his coach and the fans."

Orchid flattened her hands on her thighs and then adjusted the onyx pinkie ring that Anne had given her. "Make sure you tell him it was your decision."

I sipped the coffee that I'd brought from home and savored the cinnamon scent that wafted from the kitchen. "Mmm."

✧✧✧

The videotape of the protest lay unwatched on the coffee table next to a decimated plate of muffins and the remains of a tofu-scramble casserole.

"We should watch it without Vince," Orchid said. "It's almost noon." She took Neale's plate and stacked it atop her own empty one.

"Let's give him a few more minutes," Anne said. "He'll be here soon." The maroon scarf around her neck made her eyes seem the color of maple syrup, and she was just that sweet, always expecting the best. She leaned over her chair and petted Labrys, the huge golden retriever they'd recently adopted from the shelter.

"I'm in no rush." Neale swung her arm around my shoulders, and I leaned my head against her arm. Her hair smelled foresty and fresh. Last night I'd let her talk me out of talking and into bed. Tomorrow she'd have to head back to St. Louis.

"What are you going to do with the new room?" she asked.

Anne and Orchid met each other's eyes.

"Who knows?" Orchid said.

Something was afoot. Suddenly—after subjecting me to floor samples ad nauseum—they didn't want to talk about their new room?

"You must have some idea," Neale said.

Orchid shifted in her chair and glanced at Anne again. "Half of it might be for Anne's yoga and meditation, and the other half for my calligraphy."

A whole room for activities that Neale and I never had time for.

Anne bit the inside of her lip and adjusted her scarf. Their grandfather clock ticked, and their heat came on. "We might turn it into a nursery." She giggled and gave Orchid a nervous look.

I couldn't believe it. Anne hadn't wanted kids when we were together. Well, she'd always gushed over the cute ones in public, but that hadn't meant anything, had it?

"Wow," Neale said. "Are you going to adopt or try to conceive?"

Anne took a deep breath and grinned. "I'd like to give birth."

Orchid smiled weakly. One of the few things she and I bonded over was our attitude toward kids. Whenever our office manager brought her toddler to the station and he'd fuss or scream or try to eat paper clips, Orchid or I would whisper, "Reason 956"—meaning there are at least that many good reasons not to reproduce. "We've been talking about it," Orchid said.

No wonder they'd been stalled on their floor samples.

"I've done lots of research," Anne said.

"Good for you." Neale's voice was false perky. She didn't—thank God—want to be a mommy any more than I did.

I leaned away from Neale's arm. Anne could no longer hit the snooze button on her biological clock, but she hadn't said a word to me. We had coffee once a week, yet I knew nothing.

The doorbell rang, and Vince threw open the front door, letting in a gust of cold air. "Better late than never," he called.

Labrys bounded toward him, barking. She threw her front paws on his shoulders and nearly knocked him over. "Whoa, girl, you wag that tail any harder and you're going to lose it." Labrys loved Vince. She spent part of her time at our place because he was trying to train her to be the ring bearer for Anne and Orchid's as-yet-unscheduled commitment ceremony. Anne didn't want to pick a date until after Labrys mastered the ring-bearing trick. At least that was what she said. Maybe she was stalling, wanting to feel sure that Orchid was onboard with the parenting thing. If so, she'd bought herself a lot of time. Vince had been working with Labrys for a month—ever since Anne and Orchid had gotten her—and so far the canine couldn't go two steps without the practice ring sliding right off the soggy practice pillow.

As Vince rubbed Labrys's head, he managed to extricate himself from his jacket and hang it on the doorknob. "Pardon my tardiness, but Richard wanted to try a new scone recipe." Richard was Vince's default date, the guy he spent the night with when neither of them could find anybody better. "They were a delight." He licked his lips and patted his belly before crossing to the empty chair closest to the TV. "I'm ready for my close-up," he said. "I do hope there's good footage of me."

Labrys settled at his feet, and Anne popped in the video. I tried to imagine her pregnant, the skin on her belly stretched taut, her breasts swollen.

Neale placed a hand on my shoulder, and I leaned back into her as Orchid fast-forwarded through the early parts of the local nightly news: announcers with too much hairspray and make-up, explosions in the Middle East, a commercial for Cascade.

"There we are," Vince said.

The camera panned the sea of signs, lingering on one that said NO MEANS NO. You could hear our chanting, but you couldn't tell what we were saying. Anne hunched over a microphone held by a guy much younger, blonder, and shorter than herself. "We believe that the university's decision to allow Dave DeVoster to redshirt sends the wrong message." She glanced nervously at the camera. "It shows no consideration for women or for the victim in this case."

"Brava," Vince said.

The camera cut to Lexie. Instead of stooping toward the announcer, she gestured to the crowd. "All of us here tonight want to see Dave DeVoster brought to justice."

"She's making it sound like we're all one group," Anne moaned.

The camera lavished its attention on Lexie's castration banner, and Anne buried her head in her hands.

Then the announcer interviewed a seventyish man with a gravelly voice. "These feminists are always protesting something. They don't know what went on between Dave and that woman."

"She was bruised and bleeding when she went to the hospital," Orchid fumed.

"They're making a mountain out of a molehill," the man continued.

The camera zoomed out and showed him holding the hand of his grandson, a pudgy-cheeked lad with a winsome smile. Then it cut to a group of high school girls with pom-poms in their hair, saying that they just wanted to enjoy the game. The announcer grimly noted that enjoyment was far from the minds of the protesters, and the camera swept over us again. The segment ended with another shot of Lexie's banner.

Orchid heaved a sigh and stopped the tape.

An ad for Pampers blared from the TV.

Anne's fists were clenched and her lips were pressed tightly together. Labrys abandoned Vince and plopped her chin on the armrest of Anne's chair.

"You did a good job," I said.

Neale yawned and stretched her arms above her head.

"KCRG-TV Channel 9 returns to its special coverage of a breaking story," the TV squawked.

"No footage of my darling Hawkeye boa!" Vince said. "I can't believe—"

"Shh." The rest of us silenced him.

An announcer, a woman with big teeth and big hair, said, "The body of UI basketball star Dave DeVoster was discovered early this morning near the Duane Banks Baseball Stadium." The TV showed the scoreboard: zero to zero.

None of us moved.

"His body was found at the base of the statue known as Marilyn MonHerky, one of the Herky on Parade statues." The screen showed old footage of two football players standing next to another (more masculine) Herky. Then there was a photo of Marilyn's head. Six-inch-long eyelashes sprouted out of blue glitter eye shadow, and bright red lipstick outlined the bottom of the hooked beak (which, of course, shone Hawkeye-gold in the sun).

"Oh, my God," Vince said, "Dave DeVoster died at the feet of Drag Queen Herky. A masterpiece of aviary artwork has been sullied."

Orchid turned to Anne. "Isn't that the bird I took your picture with? You and your nieces?"

Anne barely nodded.

Neale perched on the edge of the futon, energized.

"Blood and hair was found on the bird's beak," the announcer said. "Police also found significant blood on the bird's elbow and on the concrete slab beneath the sculpture." She paused dramatically. "Blood was also spattered on the bird's dress."

As the camera showed Marilyn's white dress, all I could think about were red polka dots. I felt numb.

"DeVoster's neck was broken," the announcer continued. "His skull was badly damaged, and his back was bruised."

"I told you the Herkys promoted violence," Orchid said to no one in particular.

"Authorities report that his face was inflamed."

"Pepper spray," Neale said. "Or Mace."

"'He had it coming.'" Vince sang a few bars from *Chicago*.

"This has to be a homicide," Neale said.

When she and I first met two summers ago, we'd both been investigating the murder of my aunt's beloved partner. Like this basketball player, she too had suffered a blow to the head. My throat tightened, and I felt queasy.

"Are you okay, Mara?" Anne asked.

I nodded and tried to tell myself that DeVoster had gotten what he deserved. But that wasn't true, not really. He deserved to be in jail, not dead. Not murdered.

The camera cut to the chief of police, a square-faced man in his fifties with a wart-type thing beneath one of his eyes. "A jogger found the body around six this morning."

"Are you treating the death as a murder?" a baby-faced reporter asked.

"He suspects fowl play," Vince tossed his head back and laughed maniacally. "Get it?" He bent his arms and flapped them like a chicken. "Fowl play."

Labrys barked.

"As of this time, we haven't determined the cause of death," said the chief.

"But wouldn't you say that the death *looks* like a murder?" the reporter asked.

"There are some suspicious circumstances," the chief admitted.

"What next?"

"I'm not at liberty to discuss the investigation."

"So there's an investigation?" The reporter was practically salivating. He barraged the police chief with more questions that the cop was not at liberty to answer.

Finally, the officer said, "If it is a homicide, we'll work around the clock to bring the killer to justice."

"Nobody worked hard to help the woman he raped," Orchid said.

The announcer back in the studio noted that DeVoster was attired in running gear. "Our sources reveal that he enjoyed running in the middle of the night—especially after his legal troubles. The cement path that runs past Marilyn MonHerky and the Duane Banks Field is reportedly his favorite route."

DeVoster's lawyer, Bernardo Church, appeared on the screen.

"There's the sleaze that got DeVoster his plea bargain," Orchid said.

"Shakespeare had it right," Vince chimed in. "Kill all the lawyers."

I glanced at Neale—she'd been a lawyer, an up-and-comer in the Chicago district attorney's office, before she decided to become a cop—but she focused on the TV, oblivious to the slight against her former profession.

A reporter held a mike in front of Bernardo Church's red necktie. "This is a terrible tragedy," the lawyer said, "the death of a talented young man with a long and stellar career ahead of him in the NBA." Church had a luxurious baritone and an obvious fondness for hair gel, his dark hair slicked straight back from his high forehead. "There were lots of people who were jealous of my client," the lawyer said. "He had several enemies."

Then the TV flashed on Lexie's castration banner and on Anne speaking to the reporter at last night's protest. "We need to do all we can to stop violence against women," she said. There was also footage of her at the women's game as she stood and called DeVoster a rapist. The camera had captured me and Orchid too.

"I didn't know I was being taped there," Anne exclaimed. "They're making it look like I might have shoved him into that stupid bird."

None of us could argue with that. We knew Anne wouldn't hurt a fly—literally, it was a reincarnation thing—but Channel 9 was painting her as a homicidal feminist.

"Don't worry," I said to Anne. "Nobody is going to think you had anything to do with it."

"Yeah," Orchid said, "because she was with me all night long."

I turned my attention back to the TV. There was a head shot of Dave DeVoster. It was strikingly white: his crisp dress shirt, his Pepsodent-perfect grin, his rakishly spiked hair. "Dave DeVoster was more than a star basketball player," said a saccharine voice-over. Music swelled. "He was a teammate, a friend, a hero."

Next, there was a childhood photo of DeVoster holding a basketball that covered his entire torso. Channel 9 had obviously been hard at work since learning about his death. There was footage of him playing in grade school, high school, college—stealing the ball, dunking, shooting the three—taller and more proficient in every image. We saw him named Big Ten player of the year for the third time in a row before the music turned funky, and he sat with his attorney, his arms draped across two chairs, his blue eyes mocking the camera. Finally, he waved to cheering fans after his plea bargain.

"I don't know if I can watch much more," I said, but no one made a move to turn off the TV.

We were treated to a close-up of Coach Eldon Bly: black-framed glasses perched atop a crooked, thrice-broken nose, and wavy silver hair. "D was one of the best forwards we've had," Bly said, "and despite recent allegations, he was also a very decent young man."

"'Allegations ...'" Anne's voice trailed off.

"Now that he's dead," Orchid said, "the athletic department can get him canonized."

"I sincerely hope," Bly continued, "that university officials and the police will do everything in their power to bring Dave

DeVoster's killer to justice. Whoever killed him dealt a huge blow not just to his family and our team but to the entire community."

BS that thick drew no commentary from the living room—not even from Orchid.

Vince headed to the kitchen. When he returned with the leftover muffins, Bly had moved on to more important matters. "We're going to miss D, but everybody will step up. Ty Bennet was great in his first start last night: thirteen points and ten boards."

The screen showed a gangly red-haired Hawkeye dunking the ball.

"His chance to shine," Neale mused.

"Most guys don't carry pepper spray." Vince broke a muffin in half, and Labrys wagged her tail expectantly.

"Maybe he wanted to make it look like the killer was a woman," Neale said.

My stomach churned. If she didn't stop obsessing about DeVoster's death, there was no way we could have our serious talk before she left.

"I like that." Vince slipped a piece of muffin to the dog. "The killer would have to be big to manhandle a guy the size of DeVoster."

"There are big women," Orchid said.

Anything men can do, women can do better—even murder. That's Orchid's feminism in a nutshell.

The reporters went to work on DeVoster's teammates. One scratched his shaved head. "D's death was, like, real surprising. We gotta regroup." An African-American with huge ears said, "Somebody had it in for our man D. Our hearts go out to his family." A sinewy guy observed, "After all D's been through, this brutal murder is the icing on the cake."

"After all *he's* been through!" Orchid shrieked. "What about the woman he raped?"

The red-haired player said, "This is a tough situation for our team."

"He doesn't sound very sorry," Neale said.

Apparently done with the team, the reporters hounded other people for their reactions to the death. DeVoster's marketing professor called him a "scholar-athlete" and touted his 3.8 GPA. A cheerleader said he was a "real All-American guy." A woman walking her dog noted that the incident hurt Iowa City's progressive image. The artist who had created Marilyn MonHerky—and who looked like she had just rolled out of bed—agreed that she never expected her bird to be involved in anybody's death.

"This is going to be on all day," Vince said.

But the worst was yet to come: press coverage of Dave DeVoster's family. His father stood erect at a podium that said DeVoster Farms, reminding viewers that he, Darren DeVoster, was one of Iowa's wealthiest men and one of the university's biggest donors. He had one arm around his wife, and the other around his daughter: A tall, blond threesome clad in black. Designer mourning, no doubt. Darren and his wife, like their deceased son, were ultraphotogenic, but their daughter had tiny eyes and a chin with zero definition. I felt sorry for her, an ugly duckling who would probably never feel like a swan. Her lip trembled slightly as her father began to speak.

"Today Joyce and I have lost our only son. Darlene has lost her big brother."

Darlene gazed at the floor, her hair hiding her face.

"A killer has stolen him from our midst," Darren DeVoster said, "our golden boy who gave his all to the Hawkeyes, who helped his little sister with her homework, who raised thousands of dollars for firefighters after 9/11."

"Now *he's* the victim we're supposed to feel sorry for." Orchid shook her head in disgust.

"I beg all of you to be alert for clues that could lead to the capture of my son's murderer," Darren DeVoster said. "Anyone who calls the police with a tip that helps them apprehend the killer will receive my family's undying gratitude and $50,000."

"The police are going to get a lot of phone calls," Neale said.

When Darren DeVoster opened the floor for questions, he unleashed a journalistic feeding frenzy. "Sir, have the police officially declared your son's death a murder?"

Darren DeVoster stared straight at the camera. "I don't know about official declarations, but I know that Iowa City's fine police force will work expeditiously to achieve justice. No one wants to see a killer on the loose."

"Do you think that your son's death had anything to do with the recent charges against him?"

"It's likely," he said. "My son was the victim of a vicious smear campaign, and the people who spread the lies about him may well have killed him."

"This guy has more spin than a Laundromat," Vince said.

"What people?" asked a reporter.

"Feminists and activists." DeVoster looked like he'd just sucked a lemon. "Whatever they call themselves."

"Sir," said a woman reporter. "Are you suggesting that your son's accuser lied?"

"I don't believe she intended to." DeVoster forced a smile. "But young women can exaggerate when they don't get their way."

Neither Darlene nor her mother looked at the camera. "When was the last time you saw your son?" asked a reporter.

Mrs. DeVoster's lip trembled as her husband began answering the question. Before he finished, she was sobbing, her face in her hands.

Labrys went to the TV and started pawing the screen.

"She gets really agitated when people cry," Vince said. "She wants to comfort them."

As if to prove his point, Labrys butted her head against the screen and started whining.

Orchid turned it off, and Labrys fell silent. She cocked her head and put a single paw on the screen.

Vince knelt next to the befuddled dog and scratched her head. Then he turned to the rest of us. "DeVoster's demise," he said. "Can we say 'just desserts'?"

If only it had been that simple.

FOUR

I should've been happy, sitting on my couch, the sun streaming through the window, my girlfriend slowly sliding her tongue around the edge of my ear. But I felt restless. "Do you think the police will question Anne?"

Neale paused and exhaled gently on my ear. "Sure," she said. "As a formality." She took the bottom of my earlobe between her teeth.

"Will she have to go to the station?"

"Hey," Neale whispered, "Anne will be fine." She started nibbling.

"You don't know that."

Neale released my ear. "They'll ask her a couple questions, and then she can return to her floor samples."

I pulled away. "What's that supposed to mean?"

"Nothing, Mara." Neale sighed and rested her hand on my

thigh. A patch of sunlight covered her long fingers and her legs. Neale's wool socks were covered with pine shavings that had fallen from Vince's guinea pig cages. I moved my eyes up her leg, past the contours of her knee, the snap on her Levi's, and the cashmere sweater with tiny buttons that dotted the center of her chest. Then I gazed into her indescribably green eyes. Sometimes they reminded me of a summer lake, reflecting acres of trees in its shimmers and shadows. But now they made me think of the pine tree I lugged home last December, hoping we could spend our first Christmas together. "At least they have a life together," I said.

Neale removed her hand from my leg.

"They have friends over for brunch," I said. "They spend holidays together." My stomach clenched, and I thought about leaving well enough alone. Neale was the most beautiful woman I'd ever met, and she treated me like a queen when I visited her in St. Louis—the best restaurants, the theater, and dancing into the wee hours of the morning. Although I suspected that dancing was yet another form of aerobic exercise for Neale, another way of staying in shape so she'd be ready for "high-speed" cases when they came her way.

"Don't you wish we could just read the Sunday paper in bed?" I asked.

The radiator wheezed, and Neale's brow furrowed. "We could get a paper."

I wanted to scream that it wasn't about the paper, but I kept my voice calm. "Whenever I'm with you, I feel like we need to make love or cuddle—or at least talk—because it won't be long before one of us has to leave. I'm tired of making every moment count."

I was also tired of driving to St. Louis. When Neale moved there a little over a year ago, we agreed to spend one weekend a month at her place and one at mine. It had been four months since she'd last made it to Iowa City.

"I could come here more often," Neale said.

"When you're not working extra shifts or risking your life?"

Neale moved to the far side of the couch. "I thought you were proud of me."

I started to tell her that I was, but my throat and eyes burned. "You could have been killed."

She had saved her partner's life and the lives of a man and his five-year-old son. What had started out as a domestic dispute turned deadly when the man, who'd just lost his job, lost his head as well and decided to put himself and his family out of their misery. His wife somehow locked herself in the bathroom with a cell phone. When Neale and her partner arrived, the guy had a gun pointed to his kid's head. He kept saying, *My old man worked there his whole life.* He'd never handled a gun before, so it wasn't long before he managed to shoot Neale's partner in the shoulder. Twenty minutes later, she'd talked the distraught man out of his gun and got her partner to the ER. For weeks after her heroics, my dreams had been filled with bullets. They lodged in my arm, exploded out of my computer screen, spurted out of my toothpaste.

Neale leaned back toward me and took my hand. "It's part of my job. You knew that when we got together."

I pulled away. "You were in Aldoburg then."

"You knew I wasn't going to stay there."

Aldoburg, Iowa, is a sleepy town of 5,000. I'd grown up there, and I'd met Neale there. She'd been fresh out of the academy, determined to become a crack homicide detective without relying on the reputation of her father, the chief of police in Chicago. Together, she and I solved the murder of my Aunt Zee's partner, Glad. For me, the investigation had been about keeping Zee safe, finding justice for Glad, and giving back to the women who'd taken me in when my parents couldn't handle a sixteen-year-old baby dyke. But for Neale, it had all been about her career.

"Why didn't you want me to come to your award ceremony?" I asked.

Neale crossed her legs. "It's not that I didn't want you to come," she said. "I didn't think you'd enjoy yourself."

My muscles tightened, and I squeezed the arm of the couch.

"It was no big deal, Mara. They just slapped the medal on me, and then I had some beers with the guys."

"The guys who don't know you're a lesbian," I said.

Neale stood. "We've been over this. I keep my private life private. Cops can be really homophobic." She pushed her hair away from her face. "What do you want from me?"

The doorbell rang, but I didn't move. I'd taken so much for granted with Anne: hearing her laugh on the phone with her mother, helping her chop onions and garlic for dinner, finding my clean socks all balled up and knowing she had done it—rituals and rhythms too sweet to call routine.

The doorbell rang again.

"Do you want me to get that?" Neale asked.

I shook my head. We needed to finish what we'd started. I held my fingers to my lips.

The bell rang again and again. Somebody started pounding.

I rushed across the living room, my stocking feet sliding on the hardwood floor, and yanked the door open. Beyond the frost on my storm door was Bridget Stokes. I opened the door and stuck my head out. It had been over a month since we'd last spoken. After I interviewed her about Coach Carol's twenty-fifth year as head coach, we'd gone out for coffee. Despite Bridget's refusal to dish about Hawkeye athletics, I enjoyed my time with her—in fact, if we'd been single, it might have been one of those is-this-a-date-or-isn't-it? scenarios—but neither of us had tried to contact the other since then.

My fingers felt like ice on the metal door as I ushered Bridget in. When she pulled off her stocking cap, her short dark curls went wild with static electricity.

Neale headed toward us.

I'd have to introduce them, and I had no idea what to call Neale. My soon-to-be ex? Where was Miss Manners when you needed her?

Neale extended her hand. "I'm Neale Warner, Mara's girlfriend."

That dilemma was solved—for the time being.

"Bridget Stokes." She pumped Neale's hand and identified herself as an assistant coach of the women's basketball team. "I'm sorry to interrupt, but I need to talk to Mara in private."

Neale raised her eyebrows.

"It's important." Bridget unsnapped her coat.

Neale's eyes bored into mine.

Well, well, well. I'd waited for Neale Thursday night and most of Friday, and now the shoe was on the other foot.

"I'll make some tea." Neale took her time heading to the kitchen.

"Have you heard about the murder?" Bridget whispered.

In the midst of my own drama, I'd nearly forgotten about it.

"That's why I'm here." Continuing to whisper, she shoved her stocking cap into a coat sleeve and draped the whole thing over a doorknob. "What I have to say can't leave this room." She wasn't asking; she was telling.

I felt a wave of irritation and a flutter of excitement. "Do you want to sit down?" I asked.

Bridget removed an *Entertainment Weekly* from Vince's

chair and sank into it. "I'm sure you've heard rumors that it was one of our girls DeVoster raped."

I didn't think she'd like to hear that I'd already guessed which one, so I simply nodded.

"I'm concerned that the police will consider her or some of the other girls as suspects in his murder."

I could see where this was going. Everyone in Iowa City had heard the story about how I'd solved Aunt Glad's murder. Bridget was hoping that I'd poke around, find the real murderer, and get her girls off the hook. Nancy Drew on demand.

My pipes groaned as Neale ran some water in the kitchen.

"Any reason they'd be suspects besides motive?" I asked.

"There was a witness," Bridget said. "He saw someone sprint through the parking lot near the place where DeVoster died."

"What time?"

"A little after two in the morning." She sighed. "Close to the estimated time of DeVoster's death. He couldn't identify the person, just that they were tall and white." Bridget jiggled her leg up and down.

"Are the police sure he didn't concoct his story in order to earn the reward?"

"He came forward before it was offered," Bridget said. "And he also saw that the person was wearing sweats with a glow-in-the-dark Nike basketball on the front and on the back—the exact kind Nike just sent our team."

"That's circumstantial," I said. "Lots of people buy Nike."

Bridget shook her head sadly. "Not these. Nike hasn't released them on the general market yet."

"So it's just your women that have them," I said.

Bridget's leg took a break. "The men have them too."

"The men's basketball team?"

Bridget nodded. "Our girls each got two pairs, so the guys

would've got at least that. Some of the players might have given a pair away."

That broadened the circle of suspects. I'd need to find all those sweats. "What about the witness?" I asked. "Could he tell whether the runner was male or female?"

"Whoever it was wore a stocking cap." Bridget's leg began jittering again. "But the cops think it was a woman."

"Because of the pepper spray?"

The radiator clanked, and Bridget sighed. "After the rape, the Women's Center sent our girls a letter of support along with enough pepper spray for the entire team."

I wondered if Anne had signed the letter. She hadn't said anything to me about it, but clearly, she wasn't telling me everything these days.

"You can see why I need help." Bridget stared at me with her unflinching blue eyes.

One of my kitchen cupboards creaked. If Neale were willing to help me investigate, maybe it would bring us closer. "You know," I said, "my girlfriend is a cop."

Bridget's eyes widened.

"Not here," I said. "In St. Louis. She helped me catch my aunt's—"

"No cops," Bridget said.

"She's not a DeVoster fan like the ones—"

"My player doesn't want any more cops knowing about her." Bridget looked away and took a deep breath. When she turned back to me, her voice was gentler. "You need to understand, Mara. My player was terrified about people discovering her identity *before* DeVoster was killed. You can imagine how she feels now. If the cops show too much interest in her, there's no telling what his fans will do."

I thought about Kobe Bryant's accuser.

"She's a wreck," Bridget said. "The whole team is. But if you could find out who really did it ..." She trailed off, but her eyes held mine.

This was it. She was counting on me. I was the go-to player.

"I know it's a long shot," Bridget said.

The kettle whistled, and I could hear Neale pouring water for her tea.

I wanted to help Bridget—I really did—but then Neale and I would have even less time together.

"I'm asking a lot," Bridget said. "I know that, but the team and I really need you."

It had been a long time since I'd felt needed.

"Maybe you need some time to think it over." Bridget stood.

"No." I sprang to my feet. "I'll give it a try."

"Thank you," Bridget said. "Thank you so much." She threw her arms around me and walloped me on the back.

If I actually found the murderer, I'd have to wear protective gear.

"How about you come by my office around four," Bridget said, "and I'll tell you more. We're having a special team meeting at five, and you can meet the girls."

"Today?" The rest of Saturday was for Neale and me—whether we kept arguing about our relationship or made mad, passionate love. I was about to tell Bridget that she'd have to wait when I glanced over her shoulder. Neale was standing in the entrance to the kitchen, scowling and tapping her watch. I thought about all the hours that had ticked by as I'd waited for her. I thought about all the times she'd bailed on me.

"Four it is," I said.

✧ ✧ ✧

As Bridget made her way out, the cold made its way in.

"You're meeting her at four." Neale's voice was flat, and she stood next to my kitchen table, her hands on her hips. Her tea had a sharp peppermint scent.

"I'm sorry," I said, "but she needs my help. It's urgent."

"Urgent," Neale repeated.

She was always tossing the word around, but she didn't seem to like me using it.

"It's about that basketball player, isn't it?"

I wondered if Neale had made a lucky guess or if she'd been eavesdropping. "Forget about it," I said, "let's get back to our talk."

"Is she a suspect?" Neale asked. "Or one of her players?"

It was none of her business, but I didn't say so. Instead, I picked up a bowl that Vince had left on the table. The milk in it was a dull pink from God-knows-what sugared cereal.

"I suppose she wants you to play amateur detective," Neale said.

"I don't play. In case you've forgotten, I'm the one who solved Glad's murder."

"Think about the danger. All those angry people on TV—not to mention the killer."

I tightened my grip on the bowl. "Excuse me," I said, "are you complaining about me putting myself in danger?"

"She's hiding something," Neale said. "Why doesn't she hire a professional?"

I set the bowl on the counter and started counting to ten.

"Are you two friends?" Neale asked.

"What does that have to do with anything?"

Neale picked up her tea. "You could have checked with me before you agreed to meet with her."

"You didn't check with me before you moved to St. Louis."

Neale dumped her tea in the sink and left the kitchen.

By the time I followed her, she'd disappeared around the curve of the staircase.

"What are you doing?" I called.

A stair squeaked under her weight, and she popped into view. "I'm getting my suitcase. You're going to be busy, so I'm going back to St. Louis."

Her voice was matter-of-fact, but I felt like she'd slapped me. "But we could still have most of tonight and all of tomorrow morning together." I tried to keep the pleading out of my voice. "I won't be long."

"You don't know that, Mara." Neale leaned against the banister. She seemed far away, there on the stairs. "And in the meantime, I'll be sitting here waiting when I could be home."

Home. I hated it when she called St. Louis home. "Doing what?"

She shrugged.

"So you're cutting our time short for nothing?"

She met my eyes and looked away. "One of the guys is throwing a surprise birthday party for the lieutenant."

God forbid she should miss an opportunity to schmooze. For all I knew, Neale had been planning to leave early even if Bridget hadn't shown up. I was too angry to speak.

Neale smiled. "We're both busy. Why make a big deal out of it?"

Before I could respond to her favorite nonquestion, Neale disappeared behind the curve in the stairs.

I didn't follow her.

FIVE

The wind stung my cheeks as I dashed across the parking lot. Against a sky of gray sludge, the top of Carver-Hawkeye Arena looked like a monstrous jungle gym, its jumble of iron beams somehow supporting the arena's ceiling—one more thing I'd never understand. Like Neale. When she left, she'd given me a quick peck on the cheek as if nothing were wrong. But I couldn't help wondering: Why not a longer kiss?

A car door opened next to me, and a long pair of legs, shod in leather high-tops, swung to the pavement. The shoes were longer than my thighs, and the owner of this footwear was over a foot taller than me. She was also a student manager of the women's team. I knew this because last summer she'd done an internship with me at KICI. "Shelly," I said, "nice to see you."

That was a lie. She'd been a great worker at first, but then she'd blown off an important interview, calling in sick and leaving me to handle it myself during one of Neale's rare visits to Iowa City. After the interview, we'd seen her downtown drunk off her butt.

"The girls aren't talking to the press." Shelly's square face was expressionless, and she had the bland coloring of many Iowa girls—blue-gray eyes and hair just dark enough not to count as blond.

"Bridget invited me," I said.

Shelly raised her eyebrows. "Coach Stokes?"

I nodded. I wasn't sure how open to be about my investigation, so I didn't offer any further information. The wind whipped at the jean jacket I'd been too lazy to button. I pulled it tightly around me and tried not to shiver. "Maybe you could show me her office?"

Shelly lumbered toward the arena.

"Are you here for the team meeting?" I asked.

She nodded and held the door open for me.

"You're early," I said.

"A couple of the girls wanted to shoot."

My glasses fogged over as I stepped inside, so I paused to polish them on my sweatshirt. "Do you have lots of team meetings?"

She shrugged.

I hoped that the rest of "the girls" would be more talkative.

Shelly checked her watch—none too subtly—and clasped a clipboard to her chest. "Coach's office is on the third floor. You want the elevator or the stairs?"

Normally, I'm an elevator girl. But I wanted the time to ask Shelly some questions, so I opted for the stairs. They were concrete, and the railings were coated in chipped gold paint.

"How does the team feel about DeVoster's death?" My voice echoed in the stairwell.

"We haven't been together since it happened."

"What about you? How do you feel?"

Shelly's thin ponytail swayed as she climbed the stairs. "It's really different—knowing someone that was murdered."

Shelly had the descriptive powers of a typical small-town Iowan. "Different" was the default word for all things unpleasant. "How well did you know him?"

She started taking the stairs two at a time, and I was short of breath by the time we reached the third-floor lobby. It had CEO written all over it: marble floors, leather furniture, preternaturally green plants, and a sign that said WOMEN'S BASKETBALL. The letters were gold—not Hawkeye gold, but pirate treasure gold, money gold. The gilded age was alive and well in Carver-Hawkeye Arena.

✧ ✧ ✧

Bridget frowned at her computer, leaning in toward it as if she were coaching the final seconds of a tie game. She jiggled her leg and started clattering away on the keyboard. Was she always so intense? The wall behind her was covered with basketball photos. There was the younger Bridget dribbling the ball, sporting the same short, dark, wavy hair—her stocky frame clad in a Hawkeye uniform, one of those tight ones from the eighties. From the looks of her arms at the keyboard, she still worked out. I scanned the desk for photos from her current life, but the only one there featured Coach Carol hugging Bridget back when she'd been a player. Coach Carol was nearly two feet taller than Bridget, a supremely fit sixty-year-old. But because of the nonstop coverage about her brother's condition in Pennsylvania, I knew that she'd been out of state when DeVoster died.

I tapped on Bridget's door, and she swiveled toward me, gesturing to a couch that matched the leather ones in the lobby. Then she whipped back to her desk, punched off her monitor, and pushed up the sleeves of her sweatshirt.

"Nice office," I said. It was bigger than my living room.

"I meet with a lot of potentials." Bridget tried to smile, but she was way off the mark.

As she pulled something out of a file drawer, I thought about the hundreds of nervous teenagers who'd perched on the couch, flanked by their parents.

"Thanks for coming." Bridget rolled her chair next to me until our knees were nearly touching. "Let's start with this year's program." She opened it to the players' bios.

I reached for it, but she pulled away. "This is all in confidence," she said. "You won't tell anyone?"

"Of course not." I wondered if that counted Vince. I couldn't keep a secret from him even if I wanted.

Bridget handed me the program and pointed to a photo of a young woman with a championship grin—slightly crooked teeth but all charisma and charm. "Varenka White." Bridget took a deep breath. "That's who DeVoster raped."

Even though I'd guessed the victim's identity, I still found it hard to mesh my image of Varenka White with the media's "female athlete." She'd behaved as if she had nothing to lose. She'd gotten drunk and stayed at DeVoster's party, even after some of her teammates had begged her to leave. But Varenka White? She had everything going for her. She was the second leading scorer of a top twenty team, an Academic All-American. She was also strikingly beautiful. Her honey-blond hair was the type that most white girls try to replicate with a bottle. She was a slender-framed six foot five inches, with high cheekbones and huge eyes the color of a cloudless October sky. If her beauty and skill hadn't made her a fan favorite, her story would have. Varenka had been adopted from Russia when she was eight, and she'd quickly embraced her new country. Now she mentored younger adoptees like herself.

"I don't know what she was thinking." Bridget shook her head sadly. "Not that I'm blaming her," she added quickly. "Were you at our first game?"

I nodded.

"Then you saw what this has done to her."

Orchid had kept track, so I knew that Varenka had taken only five shots from the floor. None of them went down, and we'd barely come away with the win. "Maybe she just had an off night," I said.

"She's been like that in practice too, and she just phoned to ask if she could be excused from the meeting today." Bridget's face creased with worry. "I asked one of the other girls to sit with her, so she won't be here today either."

"Which one?"

"Kate Timmens. She lives across the hall from Varenka. They're from the same town."

I flipped back a page in the program. Timmens was a backup center, a hefty brunette. Like Varenka, she was six foot five.

Two tall white girls had been excused from the team meeting. "Where were they both last night?"

Bridget pushed her chair away from me and frowned. "None of my girls had anything to do with DeVoster's death."

"If you want my help, you need to answer my questions."

Bridget pressed her lips together.

"Surely the police have already asked about Varenka's whereabouts?"

"Both girls were at home in Independence—with their parents."

Not the world's best alibi. "Have the police confirmed that?"

"They've harassed Varenka, if that's what you mean. They showed up at her apartment while I was at your place and reduced her to tears." Bridget's tone suggested that she'd like to give the cops a taste of their own medicine.

I'd need to tread lightly when I questioned her players. "Did anybody see them in Independence," I asked, "besides their parents?" Even if someone had, Independence was not far from Iowa City. Who knows what the girls might have done while their parents were sleeping?

"Mara." Bridget said my name as if it were a command. "I need you to believe my girls."

I tried to make my tone match hers. "The sooner your players are ruled out as suspects, the easier their lives will be."

She edged her chair back toward me. "There are only four who don't have good alibis and fit the witness's description."

I pulled a pen from the inside pocket of my jacket and flipped through the program again. I checked off three black players and the two short white ones.

"Our starting center and our top reserve are out with ACL injuries." Bridget's knee brushed against mine as she reached over and turned a page. I felt a flood of warmth, but Bridget was all business. She pointed to two tall white girls, and I checked them off. Neither could have sprinted across a parking lot.

"I guess their injuries turned out to be lucky," I said.

"Lucky?" Bridget raised her eyebrows.

"They're not suspects," I said.

"As far as I'm concerned, none of my players are. You should also know that the freshmen who quit the team left long before we got the incriminating sweats."

I remembered Orchid moaning and groaning when the three rookies left.

"We've got only nine healthy players," Bridget said, "and one of them is Varenka. We get other injuries, we get in foul trouble, we're sunk."

I was about to say something encouraging when Bridget announced that the gray team was off the hook. As a diehard fan, I knew that the gray team was a bunch of guys that ran the opponents' plays against the women, but the phrase always made me picture a band of little old ladies dishing and driving.

"One of them had a birthday last night," Bridget said. "They were all at some frat house until the wee hours of the morning. So were our three male managers. There were lots of witnesses."

I thought carefully about my next question. "So, besides Varenka and Kate, who else do the police suspect?"

Bridget reached for a pen on her desk. She tapped it absently in her hand before tucking it behind her ear. "Jessie March and Win Ramsey."

You couldn't live in Iowa City without hearing about Win Ramsey, starting point guard—the tallest floor general Iowa has ever had. She led the Big Ten in scoring, assists, and steals. "Where were they?" I asked.

"At home in bed."

Healthy choices don't always pay. If they'd been out closing the bars with all the other students, they'd have alibis.

"Jessie got called for a technical, right?"

"It was her first college game," Bridget said.

Iowa had been up three with mere seconds left when Jessie got called for a block. She threw an elbow at the player she'd collided with.

"She always have a temper like that?" I asked.

"It was a rookie mistake."

If the Hawkeyes protected the ball half as well as Bridget protected them they'd be national champions. "Was Jessie close to Varenka?"

"Everybody loves V."

I squelched a wave of irritation. "Is she dating anybody? Or was she before …"

Bridget stood and flicked her eyes toward the clock that hung above her desk. "My players keep their private lives private."

I stood too. If Bridget were taller, I'd think about suspecting her.

SIX

Given Bridget's evasiveness, I was having second thoughts about sleuthing, but they vanished when I saw the sign above the locker-room door—WOMEN'S BASKETBALL PERSONNEL ONLY. Bridget punched in the secret code on the keypad. There I was—a former benchwarmer who had abandoned ninth-grade hoops for the debate team—about to enter the inner sanctum.

At the end of a long hallway was a trophy case. If you were a new recruit, its bountiful hardware would either inspire you to greatness or scare you shitless. We took a left at the trophies and entered the players' lounge. Most of them slouched on a huge U-shaped couch—leather, of course—their legs extended toward a Hawkeye logo that was woven into the carpet, their eyes glued to a football game on a big-screen TV. The only girls who weren't watching had no alibis.

Win Ramsey sat at a computer at the side of the room, her hands dwarfing the keyboard. Her deep-brown hair was pulled back into the obligatory ponytail, and her face was spattered with freckles. Jessie March, the hot-tempered freshman, sat on the floor, her back against the back of the couch, facing away from the TV, away from her teammates. If she hadn't been so intent on a huge sketch pad, she would have been staring straight at me. She and Win both had flushed faces, so I figured they must have been the ones shooting hoops with Shelly. I was scanning the room for her when Bridget touched my elbow. "Make yourself at home. I need to check in with the other assistants before we start."

She headed toward the back of the room where two lanky black women stood, studying the team. Sue and Evette—both a decade younger than Bridget—had played their college ball as Hawkeyes. Sue didn't look the least bit pregnant in her turtleneck and Levi's, but neither she nor her partner fit the witness's description. I needed to focus on someone who did.

As Jessie took a long swallow of water, I flipped through my program. In her photo, she had a huge grin, but it didn't quite reach her brown eyes. Her bio informed me that she was from Des Moines, last year's Miss Iowa Basketball, an art and women's studies major. I skipped over her high school stats and gazed at the girl herself. Except for her flushed face, she was anemically pale like me. Her auburn hair was pulled back and wound into a tight bun—same as in the photo. I wondered how it felt to be the team's only freshman. And I wondered if she always distanced herself from the other players.

From the TV, a woman gushed about her deodorant. Shelly squatted next to Win and wrote something on a clipboard. They leaned close and whispered, their eyes darting my way. I felt awkward standing against the wall, but it would have seemed intrusive to sit on the couch as if I were part of the team. I headed toward the coaches.

Sue was saying something about how you could always count on Shelly.

Bridget turned toward me. "We figured that since you already know Shelly you'd want to talk to her first."

Shelly hadn't engaged in much personal chitchat at the station. She hung out in the break room only when there were Krispy Kremes or when I was regaling the interns with my sleuthing adventures. Other than that, Shelly's entire social repertoire consisted of rehashed basketball games and the latest sale at the Coral Ridge Mall. "She wasn't very forthcoming this afternoon," I said. "Maybe I should start with someone else."

"No one else knows all the players as well as Shelly," Bridget said. "She'll open up once she understands you're here to help them."

Next to the TV, Shelly opened a high cupboard and snagged a couple bottles of water. The girl was tall. "What about her alibi?"

"The cops already cleared her," Bridget said. "She and her boyfriend were at his parents' house in Waterloo."

Waterloo was an hour-and-a-half drive from Iowa City. As Shelly reached for some more bottles, I thought about how she might have snuck out in the middle of the night.

Bridget seemed to read my suspicion. "The police checked with the boyfriend's mother. She got an emergency call around 2 A.M. It woke her son and Shelly too."

"She knows all the girls really well," Sue said. "And she rooms with Varenka. They played high school ball together."

"With Kate Timmens." Bridget pointed to a photo behind her.

Kate was snaring a rebound, face grim, elbows flying. The wall was lined with gold-framed action shots. One for each player, I figured. But none for Shelly. Her place was behind the scenes, where nobody noticed her, but where she might notice plenty. "Sure," I said. "I'll start with Shelly."

Bridget nodded and surveyed the room.

Shelly offered Jessie another water, but the freshman shook her head.

"Ladies," Bridget said. "Let's get started."

Hennah Jennings pointed the remote at the TV, and it blinked off. As the coaches and I moved toward the screen, Jessie scooted on the floor until she was facing us. Her legs jutting straight out, her back still against the couch, she didn't see Hennah scowl and edge away from her. Win stayed at the computer but turned her chair toward the front of the room. Shelly handed her a bottle of water and stood next to her. All eyes were on Bridget, wide with worry and shock. A pale girl with a knee brace chomped a wad of gum. Her chewing was the only sound in the room.

"I'm sure you've all heard that the police have questioned Varenka about Dave DeVoster's death," Bridget said.

The girls nodded glumly.

"There's no need to worry. She was with her parents."

"Where is she now?" Jessie asked.

Win shot her a dirty look, and several girls exchanged glances.

"Resting," Bridget said. "Kate is with her. They'll be at practice tomorrow." She stared at her players until they all met her eyes. Then she nodded toward me. "This is Mara Gilgannon. Some of you may have heard her on KICI."

Blank looks all around. Alternative radio is not usually popular with the jock crowd.

"She is also an experienced investigator with a strong record of success."

Now there was some spin. Sure, I'd solved my aunt's murder, and I had an inquisitive spirit, but Bridget was making me sound official—like there was a bevy of killers in prison ruing the day they'd met me.

"Tomorrow, I want you all here at 9 A.M. so Mara can interview you," Bridget continued.

The girls eyed me, game faces all around.

"You'll give her your full cooperation. Honesty is key."

Jessie frowned and examined at her sketch pad.

"When you're not being interviewed, you can use the time for lifting or studying, or you can shoot until the men show up."

Sue leaned toward me. "The guys practice in the early afternoons, and we've got late."

I wondered if the two teams crossed paths every afternoon. That couldn't be pleasant.

"You'll stay until Mara has talked with all of you in case she has any follow-up questions."

"They don't need to do that." There was no graceful way of saying that I wanted each player to leave after I questioned her. "I don't mind following up with a few phone calls."

The gum chewer stopped mid-chomp. The team's eyes darted between Bridget and me as if they'd never seen anyone challenge her before. And Bridget couldn't very well argue with me since she'd just ordered her players to give me their full cooperation.

Win Ramsey bailed her out. "When is Coach Carol coming back?"

"I talked to her this morning." Bridget's voice softened. "Her brother is doing worse."

Meaning, I supposed, he would soon die, and they would have their head coach back. Most of the players gazed at their shoes. A wiry girl with cornrows began biting a fingernail.

"What are we supposed to tell prospectives if they ask about …" Jessie hesitated.

Bridget surveyed her team and crossed her arms over her chest. "We'll get to that soon. I don't want to take up Mara's time with routine team business."

If murder was routine business, then I was ready for the WNBA. I started to protest, but Bridget cut me off.

"Shelly, why don't you make sure Mara has everything she needs."

The manager hustled to the front of the room. There was something about recruiting that Bridget didn't want me to hear.

✧✧✧

Shelly retied her shoe as I studied the reception area that led to the coaches' offices. The main desk was piled high with paper, and so was the floor behind it and the smaller desk in the corner where we were seated.

"It must take a lot of paperwork to keep a basketball team running," I said. "Do you help with all this?"

She nodded and squared her shoulders.

It probably took a lot of willpower for her not to slouch.

"About that interview last year," she said, "the one I missed. I was going through a rough time."

So rough that she'd been out bar crawling.

"I'm usually really responsible. Just ask the coaches."

"They've been singing your praises."

Her boxy face relaxed, and she squared her shoulders again.

I wanted to ask which player seemed most upset about Varenka's rape, but that didn't seem like a smart way to start. "I'm a big fan," I said. "But I don't know much about how a basketball team works. What's your role?"

Shelly smiled. "I'm kind of the head manager because I've been doing it all four years."

"Bridget mentioned that there are three male managers ..."

"Three guys and me and Chante." She pointed to a photo on the bulletin board. "That's us last Christmas."

Shelly and a tiny African-American woman grinned at the camera, decked out in Santa hats. I crossed Chante off my list of suspects.

"We get things ready for practice," Shelly said. "Mark the floors, get the balls out, the clocks ready. And during practice, we run clock or keep stats. We have to know as much about the game as the players do." Pride energized her, and she moved to the edge of her seat. "The guys run drills. They're stronger and faster, so they give the girls more of a challenge."

"You must have played in high school."

"Yeah." She folded her hands together in her lap and gazed at them.

Since she didn't seem eager to talk about her playing days, I switched topics. "What about traveling? Do you go to the away games?"

"All the tournaments. Two Thanksgivings ago we played in Denver, and we got to go skiing. I was scared at first, but now I'm dying to go back. Last year we played in the Bahamas." She pulled another photo from the bulletin board.

I held it carefully in my hand, studying the team members as they relaxed on the beach. It was hard to tell who was who amid the sunglasses and straw hats. As I returned the photo, I glanced at Shelly's bulletin board. Next to a flyer for the Fellowship of Christian Athletes was a small poster of a huge four-towered cathedral. LA SAGRADA FAMILIA, it said. BARCELONA. "Have you played in Spain?"

"I wish." Shelly grinned. "That's where Maria lives." Shelly pointed at a photo of a lovely girl with cascading dark hair. "She lived with my family my junior year of high school—an exchange student. I can't wait to visit her. We e-mail almost every day."

Our conversation was drifting from the Hawkeyes. "Where else have you traveled with the team?"

"All over. I've had lots of cool opportunities. And I get a full scholarship—just like the girls."

The girls. Despite her insistence that she was part of the team, Shelly didn't seem to see herself that way. "What are your responsibilities outside of practice?"

"Me and Chante are in the office a lot. We do most of the correspondence with potentials. They think they're getting personal letters from Coach Carol, but really Chante and I write most of them—one a week."

"Sounds like an important job."

She shrugged and smiled.

"Bridget mentioned that your number of potentials has gone down since the rape."

Her smile faded. "I'm not really a numbers person."

An obvious lie, given that she kept stats, but I let it go. "You're Varenka's roommate?"

"We share an apartment." She started straightening a stack of papers.

"You're both from Independence?" I asked. "And Kate Timmens too?"

Her nod was barely perceptible.

"You three must be close."

Shelly shrugged again.

I was losing our game of one-on-one. "What about the night Varenka was raped? Were you and Kate at the party?"

"*I* wasn't." She glanced at me and started separating a stack of papers. "I don't like big parties. I don't like going, and I don't like hearing about them."

I tried another tack. "Were you with Varenka after she was raped?"

Shelly swallowed and took a deep breath. "Yeah, me and Kate and Win. They live across the hall."

"Can you tell me a little about that night?" I tried to keep my voice gentle.

"Like what?" She absently tapped some papers against the desk even though their edges were already aligned.

"How was everybody feeling?"

"Upset." She stood and started moving stacks from the table to the floor.

I'd asked a stupid question, but I couldn't just let it go. "Crying?" I asked. "Angry?"

Shelly simply kept transferring the paperwork, slamming each stack to the floor.

"I need your perception of the team's dynamics since the rape."

She met my gaze. "What do you mean?"

"How has the team gotten along since it happened?" I asked. "Has anybody been especially outspoken about it?"

"What does it matter?" she asked. "None of the girls killed DeVoster."

"I'm just trying to eliminate them as suspects." I stood, but she still towered over me. "I'm on your side, Shelly. Your team's side."

She narrowed her eyes, stone-faced.

"Come on," I said, "the cops have already questioned Varenka once."

Shelly's eyes widened.

"Early this afternoon," I said.

"But Varenka was in Independence with Kate when …" She trailed off.

"They have only Varenka's parents to vouch for them, so the police are suspicious."

"The cops think Varenka killed DeVoster?" Shelly's voice was shrill. "Wasn't it enough that they treated her like a criminal after the rape? Now she's a murder suspect?" Shelly plopped back into her chair, her face a mass of worry.

"You could help her," I said, "if you told me a bit about your team dynamics."

She heaved a sigh. "We've all been angry. We're a team. We pull together."

"Has anyone seemed especially angry?"

"We're not the only angry ones," Shelly said. "How did you feel when you heard about his redshirt?" She didn't wait for a response. "Some of his own teammates think he should have been put behind bars."

I thought about the red-haired dunker I'd seen on TV earlier that day. "What about Tyler Bennet?" I asked. "What did he think?"

Shelly bit her lip and glanced at her watch.

"What year is he?" I asked.

"Junior."

That gave him a motive. Next year, DeVoster's redshirt year would have been over, and Bennet would have lost his starting spot.

"I don't know him real well," Shelly added. "He seems nice, but Roshaun says he keeps to himself."

"Roshaun?"

"My boyfriend." She looked at me expectantly. "You know," she insisted, "he's an intern at the station, a manager for the men's team. You might let him interview—"

"Gotcha," I said, knocking my hand against my forehead. "Coach Stokes says you were at his parents' the night DeVoster was killed."

Shelly's face grew pinched again. "I wanted to get out of town after the redshirt thing. We left right after the men's game."

"Has it been awkward—you two being together?"

"It's been kind of different," she said, "but we've known each other a long time. We started managing the same year."

"Does he have any thoughts about who killed DeVoster?"

"Yo, Shell." There was Roshaun himself. He nodded at me. "Miss Gilgannon." He stood in the doorway, his beaded cornrows at odds with the chinos and dress shirt he always wore at the station. He and Shelly made quite the odd couple. Roshaun was more than a foot shorter, wiry and graceful, with a molasses complexion. Usually all smiles and jokes, he grimly tossed a set of keys from hand to hand. "You about ready to go?" he asked Shelly.

"She was just telling me about DeVoster's backup," I said.

"Bennet," Roshaun said. "Real nice guy." He spoke deliberately, squinting at Shelly.

"That's what I said." She squared her shoulders but dropped her eyes to the floor.

I tried again. "Rumor has it that DeVoster wasn't exactly well liked by the rest of the team."

Roshaun stared at Shelly a moment longer before turning to me. "Jealousy," he said. "I don't mean to be rude, but me and Shell got a test to study for."

"About Bennet—"

"Red saves his aggression for the floor." Roshaun edged toward Shelly's chair.

"What's the buzz on your team?" I asked. "Who do they think did it?"

"We haven't had time for buzz."

"You must have some guesses about who killed him."

Roshaun tossed his keys in the air and caught them.

"From what I've heard," Shelly said quickly, "DeVoster messed with a lot of girls."

Now she offers information? When I'm questioning her boyfriend? "Do you know any of their names?" I asked.

Shelly shook her head. "I bet he didn't either."

SEVEN

Some women feel sorry for themselves because they're always the bridesmaid, never the bride. But I had no role at all in Anne's yet-to-be-scheduled commitment ceremony—unless you counted my halfhearted attempts to help Vince train the canine ring bearer. Said ring bearer was also less than thrilled with her role. Labrys gaped at the plastic ring she'd just dropped, her tongue hanging out. She sank to the floor and rested her front paws on the pillow she was supposed to carry.

I put the ring back on it.

"Come on, girl." Vince clapped his hands.

Labrys thumped her tail once and closed her eyes.

"No one is cooperating with me today," I said.

"And you call me a drama queen." Vince squatted next to the golden retriever and scratched her head. "Those players will open up once they get used to you."

"What about Bridget?" I said. "There's something she doesn't want me to know."

"Maybe she doesn't want to waste your time with irrelevant information." Vince sat all the way down on the floor and pulled his jean-clad legs to his chest. Labrys twisted her head and looked at him expectantly until he began stroking her back.

"She's bossy, It's like she's forgotten that I'm doing her a favor."

"Ooh," Vince said. "Bossy can be fun."

I rolled my eyes. Whenever Vince wants to cheer me up, he talks about sex. Actually, he talks about sex regardless.

"Seriously," he said. "I think she has a thing for you. Why else would she have asked for your help?"

"Why wouldn't she ask me?" I snapped. "I've already solved one murder."

Vince grinned. "That may have been her conscious motive, but I bet her subconscious is seething with desire for you."

"She'll just have to seethe," I said. "I'm already taken." But I wondered if that were true. When Neale left, neither of us had said a word about our next visit.

"Monogamy," Vince said. "So overrated."

Our phone rang, and I motioned him to get it. I'd been waiting for Neale to call all evening, but I didn't want her to know that.

Vince picked up the phone and shook his head no. "*I'm* the lady of the house," he said in his deep baritone, waggling his eyebrows at me.

Damn telemarketers—they raise your hopes and dash them to the ground. Why hadn't Neale called? She always phoned to say that she'd made it home safely.

"I beg your pardon," Vince continued toying with the hapless soul on the other end of the line. "I don't take care of that bill. You'll want to talk with my boy toy. He should be home soon. He just stepped out to purchase a little something at the Pleasure Palace." Vince hung up the phone and laughed. "Another one bites the dust. Truly, I am a master at torturing phone solicitors." He maneuvered into his favorite chair, a La-Z-Boy surrounded by magazines and boxes of Pop-Tarts. "You're lucky to have me."

I sighed, and he gave me a sympathetic look. "Don't fret, Mar-bar. She'll call."

"Our parting wasn't exactly sweet sorrow." I scooped the plastic ring off the pillow and sat on the futon couch across from Vince. I draped an afghan across myself. Even in sweats, I was cold because we couldn't afford to move our thermostat out of the arctic range.

Outside, a couple dogs barked, but nothing was getting a rise out of Labrys. I placed the ring on my thumb. "I just don't get her," I said. "Why do we keep seeing each other if our relationship isn't going anywhere?"

"Because it's fun?"

Silly me, I'd forgotten I was talking to a man whose longest relationship could be counted in months. "I don't understand anyone," I said.

Vince bent over and grabbed a box of chocolate Pop-Tarts. "Let's break out the treats," he said. "Somebody's throwing herself a pity party."

I glowered at him.

"What's with all the hyperbole?" he asked.

I stared out my front window. The house across the street was dark. "Did you know Anne wants to have a baby?" I asked.

Vince set the Pop-Tarts back on the floor. "Turkey baster?"

I nodded.

He clasped his hands together. "We'll be honorary aunties."

"The first I heard about it was this morning at brunch," I said.

"You know Anne," Vince said. "She probably wanted to get all centered about it before she told anybody."

He was trying to be nice, but his remark stung. "I'm not just anybody."

Labrys stood and whimpered.

Vince stroked his goatee, a sure sign that he didn't know what to say.

"Orchid is going to be a terrible parent," I said. She and Anne had been together for a year and a half, but I still couldn't believe that my sweet, gentle Anne—with her Zen-induced serenity and carefully balanced chakras—had wound up with the chronically angry and self-righteous Orchid Paine. Anne didn't care about money, so she couldn't have been drawn to Orchid's trust fund. What was it? Their shared passion for remodeling?

"Permission to point out the obvious?" Vince asked.

I sighed.

"You're obsessed."

I started to protest, but Vince moved toward me, putting a finger to my lips. "Shush. You follow their relationship more religiously than my mother tracks her soaps."

"Now who's exaggerating?"

"Not *moi,*" he said. "You talk about Anne and Orchid way more than anything else—including Neale."

"I do not."

Vince sat next to me and held out his hand to Labrys.

"I've known Anne a lot longer," I said. "I see her more."

Vince rubbed the dog's head.

"She wants to get pregnant," I said. "She never wanted to do that with me."

"Mar-Bar, you don't even have houseplants. What would you do with a baby?" He put his arm around me, but I pulled away.

"That's not the point." But what was?

The phone rang.

This time it would be Neale. We'd make up and exchange sweet nothings. Then I'd tell Vince all about it, and he'd see that I talked about Neale good and plenty. "Get it," I hissed.

Vince feigned a wounded look and headed to the phone. Labrys followed him, her tail wagging.

I'd ask Neale if she wanted me to come down next weekend. It wasn't such a bad drive—especially if the weather was good.

Vince picked up the phone mid-ring, his back to me.

Neale was always good about chatting with Vince before asking for me.

"Richard!" Vince exclaimed.

There is no justice. Vince's default date calls just to say hi, but my girlfriend can't take the time to check in before she goes drinking with her band of brothers. Maybe we were through. My eyes burned and my lip trembled.

Labrys whirled around and studied me.

Soon Anne would be pregnant, and Orchid would be shopping for politically correct baby clothes. A tear rolled down my cheek. Before I could reach for a Kleenex, Labrys lunged at me. Licking my face, she soon pinned me to the futon, her front paws on my shoulders, her hot doggy breath too close for comfort. It was no use trying to push her off, so I resigned myself to her slobbery ministrations.

✧ ✧ ✧

I told myself that visiting the crime scene would help me prepare for my interviews the next morning, but really I'd gone simply to take my mind off Neale. Vince had insisted on coming along, but he needn't have worried about me being alone. When we pulled into the parking lot, the lights of several police cars strobed the night. I drove deep into the lot before finding an empty space.

The darkness was filled with chants and shouts, but I couldn't make out any words, only garbled anger coming from the area around the Herky where DeVoster had breathed his last. The offending bird was brightly lit, but you could barely see it—there were that many people. I headed toward the crowd, shivering. Soon Vince and Labrys were at my side, the dog straining against her leash, eager to chase a terrier that yapped and darted in and out of the crowd's periphery.

"Everybody and his dog are here," he said, "literally."

On the far side of Marilyn MonHerky, a mass of Hawkeye faithful waved signs that said FIND DEVOSTER'S KILLER and AN EYE FOR AN EYE. Clad in black and gold, they chanted, "Lie, lie, you killed our guy," presumably at the smaller group on the other side of Herky. This group, mostly women, stood silently, holding signs that said RAPE DESTROYS LIVES and TAKE BACK THE NIGHT. I wondered if Anne were among them, but I couldn't spot her.

Signs on both sides of Herky read JUSTICE FOR DEVOSTER. Neither group was too close to the bird because of the crime scene tape. If I hadn't known that all such tape is black and gold, I might have thought it was designed to bolster our Hawkeye spirit.

The cops who surrounded the crowd mumbled into their walkie-talkies and eyed each other nervously. One of them lifted a bullhorn and shouted at the crowd to break it up and go home, but all he got in response was heckling. "Stop dicking around," shouted a voice from the bumblebee side. "Go catch the killer."

A toddler in a stocking cap with bunny ears tugged at the bottom of her mom's coat. "Mommy, can we get some popcorn?"

I saw more kids—on both sides of the crowd—as Vince and I worked our way toward Herky. Three boys who were playing tag nearly upended an elderly woman who held a sign that said WE MISS YOU, DAVE.

Herky was waist-high in flowers and black-and-gold kitsch. A toddler tried to place a miniature basketball atop the makeshift shrine, but it rolled back to his feet. His father picked it up and shoved it in between some gold mums and a game program. On the sidewalk in front of the statue, votive candles flickered on framed photos of DeVoster and high-tops of all sizes. There were also empty pop cans, but they were probably just litter.

Labrys sniffed at a sneaker and squatted. I yanked her chain, and just barely kept her from desecrating the sacred space. "Vince!" I thumped him in the chest. "Do you want to start a riot? Watch the dog!"

He reluctantly abandoned some frat boys he'd been ogling and dragged Labrys toward a huge pine at the back of the crowd.

As Labrys did her business, I pointed at the dark side of the tree. "The killer might have hid there, waiting for DeVoster."

"Unless it was a chance encounter," Vince said. "It seems unlikely that anyone would choose to attack DeVoster here." He gestured toward Marilyn. "She's one well-lit bird."

I watched the cars streaming into the parking lot and lining Hawkins Drive. "It's hard to see her from the street," I countered. If the murder had been premeditated, then I could narrow my list of suspects by discovering who was privy to DeVoster's running habits.

"We should have brought hot chocolate," Vince said. "I'm catching my death in this cold."

Labrys yanked on Vince's arm and started barking.

"She votes for staying," I said.

"Of course she does. She has fur." Vince sulked as the dog lead us back into the crowd. A gaggle of undergrads were engaged in a game of protest one-upmanship. "I've marched in Take Back the Night since I was twelve," said a girl with black lipstick.

A skinny guy with wheat-colored dreadlocks smiled smugly. "My moms brought me when I was a baby."

"What time is it?" asked someone with a blue mullet.

"I haven't worn a watch for, like, five years." With that proclamation, Black Lipstick silenced her comrades.

My own watch said 10:15. Neale might have phoned right after Vince and I left. I was about to dig my cell phone out of my pocket and check when a bullhorn blared, "DeVoster got what he deserved."

The crowd hushed for a moment, stunned.

"DeVoster got what he deserved," Lexie repeated and strode toward the crowd with some twenty people in her wake. "DeVoster got what he deserved." She towered over the two guys who marched at her side.

"She's got balls," Blue Mullet said.

"Why equate balls with bravery?" Black Lipstick retorted.

Her feminist commentary was drowned out by the decidedly unfeminist shouts from the other half of the crowd. But Lexie was undaunted. "DeVoster got what he deserved."

If she had murdered DeVoster, she sure wasn't worried about making herself look like the prime suspect.

"DeVoster got what he deserved." Black Lipstick and crew joined in, pumping their fists in the air.

Vince grabbed my shoulder. "Let's get out of here."

As we dashed away, the cops were barely managing to stem the black-and-gold flood that rolled toward Lexie.

EIGHT

I was tired of the windowless reception area of the women's basketball offices, and I was tired of Win Ramsey. So far, she hadn't been any more helpful than her teammates. She was simply giving me the Dixie version of the team's party line. "We've all been shocked by recent events," she said, her Southern drawl spinning the last word into three syllables: *ee-vay-ents*. But other than the extra syllables, the story was the same. She couldn't imagine any of the girls hurting anybody—especially not V. She hadn't noticed that some of the girls seemed to dislike Jessie. They'd all been upset about DeVoster's plea bargain and redshirt—they were a team, after all. She didn't have any guesses about who killed him—none at all—but she couldn't believe that one of his own teammates would have. Teams pull together. With that last bit, she leaned forward in her swivel chair as if she were granting me the final piece of the puzzle.

"Even if someone on the team is a rapist or a murderer?"

"No one on our team killed anybody." She folded her hands on the table in between us, her hazel eyes never leaving mine. They were round like her freckled face, and one of them had a streak of brown. "We're family."

I shifted my focus to her tight pumpernickel French braid. Behind her hung a photo of a rock climber scaling a sheer cliff. DETERMINATION, it said. That's what I needed. "The team must be extra important to you since you're so far from home."

Her brows squeezed together. Worry lines cut deep into the middle of her forehead. Something had been burdening this girl for a good long time. "What drew you to Iowa?" I asked.

"You ever been to West Virginia?"

I shook my head.

"It used to be real pretty—that's what Mama says—but there ain't nothing there now. The mountains have been all cut up. There's no coal and no jobs. No trees hardly." She unclasped her hands and put them in her lap. "I wanted to get me and my baby sister out of there. Coach Carol, she said if I came, she'd get Mindi—that's my sister—a scholarship as a manager."

"Your sister is a manager?" Was there yet another tall girl I needed to interview?

"Next year," Win said. "We won't be here at the same time, but the coaches will look after her—the other girls too."

"You're hoping to go pro?" I prompted.

"If I could get a good pick—second round even—I could afford to bring Mama up here."

I was beginning to understand those worry lines. Win had been carrying her family on her back long before she carried the Hawkeyes. "How are things looking for you?"

She hung her head and swiveled from side to side in her chair. "It depends on the team. We need to make it deep into the tournament."

Her chair squeaked, and the clock over the secretary's desk ticked loudly.

"You played well in the first game."

Win frowned. "I could be an assist leader if my teammates made their shots." Her voice grew bitter. "I can understand V having a bad game. But everybody else? They're letting themselves get rattled. They shouldn't even be thinking about DeVoster. We got business to take care of."

This was the first complaint about the team I'd heard all morning. "Who's having a particularly hard time?"

"I'm not going there," Win said, "but I'll tell you this. It's *her* fault." She jabbed her finger at the newspaper that lay between us. On the front page was a photo of Lexie Roth with her bullhorn. "She won't leave us alone. When it first happened—when V was, you know—that reporter found out it was one of us, and she called us all the time. Then she just kept fanning the fire, following DeVoster around like that. We were trying to move on. Why couldn't she? She's made our team look really bad."

Baa-yad. I was swimming in vowels.

"She won't let anybody forget."

"Do you think you should?"

"Won't do any good to remember." Win shoved up the sleeves of her sweatshirt and folded her arms over her chest.

I didn't want her to shut down. "What did Lexie ask when she called you?"

"All kinds of stuff. I don't remember."

"You must remember something."

"You should interrogate her."

"I plan to."

That calmed Win down. "She mostly called our freshmen. I guess she thought they'd be more likely to blab."

"Do you think it's her fault they left?"

Win studied her lap and took a deep breath. When she looked up, her cheeks were red. "They were already homesick," she mumbled.

Someone knocked, and Win gave the door a thankful glance.

Shelly stuck her head in. "I've got the info you wanted." She nodded to the file folder in her hand.

"Come on in," I said. "Win and I were just talking about why the freshmen left."

Shelly remained at the door. Her eyes flicked toward Win.

"I told her to question Lexie Roth." Win nodded toward the reporter's photo. "She's obsessed with him."

Gazing at the newspaper, Shelly tugged at her sweatpants and retucked her T-shirt. SPAIN, it said, above a gorgeous snow-capped mountain range.

"What do you think?" I asked.

Shelly kept her eyes on the paper. "She'd have known his running route since she stalked him."

Win stood.

"About those freshmen," I said.

"We hadn't gotten to know them very well yet," Shelly said.

"They kept to themselves," Win added as she headed to the door.

"Speaking of freshmen," Shelly said, "do you want me to get Jessie for you? I think she's the only player you haven't talked to yet."

These girls sure didn't want to discuss the freshmen who left the team. I picked up the folder that Shelley had brought me. Maybe its contents would help me ask better questions. "I'll come get her myself," I said. "I need a break." I did indeed need a break—just one girl who was willing to be straight with me.

✧ ✧ ✧

The clock next to the rock-climber poster said 11:05. Time for Vince to awaken if he hadn't already. I was surprised that the phone on the secretary's desk wasn't black and gold. Everything else was: the paperweight, the pencil holder, the calendar with the season's football schedule at the bottom. There was also a package of Herky on Parade trading cards. CELEBRATING 75 YEARS OF KINNICK STADIUM, the shiny wrapper said. Samurai Herky pumped his tiny fist in the air. His brows were drawn into a sharp V over his beak, his eyes rolled heavenward, and his mouth—complete with gargantuan teeth—twisted downward into a grimace that signaled either ferocity or debilitating constipation. Like any self-respecting mascot, the bird had his own Web site. Since the package was open, I dumped the deck into my hand: Air Passenger Herky, Harley Herky, Da Herkinator. In the middle of the deck was Eldon Bly Herky, its massive silver hair and black-rimmed glasses a tribute to the men's basketball coach. The man who—mere hours after DeVoster had been accused of rape—went on record saying that he was "110-percent certain" that his player was innocent of all wrongdoing. He also declared that it was hard for a young male athlete when girls constantly threw themselves at him. "Who really is the victim here?" he'd asked. The question unleashed a spate of vandalism on his Herky. The sponsors of the parade finally had to remove the avian Eldon to a storage facility in an undisclosed location.

I wondered what would happen to Marilyn MonHerky now that she'd played a starring role in DeVoster's death. According to the morning paper, some fans believed that the bird should be auctioned off as planned because it would attract even more bidders now that it had "a history." Others wanted Marilyn to remain where she was as a tribute to DeVoster. What a memorial—a gender-queer Plexiglas raptor!

I went back to the table where I'd been conducting player interviews and reviewed the paper's front page. Next to a photo of DeVoster helping to build a Habitat for Humanity home, an article quoted some of his fans calling for the death penalty—apparently unaware that Iowa doesn't have one. If the cops didn't arrest someone soon, they'd have vigilantes on their hands.

That would be bad news for Anne.

She'd been painted as DeVoster's nemesis in several venues. First by Lexie in *The Daily Iowan,* then on the TV news, and now in the Sunday *Press Citizen.* Embedded in a story headlined "Killer Uses Pepper Spray" was a head shot of Anne that made her look like the stereotypical humorless feminist. Her name appeared in the story's second paragraph: "Under the directorship of Anne Golding, the Women's Center at the University of Iowa donated several units of the spray to female students." I could only imagine how the DeVoster faithful would react. At best, Anne and her center would be scourged in letters to the editor.

She'd need lots of support. The least I could do is call and see how she was. As I headed back to the phone, I remembered Vince saying that I spent too much time on her. That wasn't true, of course, but I'd call him first to see if Neale had finally phoned, and then I'd call Anne. Nobody could accuse me of having messed-up priorities.

Vince picked up in the middle of our answering-machine message—an epic saga that featured other numbers where he might be reached. "Mar-Bar," he croaked. "Do the words 'beauty sleep' mean nothing to you?"

I felt more than a twinge of irritation. While he'd been cozy under a mound of quilts, I'd been questioning sullen young hoopsters. "Has Neale called?"

His hesitation gave me my answer.

"She might have while I was sleeping and not left a message," he said.

"Right," I said, "and when I get home, I'll put our Sunday pot roast in the oven and iron your shirts."

"She just needs to sulk a couple days."

I heard Vince open the refrigerator, and my stomach rumbled. The stale granola bar that I'd scarfed down on the way to the stadium was but a faint memory.

"Anne hasn't called either," he said.

Vince was always so damn sure he knew what I was thinking. I wouldn't call Anne at all. Instead, I'd skim through the folder that Shelly had brought me, and I'd interview Jessie. I was bound to find a lead sooner or later.

"How goes the sleuthing?"

"It could be better."

"Look on the bright side," Vince said. "That sweet morsel of a coach will be forever in your debt."

"Not if I don't get her players off the hook."

"You should interview her again, have a tête-à-tête over a glass of wine."

For Vince, the world is one big singles club. I opened the folder and thumbed through its top pages. As per my request, there was contact info for all the players—women and men—and their parents. But there was nothing about the freshmen who'd left—not even their names.

"Mar-Bar," Vince moaned, "you used the last of the coffee."

I'd asked for those names more than once. I was sure of it. So much for Shelly's highly touted responsibility.

"Will you get some more on the way home?" Vince asked. "Pretty please? And some milk? I'm going to use the last of it to make pancakes."

I set the addresses aside and skimmed the next list. The players had given their spare glow-in-the-dark sweats to nearly thirty people. Any of these recipients who were white, over six feet, and capable of sprinting had to be considered suspects.

"I'll save some batter for you," Vince cooed. "What do you say?"

I couldn't say anything. All I could do was stare at Anne's name. My ex had received a pair of sweats from the entire team, probably as a thank-you to the Women's Center for the moral support and the pepper spray. But the gift would not serve Anne well, not well at all.

NINE

As the women scrimmaged in the empty arena, the ball slapped against their hands and boomed against the floor. Win found a space in the lane and made an easy layup. When these women were on the court, they were so graceful and purposeful—it was easy to forget they were just kids. But off the court, you saw their braces and their acne. You felt their pain as they tried to use words like "rape" and "murder" to describe their own world.

I hoped Jessie March would be more forthcoming than her teammates. From the back row of the arena, I watched as she passed the ball to Hennah Jennings, and I started down the concrete stairs. When I'd asked Hennah whether there was any racial tension on the men's team, she said that DeVoster was an equal opportunity asshole. Her honesty was refreshing, but it didn't help me narrow my circle of suspects. And she'd clammed up when I asked how she and the rest of the team felt about Jessie.

Shelly emerged from the tunnel to the locker-room area, pushing a cart with a water container. I paused near the bottom of the stairs and checked my watch. Just half an hour until the men's practice. I'd need to make my time with Jessie count.

The ball flew out of bounds on a bad pass, and I called her name. Focused on the court, she bounced up and down on her toes, but Shelly waved to her and pointed at me. Jessie said something to one of her teammates, grabbed her warm-ups and water, and jogged toward me. As she bounded up the stairs, I lowered myself into one of the seats, deciding not to waste time taking her back to the office.

She wiped her hand on the side of her shorts and extended it to me, her grasp sticky and painfully firm. "Thanks for trying to help V and our team."

Jessie was the only player who'd treated me as anything other than an intruder.

She slipped into her jacket and sat on the concrete steps. Resting her elbows on her knees, she seemed at home in her body and unaware of her beauty—her dark coffee eyes and creamy cheekbones. "What do you want to know?" she asked.

"Let's start with how the rape has impacted the team."

Jessie uncapped her water and took a long swallow. "We keep the focus on our game."

"That must be hard," I prompted.

"We're a team despite our differences."

Here was something promising. "What kind of differences?"

Jessie watched her teammates. A few practiced jump shots, and the rest stretched nearby. On the other side of the court, near the top of the key, Shelly removed some tape.

"Behind V's back, a lot of the girls are like, 'Let's not pick sides,' or 'We don't know what happened in the room that night.'" She shook her head in disgust. "Please, give me a break."

"Some of your teammates don't believe her?"

"They can't deal with it. They're babies."

That attitude no doubt endeared her to the team's veterans.

"Who knows?" Jessie said. "Maybe they do believe her, but they don't want to make waves with the men's team." Jessie sealed her drink. "But somebody made waves—big-time waves." She smiled faintly.

"You think DeVoster got what he deserved?"

"He deserved worse." Her smile vanished. "Now the media will turn him into some martyred saint struck down at the beginning of his brilliant career—blah, blah, blah."

Jessie sure wasn't worried about being a suspect. "You were home sleeping the night he was murdered," I said. "Alone?"

"That's right, no alibi for me." She zipped up her jacket. "But I didn't do it. Trust me, if I had, he would have suffered more."

There was no bravado in her statement. She meant every word. "Do you think Varenka had anything to do with his death?"

Jessie stared across the arena at the empty stands and sighed. "She's barely been able to make it to class and practice."

A ball hit the back of the rim and arced through the air, landing with a sharp bang near a player who was doing a lunge.

"What about her close friends?" I asked.

The ball kept bouncing, a fading drum roll. I was about to repeat my question when Tyler Bennet and three of his teammates strolled into the arena. Jessie glared at them. "Talk to Bennet," she said. "He and V had a thing."

Wow. That gave him two motives. "Were they serious?"

Jessie shrugged, her glare growing more intense.

I watched Bennet myself. He picked up a stray ball, palming it. I thought about those huge hands around DeVoster's neck. "Did you ever hear him threaten DeVoster?"

She finally looked away from the court. "I don't hang with the man."

"Why'd they break up?"

"No idea." Jessie reopened her water.

"Do you know when they split?"

She shook her head. "Sorry."

As Coach Eldon Bly entered the arena, some of the female players left. Win bounced a ball to Shelly, who lodged it in a cart.

I wondered why she hadn't told me about Bennet and Varenka. "It must be hard for Shelly," I said, "dating a manager from the men's team."

If Jessie was puzzled by my abrupt change of topics, she didn't show it. "Roshaun couldn't stand DeVoster." She glanced at Bly and lowered her voice. "None of the managers could. He treated them all like peons."

Shelly abandoned the ball cart and snagged a rebound for a hapless free thrower.

"Besides," Jessie said. "Shell is totally devoted to our team—especially to V. They played high school ball together."

I thought about Shelly's resistance when I asked about her playing days. "Did she ever have a chance of playing for Iowa?"

"The way I hear it, all she had going for her was her height. That can get you by in high school, but not in Div. I."

Shelly grabbed another rebound. Her wingspan was the longest in the arena.

"Too bad," I said.

"Shell doesn't mind. She's all about managing. When she first became a manager, she vowed never to shoot again because it wasn't her job anymore. That's what Win said anyway." Jessie shook her head in disbelief.

"Is Win your closest friend on the team?" I asked.

Jessie raised her arms over her head and folded herself over her legs, stretching.

I wished I could see her face. "I couldn't help noticing in the locker room," I said. "There's some tension between you and your teammates."

She sat back up. "They're just jealous."

I doubted that Win was jealous, but I let it go. "What about the freshmen who left?" I asked. "Were you close to any of them?"

Jessie rolled her eyes. "They were totally small-town. One of them was homesick even though she lived, like, half an hour away."

"Where was she from?" I tried to keep the eagerness out of my voice. It would be great if I could get the freshmen's names and hometowns without having to go online or ask Orchid.

"Atalissa," Jessie said. "Population 203."

Since I hail from a small town—albeit not that small—such jabs usually piss me off. But I was on a mission. "Which one is from there?" I asked, as if I knew all the freshmen on a first-name basis.

"Gina Hofmeyer. She was a decent point guard. Would have learned a lot from Win if she'd stayed."

Another couple questions, and I knew the names and hometowns of the other two freshmen. "Why'd they leave?"

"Stupidity."

As I waited for her to offer another reason, I felt someone watching us. Eldon Bly.

"They were homesick," Jessie said. "Upset about what happened to V." Her explanation sounded reasonable, but her eyes darted around the arena.

Maybe she found Bly's stare as unnerving as I did. "Your

teammates didn't seem to want to talk about the freshmen," I said.

"They bailed on us." Jessie stood and stretched her arms behind her.

I stood too, the top of my head barely reaching her shoulders. I thought about how she'd nearly shoved DeVoster during the season opener. Was she strong enough to choke him, to make all those bruises? My stomach knotted. I looked away from her, trying to regain my composure.

Bly was still watching us.

"Let's finish our conversation somewhere else," I said.

Jessie sprang up the stairs without answering, and I followed her, amazed by the size of her calves. When she stopped, we were nearly all the way to the top. "They look small now, don't they?" she said, nodding at Bly and his boys.

They did indeed, but I hadn't winded myself simply for the view. "What do you think about Lexie Roth?"

Jessie grinned. "I love the way she stuck it to DeVoster."

"Your teammates think she's made things harder for Varenka." I was also thinking about how hard she'd made it for Anne.

"No way. *The Daily Iowan* is the only paper that's taken V's side." Jessie took a sip of her water. "The others just go on and on about DeVoster—scholar athlete, all-American boy, sweeter than Mom's apple pie." She stuck her finger in her mouth and made the universal gagging gesture. "Can we say purple prose? Can we say sexist?"

The girl was born to rant.

"Did you see today's *Press Citizen*?" she asked.

Before I could nod, she was off to the races. "The suspect's gender is supposedly unknown, but they kept using female pronouns. 'She' was seen running across the parking lot. 'She' was over six feet tall. Let's use the generic male pronoun unless we're talking about the murder of a golden boy. Then it's 'she, she, she.' You don't see that kind of sexism in Lexie's writing."

"Who would have known about DeVoster's running habits?" I asked.

"Duh!" Jessie gestured to the court. "His teammates."

While she was feeling smug, I tried to catch her off-guard. "What about recruiting? How has that been since the rape?"

"Don't ask me. I'm just a freshman."

She seemed to be trotting out her lowly status to avoid my question. "You were just recruited yourself. You must know something about it."

"Not from this end."

Nobody—not even this opinionated frosh—wanted to talk about recruiting. It looked like I had two mysteries on my hands.

TEN

"Discretion is the better part of valor." Vince waved his finger in my face as I pulled out of the McDonald's parking lot.

"*You* telling *me* to be discreet," I said, "that's rich."

He unwrapped his Big Mac. "I have no need for discretion, but you, my dear, you were on TV, immortalized with Anne and Orchid as Anne screamed that DeVoster was a rapist. Then Eldon Bly starts stalking you."

"He was just watching me at the arena."

"Wondering what you were up to," Vince insisted.

I braked at a stoplight, feeling sorry I'd told him about Bly.

"You could be in danger," Vince said. "That's why I'm sacrificing my Sunday afternoon. Someone needs to watch your back. Bridget shouldn't expect you to do all this on your own. Not even for love."

My defogger couldn't keep pace with Vince's hot air, so I

rubbed my hand against the window. "As long as you make yourself scarce when I'm trying to question people."

"Say no more," Vince said. "I understand the delicate nature of your interviews." He placed the fries within my reach. "While you talk with Varenka, I'll canvass the rest of the apartments."

It was a good plan, but it appeared that the police had beaten us to it. There were two black and whites right in front of the building where Varenka lived. If they were indeed there for Varenka, then my sweet Anne was off the hook—for a while at least. I reached for some fries and tried to ignore my slowly mounting guilt. There I was, hoping that a young rape victim was being interrogated. It was official: I was a terrible person. Licking the salt off my fingers, I eased past the cop cars and looked for a parking spot. I was likelier to find nutritional value in my Happy Meal, but you can't blame a girl for trying.

Two spandexed girls jogged past, laughing. One of them had Greek symbols on the back of her jacket. Varenka lived only a few blocks away from sorority row. Her building was one of those hideous boxy types where the second-story windows peek out of the oversize roof. The rest of the neighborhood was much like my own, mostly run-down Victorians that had been carved up into apartments. A canopy of bare tree branches gave the street an air of dignity. God save us from neighborhoods where the people are taller than the trees.

Vince patted his mustache with a napkin. "I wonder how long our boys in blue will be."

My dashboard clock said 12:10. I pulled into a driveway, turned around, and headed back toward the cop cars. I'm not the world's most patient person, but waiting for them to leave would be easy compared to interviewing Varenka. "I've never interviewed a rape victim before," I said.

"You've interviewed lots of other people in painful situations," Vince said, "and what's more, you've observed Detective Olivia Benson on *Law & Order: Special Victims Unit*."

"My attention hasn't been very focused on her interviewing techniques." It felt good to smile. My grin broadened when not one but two vehicles pulled out, leaving me a wide opening behind the cop cars.

"You should park farther away so they don't see you or your car when they leave," Vince said. "You don't need them recalling your recent TV appearance or linking you with Varenka."

But it was too late. A pizza-delivery car pulled within inches of my back bumper as three stern-faced cops exited Varenka's building. One of them—a woman who looked no older than a college student—had gold sweats draped over her arm. They were wrapped in plastic, ready for the crime lab. The oldest cop, a bowlegged man, scanned the street.

"Quick!" Vince reached into his coat pocket and extracted a pair of rhinestone-studded sunglasses. "Put these on."

I hesitated for a moment, but when the cop strode toward us, I traded my own glasses for Vince's fashion mistake. The world blurred, and I accidentally knocked an open ketchup packet onto my thigh.

The cop rapped on my window.

My heart raced as I opened it. "Oh, Officer," I giggled, hoping to seem like a dumb blond despite my red hair. "I hope I'm not blocking you, but something awful just happened. I was driving along, and I spilled on my brand-new jeans."

I imagined him glancing at my thigh, dubious.

"I know they don't look new." I grabbed a napkin and attacked the offending condiment. "That's the point. They're vintage. That's why there's this super-cute rip on the left knee."

I'd literally left him speechless.

"There's also a really darling rip down by her calf," Vince added.

I went for my door as if I were eager to show him my leg in its entirety.

"Stay in your car," he said. "There's no parking this side of the street today. You need to move on."

"Sure thing, Officer, right after I find my stain remover." I batted my eyes. Sometimes my theater major is worth every penny of the interest I pay on my student loans.

✧✧✧

The stairs inside Varenka's apartment building were covered with mud-stained carpet, and the dingy walls were riddled with scrape marks. On the top floor, someone was cooking with curry. I took a deep whiff and started checking the numbers against the addresses Shelly had given me. Jessie lived in apartment 12 by herself. Win and Kate were in 5, and Varenka and Shelly, across the hall in 6. I paused outside Varenka's door, hoping for a snatch of conversation, but all I heard was some music from down the hall. I knocked.

Kate Timmens filled the doorway, remaining in position as I identified myself. "C-can I s-see some i-i-i …" Her face twisted and puckered as she tried to work through her stutter.

"One ID," I said, "coming right up." I riffled through my backpack for my wallet and held it open for her.

I wondered how many reporters she had turned away. She looked back and forth between my face and my driver's license as if she were watching a tennis volley. Finally, I passed muster, and she stepped aside. Varenka was balled up on the couch, her blond hair streaming over her legs, her shoulders heaving.

"Sh-she's upset because the p-po-lee-leess …"

"I saw them," I said.

"They had a search warrant." Varenka raised her head slightly. Her eyes couldn't have been any redder or puffier.

"Did they find anything besides the sweats?" I asked.

Varenka dropped her head back to her knees.

Kate stood frozen near a table with slanted chrome legs. None of the chairs around it matched, and one of them looked like it belonged on a patio. Women's athletic scholarships did not preclude thrift shopping.

I repeated my question, but neither girl stirred.

"It must have been quite a shock to have your apartment searched," I said.

"Th-they found p-pepper spray in Varenka's p-purse."

It was hardly surprising that a rape victim would carry a means of self-defense. "Did they take it with them?" I asked.

Kate nodded, her long arms hanging helplessly at her sides.

The cops probably had some way of telling whether the spray had been used. Not that it would prove anything if it had, but it would be a strong piece of circumstantial evidence against Varenka.

She eased her head off her knees. "I wanted to try it out," she said quietly. "To make sure I could really use it."

"M-most of us tried ours," Kate added. "N-not just V-Varenka. We had the w-wind behind us, j-just like Anne said."

There was Anne again, right in the thick of things, but at least it hadn't been her place the cops had searched. "Do you think you could try to answer a few more of my questions?" I asked. "Both of you?"

"You c-can talk to me first," Kate said. "M-my apartment is across the hall." She walked over to Varenka and rubbed her back. "She needs time to re-re-recover."

✧ ✧ ✧

Kate and Win's apartment had the same thrift-shop ambience as their teammates', minus the patio furniture. The far wall was covered with a beautiful quilt that spelled out IOWA HAWKEYES in a wild variety of fabrics.

"W-Win's mom m-made that for me." Kate was supposed to use it as a bedspread, but she thought it was too pretty for sleeping. She was sorry about her stutter. It wasn't usually this bad. Stress made it worse. Did I want some tea?

She didn't wait for an answer, but retreated to the kitchen alcove. I stepped away from it to give her some space and studied the knickknacks atop a bookshelf. There were some miniature pumpkins and squash and some cutesy mice figurines. Next to the kitsch was a photo: Kate and Win, a huge Christmas tree, and a couple that had to be Kate's parents. They both had her moosey build, and her father had Kate's shy smile. She stepped into the living room and asked if I wanted cream or sugar. On or off the court, she wore her hair in a stubby ponytail at the nape of her neck.

"Does your roommate always go home with you for the holidays?" I asked.

"She stays with Shelly's family s-sometimes." Kate was back in the kitchen opening and closing cupboards.

"What about Varenka's?" I called.

A drawer squeaked, but then there was silence. Something about my question had made Kate pause.

"Does Win spend much time with Varenka's family?" I asked.

No answer. No kitchen sounds.

"You and Varenka and Shelly are all from the same town, right?"

"Y-yeah." The teakettle went off for a couple seconds before

Kate removed it from the heat. "Varenka's p-parents work a lot of overtime at the p-packing plant." Kate appeared with two steaming mugs. She handed me one and gestured for me to have a seat on the couch. "M-my mom and dad are teachers."

I perched on the edge and clasped my tea with both hands. Letting it warm my fingers, I inhaled the sweet scent of orange spice.

"S-so is Shelly's dad. He w-was our coach."

Poor Shelly, six foot five inches and the coach's daughter.

Kate set her drink on top of a *Sports Illustrated* and told me that Shelly's mom was a radio announcer just like me—except she never investigated any crimes. Kate would be happy to answer every single one of my questions so that I wouldn't have to upset Varenka any more than she already was.

"You and she were at her parents' house the night DeVoster was killed?"

Kate explained that Varenka was upset with her play in the opening game and needed to get out of town. They borrowed Shelly's car and left after practice on Friday—just for the night.

"Who did you see while you were there—besides Varenka's parents?"

"N-no-nobody."

I sipped my tea. "You didn't go out that evening? Meet up with some old high school friends?"

Kate said that Varenka just wanted a quiet night with her parents. They had the night off, so all four of them played cards.

"What about when you arrived or you left? Maybe somebody saw you then—somebody walking their dog or running an errand."

She didn't remember anyone, and her stutter was getting worse.

"Don't worry," I said. "A neighbor will have seen Shelly's car parked in the drive." Kate gazed at the tea she hadn't touched, probably thinking the same thing I was: No neighbor would have seen the car in the middle of the night. Varenka's alibi was far from solid.

"What about your own parents?" I asked. "Did they see Varenka?"

They hadn't even seen Kate. They were out of town, so she'd spent the night at Varenka's where, after cards, Varenka and her parents and she had stayed up past 3 A.M. watching old movies—really old ones, the black-and-white kind. Varenka couldn't sleep, but Kate had crashed during the trial scene in *To Kill a Mockingbird.* Had I ever seen that? she asked.

Kate's teammates had described her as quiet, but the girl was chatting up a storm with me. She was hiding something—I was sure of it—but if I asked her any more alibi-related questions, I'd lose any trust she'd placed in me. "What do you think about Tyler Bennet as a suspect?"

Kate looked at me as if I'd just suggested we go drown a bag of kittens. "He's one of the n-nicest guys on the team."

"I heard he used to date Varenka."

"They b-broke up last s-spring."

"Who broke it off?"

Kate wasn't sure, but there were no hard feelings. They hadn't gone out that long—maybe, like, a year. Varenka and Tyler stayed friends—talking all the time, shooting hoops.

When I asked if they still hung out after the rape, Kate sidestepped my question. Tyler would never hurt anybody, not even an animal like DeVoster. She'd never seen Tyler lose his temper—on or off the court. He took all the younger players under his wing, and he volunteered at some place like Big Brothers/Big Sisters, where he taught little kids to deal with their anger. Did that sound like a murderer?

I admitted that it didn't. "Did any of your teammates seem especially upset about the rape?"

She reached for her tea and peered into her cup. "W-we were all st-stunned."

"Any differences of opinion?"

Kate shook her head and set her tea back on the coffee table. Her hand was shaking.

"I heard that some of the girls weren't exactly sure that Varenka had been raped."

Kate glared at her trembling hand. "J-Jessie t-tell you that?"

I hoped I'd finally hear why the freshman was on the outs with her teammates.

"She's a t-trouble causer." Kate reached behind her head and tightened her ponytail. "And she has a b-bad t-temper—a really bad temper." For the first time in our conversation, Kate held my gaze.

"Are you suggesting that she killed DeVoster?"

"She said he deserved to d-die."

"None of your other teammates said something like that?"

"N-not like Jessie. Y-you should have heard her."

I could hardly base a murder investigation on tone of voice. "Is she close to Varenka?"

Kate folded her arms over her chest and stood. "Varenka is n-nice to everyone. She's the only one who can stand J-Jessie and her big head."

I rose from the couch, stymied. None of Kate's teammates liked Jessie, but Kate was the only player eager to cast suspicion on the freshman.

ELEVEN

It took some convincing to get Kate to leave me alone with Varenka, but there I was, sitting in a rocking chair across from Varenka's bed. She was huddled under a massive pink comforter, her hands clutching the top of it to her chin, her knees drawn to her chest. Her eyes were swollen with crying, and her breath was uneven as if she'd just gotten herself under control. The last thing she needed was some stranger asking her questions. And let's be frank, I was less than thrilled about delving into her pain. If only I could find a gentle way to start the conversation, maybe things would go smoothly—no crying on her part, no guilt on mine.

Her room smelled strongly of vanilla. Except for the standard beige carpet, it was femme all the way. The furniture was white with bubble gum-pink trim, and the lampshades and curtains were a deeper pink, the same as her comforter. There was even a rosy ruffle around the top of a cage that presumably housed some small animal.

"My hamster," she said. "Hello Kitty."

I was surprised she'd been watching me. "My housemate has guinea pigs," I said.

"Hello Kitty sleeps during the day." Varenka looked like she needed to do the same. Gray-purple bags weighed down her bloodshot eyes.

"I'm not sure when pigs sleep." How long could we chitchat about rodents? I took a deep breath, trying to think of a question that wouldn't upset her too much. "It seems like your teammates have really rallied around you."

She smiled faintly and released her hold on the comforter.

"But there seems to be some tension between Jessie and the rest of your team."

She hung her head, and her face vanished behind her hair.

"You know anything about that?" I asked.

"She's cocky. That's all."

"I heard that she might have killed DeVoster."

Varenka's head shot up. "Who said that?"

I didn't want to create more tension between the players, but if I wanted Varenka's honesty, I needed to return the favor. "Kate."

"This is all my fault," she whispered.

"Do *you* think Jessie did it?" I asked.

"Of course not!" She hugged her comforter as if it were a life preserver.

"Why do you think Kate said that?"

Her face puckered, and she pulled the comforter over her mouth.

"I'm sorry to upset you. I know you've been through a lot."

There was a rustle from the hamster cage, and Varenka glanced toward it.

"For what it's worth, I don't think Jessie did it either." I had no logical reason for dismissing the freshman as a suspect. I simply liked her.

"Who do you think did?" Varenka asked.

I'd hoped to be the one asking the questions, but at least we were talking about the murder.

"Tell me." She straightened herself against the headboard—a glimpse of her on-court relentlessness.

I decided to start with the person who would be least likely to upset her. "Lexie Roth."

"Right." Varenka laughed bitterly. "And lose the fun of writing about him every single day?"

"You don't think too highly of her," I said.

"I just want this to be over." Varenka rested her head on her knees again.

I gazed at the jumble on her vanity. A jewelry tree rose out of a clump of photos. There was Varenka with Kate and Shelly back in high school, sweaty and grinning, holding aloft a state championship trophy. Another picture was a wacky group shot featuring many of her current teammates and a bunch of cheerleaders. Varenka was cross-legged on the floor. Making bunny ears behind her head was a petite chocolate-colored girl with pom-poms atop her braids. In the largest photo, a young pigtailed Varenka stood shyly between her mom and dad. They were in front of a colorful building with onion-shaped domes somewhere in Russia, perhaps when Varenka had first met her adoptive parents. Next to the photos was a framed collage that featured WNBA players—Svetlana Abrosimova, Elena Baronova, Camilla Vodichkova, Maria Stepanova. All Russian.

"Kate made that for me last year," Varenka said. "We've been friends ever since I first came to America. Because of her stutter, she spoke slowly, and I could understand her." Varenka smiled slightly, revealing overcrowded teeth.

When she wasn't ravaged by grief, she was someone you'd look at twice. The first time you'd be wowed by her beauty, and the second time, you'd notice a few so-called flaws—crooked teeth, droopy eyelids—but they'd only make her all the more interesting.

"Kate is protective of you," I said.

Varenka's smile faded. "We look out for each other—all of us, the whole team."

Despite her depression, Varenka could muster plenty of energy on behalf of people she cared about. I hoped she didn't still care about her ex-boyfriend. "What about Tyler Bennet?" I said. "Does he look out for you?"

"Ty would never hurt anybody," she said firmly. Her hamster emerged from beneath a pile of shavings, nose twitching furiously.

"Why did you two split?"

"We didn't have much in common."

An unlikely dilemma, given that they were both Division I basketball players.

She must have read my skepticism. "We were never super-serious."

"But you remained friends?"

She nodded.

"Did you talk to him about the rape?" There, I'd said the *r* word and she hadn't fallen apart. She simply stared at her hamster running in his wheel. It was in major need of WD-40. "How did Tyler feel about DeVoster before the rape?"

"Tyler's not a violent guy."

Our conversation was going nowhere fast—just like the squeaky hamster. "I understand your hesitance to point fingers, but someone killed DeVoster. You've got to help me if I'm going to help you."

"Maybe his death had nothing to do with me."

"Why else might someone have killed him?"

"How should I know?" she snapped. "He and I didn't have a deep soulful talk before he raped me." Her hamster kept squeaking. Varenka threw her comforter to the foot of the bed and struggled with the locks on his cage. When she finally rattled it open, she nudged the fur ball off his wheel and removed the offending machinery. Then she collapsed on the far side of the bed. The back of her pajama top said GIRLS RULE.

I thought about giving her a break and leaving, but then I'd have to bother her some other time. "Just a couple more questions," I said gently.

She idly spun the wheel with her long fingers.

"No one wants to talk about recruiting or the freshmen who left," I said.

The hamster stuffed his pouches with food from his bowl and disappeared back into his nest. Varenka turned farther from me, and her shoulders started heaving. "It's all my fault," she said. "We can't recruit anybody because of me."

I grabbed a box of Kleenex from her vanity and moved to her side of the bed.

"I've wrecked our season. I've wrecked the whole program."

"Shh. That's not true."

"I was so stupid."

"Listen," I said. "It's not your fault. You were the victim."

She gave me an odd look—was it puzzlement?—and kept crying. I wanted to put my arm around her, but I was afraid that might upset her more.

"I drank too much." She wiped her eyes with the back of her hand.

"It still wasn't your fault."

"That's what everyone says, but they don't mean it. I've let everybody down."

I couldn't think of anything to say, so I handed her another tissue.

"They treat me different now—like there's something wrong with me." She was sobbing so hard, she could hardly catch her breath. "Kate treats me like a baby, not wanting me to read the papers or watch the news, and Shelly, she spends all her time with Roshaun now. Her dad won't look at me."

"Shelly's dad?" I asked.

"My coach," she moaned. "From high school. I've disappointed him too." She sniffled, and I handed her the entire box of Kleenex.

I wished that Kate would come to check on her or that the phone would ring. Anything to distract Varenka from her grief. "It's nice that you were able to go home after the last game." Yes, I was fishing for more scoop on her alibi, but the only way I could bring Varenka any lasting comfort was to clear her of DeVoster's death. "I bet they were glad to see you."

She nodded and blew her nose.

"Did you see any friends when you were home?"

"I didn't feel like it." She took a deep breath. "Me and Kate played cards with my mom and dad, but I didn't think I could sleep so we started watching old movies—the black-and-white kind. Me and my parents stayed up past three watching *To Kill a Mockingbird,* but Kate crashed during the trial scene."

That was the longest answer I'd gotten from Varenka, and it followed Kate's description of the evening almost word for word.

TWELVE

When Vince and I exited Interstate 380 for Varenka's hometown, he was on his cell with Richard, mostly listening, leaving me to ponder at field after field of withered cornstalks. A cop car zoomed past, and I eased my foot off the gas. I wondered why Neale hadn't called me yet, but before my imagination launched into warp speed, Vince hung up.

"Richard has been busy surfing," he declared, clasping his hands in his lap.

This was hardly news. If ever there was a geek, it was Richard.

"He's been checking some Hawkeye message boards. They're all abuzz with theories about DeVoster's demise. There's already a huge thread about a feminist conspiracy."

I tightened my grip on the steering wheel. "Has anybody mentioned Anne?"

His silence gave me the answer.

"What are they saying?"

Vince gazed out his window. We passed a dilapidated barn on his side of the road.

"Tell me," I said.

"They're talking about how they'd like to teach her a lesson."

My adrenaline surged. "I've got to warn her."

"Richard already did," Vince said soothingly. "The reason he called was to make sure you knew that your name had also come up."

"My name!" I sputtered. "I don't even fit the witness's description. I'm too short."

"They're saying you helped Anne plan the murder."

"How would these-these—," I grasped for words, "libelous cretins even know we're friends?"

Vince sighed. "You were on TV with her," he said. "You were at the protest together."

My heater made a clicking sound as if something were lodged inside it. I turned it off and pulled my coat collar up around my neck. "Who else is in on this feminist conspiracy?"

"Who isn't?" Vince said. "Orchid and Lexie, all the female athletic teams at the university, Hillary Clinton."

"Was the basketball team singled out?"

Vince nodded, and we drove in silence for a few moments. A huge flock of birds churned tornado-like from a stand of trees before dispersing into the sky. A sign said INDEPENDENCE, 5 MILES. "You don't need to do this, Mar-Bar."

I was touched by Vince's concern, but if I acknowledged it, I'd also have to acknowledge my own fear. And the exhaustion and pain that had burrowed deep inside me after I talked with Varenka.

✧✧✧

I pulled to the curb in front of the house next to Varenka's parents' and left the engine running. "Please," I said to Vince, "go get us some coffee. I'll be fine."

My wanna-be bodyguard said nothing.

I returned the favor and headed toward the Whites' bungalow. Its fake wooden siding matched the gray sky. Purple and orange mums lined the foundation, and there were pots of them on the front porch too. Inside, a dog barked and clawed at the door.

I turned toward my car and motioned Vince away.

He simply stared back.

When I knocked, the dog went ballistic, evoking a flood of "hushes" and "shushes."

Paulette White cracked open the door, and I was amazed to see how closely she resembled her adopted daughter. Paulette was a washed-out version of Varenka, her long golden hair losing its battle with white and gray, her eyes the color of faded denim.

I introduced myself and told her that Coach Stokes had asked me to try to find DeVoster's killer. "So Varenka and the team can have closure," I said. I wasn't sure whether she knew that her daughter was a top suspect, and I didn't want to be the one to deliver the news.

The dog barked louder as Paulette opened the door and let me in.

"Sit, Henry," she said.

Henry was a medium-size mutt with a missing back leg. He let out one more yip and obliged.

"Don't mind him," she said. "He just wants out. We were about to go running, weren't we, boy?"

I couldn't help but gaze at where his fourth leg should be.

"He gets on just fine with three, don't you Henry?" She patted his head with cigarette-stained fingers. Then she straightened up to her full height—over a foot taller than me. Her mouth had the wrinkles of a heavy smoker. "The coaches have done a good job protecting Varenka's privacy," she said.

"I'll do the same. You have my word."

"I've been so afraid for her. Some people think DeVoster can do no wrong. And now that he's dead ..."

Henry started inching to his feet, and she snapped her fingers at him. He lowered his rear and started whining.

"I want to help your daughter," I said. "I won't repeat a word of our conversation to anyone but the coaches."

She grabbed a leash that hung on a coat tree, and Henry perked right up. He clawed at the screen door and started yipping again.

"I understand that Varenka was dating Tyler Bennet."

Paulette attached the leash to Henry's collar, but he kept barking.

"Damn it, woman. Can't you keep him quiet?" Mr. White swayed into the room, a bottle of Bud dangling from one hand, his face red. "First, the cops barge in here and call me a liar, and then this fool dog barks his head off."

Henry upped the volume.

Paulette scowled, her mouth a piece of dried fruit. "Hush, Zach. I've got company."

He swung his gaze around the room and blinked at me. "What's she want?"

"Nothing. She's just a friend."

Zach took a swig. "Never saw her before."

"I'm a friend of Varenka's," I said.

He raised his bottle above his head. "Then let's drink to the death of Davey DeVoster. May he rot in hell." Zach stumbled. "Get the girl a drink, Paulette. The sonofabitch is dead."

"She's trying to find out who did it," Paulette hissed.

Zach gave me the once over and chuckled. Then he drained his bottle. "Lemme know when you find out, so I can throw the guy a party."

"No one's throwing any parties," Paulette said. "Let's get you settled back in front of the TV." She handed me Henry's leash. "Scratch his head. It keeps him calm."

Zach demanded another drink as she led him toward the back of the house. It was probably a common trek. The tall, muscular man had no beer gut to speak of, but veins had etched curving roads across his nose and cheeks.

Henry butted his nose against my hand, so I scratched him. His panting muffled faint protests from Zach, but after all the commotion, the room seemed strangely quiet. In a far corner, next to an impressive cluster of ferns and houseplants, the pendulum of a grandfather clock ticked hypnotically. It was easily the most expensive item in the room. A scarred wooden coffee table was adorned with a huge vase of mums. The sofa doubled as a cat's scratching post, and one of its corners rested on a woodblock that had been finished to match the other legs. "Your kind of sofa, Henry." The dog wagged his tail against a nearly empty laundry basket and an easy chair where Paulette had been folding clothes. At the top of her pile was something black and gold. Zach was still grumbling at Paulette, so I stood and unfolded it.

A sweatshirt with a glow-in-the-dark Nike basketball on the front and the back. Below, still on the pile, were the matching pants.

I slung my backpack off my shoulder and pulled out the papers that accounted for all the sweats. Not surprisingly,

Varenka had given her extra pair to her parents.

And one of them had already worn the new gear.

"I'm really sorry you had to see that," Paulette said.

I prayed she wouldn't notice that I'd been messing with her laundry, but I needn't have feared. She was focused on her dog.

"Come here, Henry." She patted her knees. "You want some fresh air, don't you?" Paulette no doubt wanted some time away from her drunken hubby, so I braced myself for the cold.

The moment we were outside, I saw that my car was gone, and I wondered what Vince was up to. No way had he simply gone on a caffeine run.

Henry strained at his leash, ready to sprint down the driveway, but Paulette asked me to hold him while she lit up. The three-legged beast was freakishly strong. Fortunately for my shoulder sockets, he decided to take care of some business. When I surrendered his leash to Paulette, she let Henry pull one arm taut as she took a long drag. Her smoke hovered, white, just like my breath. I sank my hands deep in my pockets, resolved to let her break the silence. A car roared by, and we passed two houses with Hawkeye flags flying next to their front doors.

"Twenty-four years," Paulette said. "That's how long Zach kept away from the bottle. When we found out we couldn't have children of our own, I begged him to quit so we could adopt." She smiled sadly. "And he did. He joined AA and never touched the stuff again until ..." Her voice caught. "He loves Varenka so much. You should have seen him the day we left Russia with her."

The wind whipped my hair across my face and made my eyes water. What an irony that Varenka had been drunk the night DeVoster raped her.

"He didn't have a drinking problem when I married him,"

Paulette said. "He had a full ride to UNI. A basketball scholarship. But his freshman year, his parents were killed in a car accident. Zach was driving. It wasn't his fault, but he was driving. One of his arms got messed up real bad, so he couldn't play for a while. All he did was drink." She stopped and yanked on Henry's leash. "He's not usually as bad as he was today." She leaned over and ground out her cigarette on the sidewalk. Then she handed Henry's leash to me and dropped the butt in a neighbor's trash can. It clanged hollowly when she replaced its lid.

"Does Varenka know about his drinking?"

"The police got him all riled up today," Paulette said, "and they haven't treated our Varenka well to begin with."

"Does she know about her dad?"

Paulette looked past me, toward the other side of the street.

"Does she?"

"I hope not." Paulette reached for Henry's leash. "She's just like him. Always blaming herself for things that aren't her fault."

"So he was sober the last time Varenka and Kate visited you?"

"Oh, sure," she said quickly. "We played spades and stayed up until some ungodly hour—past three—watching Gregory Peck in *To Kill a Mockingbird.*"

This was the third time I'd heard the *Mockingbird* story, and it had never rung more false. "It must have been hard for your husband not to drink right after learning about DeVoster's red shirt and watching Varenka struggle in her first game."

Paulette pulled her pack of cigarettes out of her pocket and shoved them back in. Across the street, a huge black dog barked, pacing along a chain-link fence.

"Zach couldn't bear it if Varenka lost respect for him." Paulette held the leash with both hands as Henry leaned toward his nemesis. "He always wanted to be her hero. It was hard for him to see how much she admired Coach Swanson."

I decided to let Paulette lead the conversation away from the night of the murder. "Her high school coach?" I prompted.

"He was good to her, took her under his wing. Of course, she was the best player he'd ever had."

My car crept past with Vince at the wheel.

"One night Zach overheard Varenka telling me that Coach Swanson was like a father to her." Paulette shook her head. "Cut him to the quick. He couldn't compete—not with someone who made twice as much money and who was shaping Varenka into a star. That's how he saw it anyway."

Vince turned right at the next corner. I had a sinking feeling that it wouldn't be long before he'd drive by again.

"James Swanson was real torn up about what happened to Varenka."

Paulette's comment was a transparent attempt to cast suspicion outside her own family. "Shelly's father," I said. "A tall man?"

"Got at least three inches on Zach." Paulette's voice brightened.

"He was torn up?"

"We don't run in the same circles, but I heard he was furious. And I believe it. Right after it happened, he wrote a letter to the editor, saying that all decent folk should stay away from the men's games at Iowa."

A measured, intelligent response, I thought. Far from murderous.

"I wish he hadn't done that," Paulette said. "Lots of fools wrote back. There were dozens of letters defending DeVoster—innocent until proven guilty and crap like that. It just made things harder."

It probably also made Zach feel all the more inadequate.

Varenka's former coach had made a public stand against DeVoster while he—her own father—had done nothing.

Henry sniffed the base of a tree, and Paulette once again turned his leash over to me. The wind made it difficult for her to light up, but she finally managed, her reddened hand cupped at her mouth.

Vince drove by again, slower this time. What was he thinking? That Paulette White and her three-legged mongrel would attack me in broad daylight? More likely, he'd give her an excuse to end our conversation. I needed to finish my questions before she noticed him. "How serious was Tyler Bennet about your daughter?"

Paulette slipped her lighter into her pocket and resumed control of Henry. "You're wasting your time if you think he killed DeVoster. You couldn't ask for a nicer boy. Gentle and considerate. Too gentle for his own good, maybe." Paulette exhaled a cloud of smoke. "Varenka told me that the reason he didn't get more playing time was because he wasn't aggressive enough. She said he 'lacked the killer instinct.' Those were her exact words."

I figured a guy could develop such an instinct pretty quickly if a woman he loved were raped. "So what happened with them?"

"I wish I knew." She flicked her cigarette, and the ashes whirled away, never making it to the ground.

"Did he talk much about DeVoster or his teammates?"

"Not really," she said. "He was closest with one of the managers. Roshaun."

Vince again, slower still.

Paulette frowned at my Omni. "That poor man must need directions," she said.

As she headed to the curb, I gave Vince my laser glare.

Lucky for him, Paulette quickly returned after giving him directions to Casey's (which, in her opinion, had the best coffee in town), and I made one last attempt to learn more about Varenka's former boyfriend. "Some of your daughter's teammates believe that Tyler Bennet killed DeVoster."

"I'm sure they do." Her voice had a nasty edge.

"What do you mean?"

Paulette paused and took another puff on her cigarette. "You know some of them are lesbians. Like it or not—that's just how it is."

I was lost, and it must have shown.

"Come on," she said, "you know how they feel about men."

I clenched my teeth and forced a smile.

We passed two completely dead lawns. Henry barked at a cat that vanished behind a row of mums, and Paulette nodded toward the flowers. "Zach planted ours," she said. "He knows they're my favorite. He's a good man." She inhaled the last drag of her cigarette. "You won't tell anyone about today, will you?"

THIRTEEN

After Vince and I discovered that Kate's and Shelly's parents weren't home, he wanted to go back to Iowa City (so he could spend the rest of Sunday with Richard), but I wanted to interview Roshaun's parents in Waterloo. I was sure they could tell me something about their son's friend, the too-good-to-be-true Tyler Bennet. Unimpressed with my plan, Vince kept grumbling about how the Andersons might not even be home, and he refused to be mollified even after I told him he could come in with me. He abandoned his grousing only when a rock DJ mentioned Marilyn MonHerky.

"Un-be-lieve-able," the DJ boomed. "One family drove ninety miles just to get their photo taken with the now-infamous bird."

"What a boon to Iowa's sagging tourism industry," Vince commented.

"It's good clean family fun—a crime-scene photo op," the DJ guffawed.

Sometimes I envied people who worked at stations where they got to make jokes out of everything. Alternative radio can be a little short on humor.

"Speaking of raptors," the DJ said, "let's listen to some Eagles."

As they strummed through "Hotel California," we drove through Waterloo trying to find the Andersons' street. We passed a chiropractic clinic, a violin shop, a nail boutique, and a falafel joint. Finally, we took a left at a bus stop and about a mile later found ourselves in a neighborhood not unlike our own. Victorians had been converted into apartments, cars lined both sides of the narrow street, and house numbers were harder to find than parking spots. We pulled over, only partially blocking a driveway, and walked toward the Andersons' three houses down.

Francine Anderson had her son's wiry build and ready grin, but she was lighter skinned, a cinnamon to his molasses. She also moved and spoke much more quickly. I'd barely begun to explain our presence when she threw the door open wide. "Come in, come in before you heat the whole neighborhood. Mind the pumpkins." She darted in between the orange construction-paper orbs that covered her living room carpet. Some had peace signs drawn with wide, wobbly magic markers. "My little ones did those," she said over her shoulder. "We're decorating the center for Thanksgiving."

"The center?" I asked.

"The youth center," she said, "where Regan and I work." Before Vince or I could comment, we were in her kitchen, and she was peering into her oven. Francine was the kind of woman who expected you to keep up. "Regan is my husband," she explained. "He's *not*—absolutely *not*—named after the so-called president." She headed toward a table strewn with papers and removed what looked like a papier-mâché turkey from one of the chairs. "Magnificent, isn't he? Roshaun and Shelly made him for me when they were here. He'll be our Thanksgiving piñata. The littlest Rivera boy asked why we had one at Christmas but not Thanksgiving, and I told him there was no reason in the world why we shouldn't have a piñata for every holiday." Francine lifted the bird and studied its underside. Her hair was closely cropped with just a trace of white near her temples. "They did a good job," she declared. "It'll take some mighty whacking to get the best of this guy." She set the doomed creature on the kitchen counter. "I'm heating up a frozen pizza," she said. "Care to join me?" She pulled some plates from a cupboard. "I know it's too early for dinner, but believe it or not, I forgot to eat lunch."

I caught Vince's eye and smiled. At least I'd have a chance to question Francine once she started eating.

"Frozen stuff is all I've had time for," she said. "I didn't even cook for my baby the last time he was here."

"When was that?" I knew full well, of course, but I wanted to hear Shelly's alibi for myself.

"Friday night. With his girlfriend I didn't even have any milk on hand. He and Shelly got woke up in the middle of the night when Ida called, and all they had to drink was—"

"Who's Ida?" Vince asked.

"Regan's great-aunt. She's got Alzheimer's, but no one will admit it, least of all her, so Regan goes to Chicago and tends to her when we have only two and a half days to finish a grant application for the center."

Vince nodded politely, no doubt sorry he'd asked.

"Regan is with Ida, and I'm sitting here in the middle of the night working on the grant when Ida calls—"

"What time was that?"

"Around two. Just like I told the police. I remember saying, 'Ida, it's nearly two in the morning,' but she doesn't care. She says there's a strange man in her house. I try to tell her it's Regan, her softhearted nephew, my husband who's too kind for his own good." Francine shook her head and pulled the pizza out of the oven. "Point being, Ida's call woke up Roshaun and Shelly, so they came into the kitchen and started eating Oreos." She turned to Vince and me, her eyebrows raised.

It was our turn to comment, but I was at a loss.

"There was no milk!" she said. "No milk at all for my sweet son and his girl. That's how busy I've been." She sliced through the pizza as if it were to blame. "Grab a plate," she ordered, dashing to the table.

As we seated ourselves, she noted that she'd never forget what she was doing when she first heard about DeVoster's death.

I gamely took the bait, hoping to steer the conversation toward some of my suspects.

"I was at my kitchen window," Francine said, "watching Roshaun and Shelly play H-O-R-S-E in the driveway. They'd gone and got some milk, bless them, and some bacon. I was about to fry it up and make pancakes when the phone rang. I thought it would be Regan or Ida, but it was . . ." She curled the tip of her tongue around the bottom of her front teeth, thinking. "One of the women players. With a stutter."

"Kate Timmens," I said.

"That's right." Francine served the pizza. "When I finally figured out what she was saying, I thought, *Oh, my Lord, it's really going to hit the fan now.* A rich white athlete—the cops are going to be falling all over themselves trying to find out who did it. Reminds me of the time my cousin Fred—"

"What exactly did she say?" I asked.

"She just wanted to make sure Shelly knew there was going to be a team meeting that afternoon."

"Did she use the word *murder*?" Vince asked.

"Goodness, I don't remember," she said. "I was worried about how my baby and his girl would take the news. Roshaun wasn't real close to Dave, but still ... I couldn't bring myself to tell them right away. They looked so happy out there in the driveway.—I just wanted to give them a moment's peace."

Francine's voice caught. She seemed to need a moment herself, so I studied the objects on the buffet behind her: a delicate blue glass vase with dried flowers, a wooden giraffe that looked like an African carving, and several photos. Most of them featured her and a man I assumed was Regan with kids from the center, but there was a childhood one of Roshaun, both his tiny arms wrapped around a basketball. There was also his senior portrait and next to it, the senior portrait of a girl with the same smile and lots of braids. She seemed vaguely familiar. "Your daughter?" I nodded toward the photo.

"My youngest." Francine struggled with her crust, and as her fork finally sliced through it, a piece shot across her plate. She prodded it back to the center, her mouth tight.

It must have been hard, having to tell her son about DeVoster. "How did Roshaun and Shelly react after you told them?"

"They stood there a few moments. In shock, poor things. Then they started packing their bags. Wouldn't even eat breakfast."

"What did they say about it?"

"Shelly is always real formal and reserved around me. You know, wanting to make a good impression."

"Maybe you overheard her and Roshaun talking?"

As Francine shook her head again and gazed at her plate,

Vince pointed at his watch.

But I wasn't ready to give up yet. "Do you know anything about DeVoster's relationship with his teammates?"

"He made sure they all knew it was his team." She frowned. "Why? Do you think one of them did it?"

Finally, the opening I needed. "I wonder about Tyler Bennet." I paused for a moment, careful not to reveal Varenka's secret. "He played behind DeVoster. Maybe he wanted to keep DeVoster from returning to the team."

"But we keep hearing what a nice guy he is," Vince said.

"Oh, he is," Francine gushed, "he is."

"He's friends with Roshaun?" I prompted.

She nodded. "Red—that's what they call him—he's come home with Roshaun a few times. Gave me quite a surprise the last time. He'd turned vegetarian. A big Iowa boy like him—imagine! But he told me my ham *looked* delicious. That's how polite he is. Helped me with the dishes after every single meal."

"Have you seen him since the rape?"

"No." Francine sighed. "His last visit was about six months ago. I keep telling Roshaun to bring him, but he says Red isn't tight with anybody on the team anymore." If Bennet were a nice guy, it wasn't surprising that he'd shun DeVoster, but his distance from the entire team seemed odd.

"He gets along with everybody just fine and mentors the younger players," Francine said. "Just likes to keep to himself, I guess."

He didn't sound like a killer—not like Lexie Roth with her penchant for stalking and castration. Or Zach White with his empty bottle and full heart. I didn't want Varenka's father to be guilty. It would be too large a burden for a young woman to bear—knowing that her once sweet and gentle father had killed on her behalf.

"Who else do you suspect?" Francine asked.

"We just started our investigation," Vince said.

I was glad I could trust him to keep quiet about things that mattered. I knew he'd never tell anybody about Varenka or her father's drinking.

"Do you have any thoughts about who did it?" I asked Francine.

"No, not really." She tapped her tongue against the bottom of her front teeth.

"You must have some," Vince said.

"This is third hand," she warned. "something Roshaun told me, not exactly in confidence but—"

"We're not interested in spreading rumors," I assured her.

"When Roshaun was bringing Coach Bly a tape, he overheard a phone conversation. Coach was saying stuff like 'My player did nothing wrong' and 'Your daughter crawled into his bed drunk.'" Francine met my eyes. "Right before hanging up, Coach said, 'You threaten my player one more time, and you'll be sorry.'"

FOURTEEN

Tyler Bennet's reputation for politeness had been greatly exaggerated. He stood in front of his door, propping it open an inch or two, denying me even a glimpse of his apartment. And this was after I explained that I was trying to help Varenka.

"We're not together anymore." He interlaced his fingers and cracked his knuckles. The slow staccato mingled with the potpourri of sounds from other apartments: a blaring TV, a thumping bass, and a whining food processor. "It's loud out here," I said.

He simply shrugged.

The top of my head came to the middle of his chest. I craned my neck slightly and asked him for a drink of water, hoping he'd invite me inside. But he shut the door in my face and retreated—presumably to get my beverage.

Vince peeked his head around the corner of the stairwell. "Are you crazy?" he hissed. "Why would you want to go in there?"

I shushed him, and as Bennet's door creaked open, Vince ducked back into the stairwell.

Bennet resumed his position in front of the door, and I tried not to be distracted by the white particles swirling around in the water he'd given me: Iowa City tap water. I'd have to buck up and take a swig if I wanted to ask him any questions. "What happened with you and Varenka?" I asked. "Why'd you break up?"

"None of your business." His freckled face reddened.

"Did she ever say anything to you about the night DeVoster—"

"That's between me and her." He reached for the doorknob.

"I'm sorry," I said quickly. "Of course, you want to protect her privacy—especially with all the media hoopla. In fact, some people see Lexie Roth as a strong suspect."

"The reporter?" he said. "How come?"

His question surprised me. "Because of all she's written. The stalking. The protest."

He cracked his knuckles again, and I pretended to sip my water.

"Did DeVoster ever say anything about her?" I asked.

"I pretty much ignored him when we weren't on the court." Tyler pressed his lips together.

"Maybe you overheard something."

"Nope." Down the hall, a phone rang. Tyler scowled at me and rubbed a hand over his receding hairline.

"He never complained about any of Varenka's teammates bothering him? Or maybe Varenka's parents?"

Tyler dropped his eyes.

"Did you know them very well?"

"Nah." His gaze remained on his humongous sweat sock-clad feet.

"Varenka's dad is really torn up—"

"Of course he is," Tyler snapped. "I gotta go." He extended his hand for the glass.

"Where were you the night DeVoster died?" I asked.

"This is harassment," he growled. "If you don't leave, I'm calling the police."

A bluff if ever there was one. "You must be worried that they suspect you. You dated Varenka. And you wouldn't have gotten much playing time your senior year with DeVoster back on the court."

Tyler clenched the doorknob. His other hand was a tight fist.

Vince appeared in the doorway to the stairwell, holding a Domino's Pizza box aloft, then lowering it dramatically in front of us. "Excuse me," he said. "Did you order a pizza?"

Could Vince's timing be worse? I'd nearly goaded Bennet into blurting important information, but now his anger was diffused. He simply asked "the pizza deliveryman" what apartment he wanted. Vince gave Bennet's number, Bennet insisted that he hadn't ordered a large Italian sausage pizza, and Vince asked if he could use Bennet's phone to check the order.

That, I had to admit, was an impressive bit of trickery.

But Bennet simply returned with a cell and folded his arms across his chest.

While Vince faked a call to Domino's ("Girlfriend, this pizza isn't getting any warmer"), I studied Bennet. He was thin compared to other ballplayers, but far from scrawny. His shoulders nearly spanned the doorway. A vein that pulsed atop one of his hands was nearly as wide as my pinkie. I imagined his huge palms pushing against DeVoster, his long finger gripping DeVoster's neck.

By the time Vince hung up, I was almost grateful for his interruption.

"A thousand apologies," he said, giving the phone back to Bennet. "I'm so sorry I interrupted your tête-à-tête."

"She was just leaving." Bennet's voice was firm.

When Vince and I reached my car, he took a deep bow and tossed me the empty pizza box.

FIFTEEN

So much for Sunday as a day of rest. After questioning an entire women's basketball team, three parents, and (as Vince put it) "a terse and inhospitable male athlete," I psyched myself up for yet another interview, this one without my thespian bodyguard. Vince was enjoying the evening with Richard while I drove through the dark streets of Atalissa, Iowa—lonely and exhausted—seeking Gina Hofmeyer, a freshman who'd quit the team.

The streetlights in her neighborhood revealed a few harvest displays—bales of hay decked with gourds, pumpkins, and an occasional cutesy scarecrow. A corner yard featured a huge bare tree with a yellow ribbon tied around it. When I finally spotted her house number, I saw a basketball hoop at the far edge of their driveway. Gina would have had to shoot the three-pointer from the middle of her front yard. If I were lucky, she'd be lolling on the couch in front of ESPN, or at the very least, one of her parents would be home, drowsing after a cholesterol-laden Sunday dinner.

The woman who answered the door was anything but drowsy. She held a huge bowl of batter in one arm, and she was beating it furiously with the other. "Come on in. Pardon me if I keep at this batter. If you let up for a sec, your cake is never quite as fluffy—know what I mean?"

I nodded as if I did and glanced around. The tiny living room was crammed with overstuffed furniture. A throw on the largest sofa said, "God bless this home and all who enter it." Above the door to the kitchen was a wooden plaque that at first seemed like nothing more than a geometric design, but, if you squinted at it, you'd see that it said JESUS. I'm never good with optical illusions, but I'm great with context clues. "Sorry to bother you," I said. "I'm looking for Gina Hofmeyer."

The woman's arm jiggled as she stirred her batter. "I'm Gina's mom." She looked up. "Becky."

Becky was about my age with bright blue eyes and lipstick that hovered between pink and white. I'd never thought of myself as old enough to be the mother of a college student. Becky must have gotten pregnant right out of high school. "And you are?" She finally let the spoon rest against the side of the bowl.

"Mara Gilgannon," I said. "I'm a journalist."

Becky narrowed her eyes at me and wrapped both arms protectively around her bowl, so I decided to embellish the truth. "I work for the publications department of the Fellowship of Christian Athletes," I said. "We're doing a feature on athletes who've left Division I schools."

Becky smiled. "Gina's not here, so I'll have to do. Put your coat on a chair and come on back to the kitchen." She nodded toward a photo on a shelf to my left. "That's Gina her senior year."

Gina was wearing her basketball uniform and enough jewelry to make a drag queen jealous—bangles, a heart-shaped locket, and sparkly earrings. She was also in full makeup, and her hair, which hung loose, had spent significant time with a curling iron. It was a photo that flaunted the athlete's femininity. Orchid would have declared it oppressive and sexist. Me, I just found it tacky. But I was glad I'd femmed it up, opting for the form-fitting sweater that Neale had given me last Christmas instead of a baggy sweatshirt. I'd also unbraided my hair and added tortoiseshell combs. I must have looked trustworthy if nothing else, because there I was in Becky Hofmeyer's kitchen, watching her maneuver a pan of brownies from the oven.

A wave of chocolate heat enveloped me, and I closed my eyes against her rooster-patterned wallpaper.

"You can try one when they cool," she said. "I'm making lots of extra because our church is having a big bake sale next weekend. A little fellow the next town over needs a bone marrow transplant, and his folks don't have insurance."

They'd have to sell barrels of cookies to cover even one night in the hospital. "Do you know how I can reach Gina?"

"She's not going to want to talk to you."

My first obstacle. I waited, hoping for an explanation.

"That whole experience really hurt her bad." Becky began pouring her batter into a Bundt pan.

"I'm sorry to hear it."

"My little girl would just as soon forget all about it."

The stream of batter grew thinner, and my curiosity grew sharper. Still, I managed to hold my tongue.

"I keep telling her she's got nothing to be ashamed of. She

did the right thing."

"Surely she doesn't blame herself for the rape."

Becky shook her head and attacked her bowl with a rubber scraper. "Dave DeVoster would never do a thing like that."

"Mom, can I go over to Ryan's?" A spindly prepubescent boy stood in the doorway of the kitchen. He had a concave chest and a purplish birthmark the shape of South America on his left cheek. When Becky gave her permission, he grinned and dashed away.

"That's my youngest, Roger." She waited until he was out of earshot. "He had no confidence until we sent him to basketball camp." Becky reopened her oven and in went the cake. "Dave took Roger under his wing and showed him how to win and how to be a man."

My stomach turned queasy.

"I tell you, that camp was worth every penny we scrimped and saved." Becky started rinsing her mixing bowl, and steam rose from the sink. "Roger will never be a basketball star like his sister, but he holds his head up high now, thanks to Dave. Poor thing, he was beside himself when he found out about the murder."

I struggled to find words. "DeVoster's death has caused a lot of pain."

"At least he's in a better place now."

If you believe God lets rapists into heaven. That's what I wanted to say, but I kept mum. I could learn a lot from this woman even if we didn't agree on DeVoster. "I bet you're glad that Gina's not at Iowa anymore."

"I told her—" Becky stopped herself and started filling one side of her sink with water. A few bubbles drifted into the air.

"Whatever you tell me, I promise I won't identify your daughter or the Hawkeyes in my story."

"I'm no gossip," Becky insisted.

"Of course not."

"The Bible says, 'The tongue is a restless evil, full of deadly poison.'"

Personally, I thought tongues were lots of fun, but I nodded somberly as she dropped a set of measuring spoons into the growing mound of suds.

"You won't bother my daughter if I talk to you?"

"I won't even try to contact her." I would have crossed my heart, but Becky might take it as some sort of sacrilege.

She turned off the faucet and faced me. "I never wanted Gina to go to Iowa in the first place, but Roger—my husband, not my son—he said there were lots of small-town girls on the team and she'd do just fine. I said she'd be happier at Iowa State with that sweet male coach—Catholic, but a decent man."

I forced myself to smile and nod.

Becky leaned against the kitchen counter and sighed.

"So Gina wasn't happy at Iowa."

"At first she was. All she could talk about was playing with Win Ramsey—that was a big reason she wanted to go there. And she was handling the practices just fine—she's a tough girl, my Gina. She liked Iowa City in the summer, and she was even looking forward to classes."

I leaned against the opposite counter.

"I tell you, I was happy to be wrong, and I was saying as much to Roger when Gina called." Becky grabbed a dish towel and started twisting it in her hands. "I never heard her so upset. There'd been some funny business."

I wondered if that was a euphemism for the rape.

"Between two of the girls." Becky widened her eyes. "The freshman from Des Moines, Jessica March, she—what would you call it? Seduced, that's the word—she seduced that Russian player." Becky shivered in distaste. "The one that was supposedly raped: Varenka White. Can you believe it?"

What I couldn't believe was my own stupidity. I hadn't considered the possibility that Varenka might be involved with one of her teammates. But obviously, Bridget hadn't either. "How did Gina find out about it?"

"She and two other freshmen—not Jessica—were out driving around and they decided to see if Varenka and Win wanted to play pickup at a park nearby. They were about to knock on Varenka's door when they heard her crying. You know how thin apartment walls are. She was saying how dirty she felt—how guilty—how she'd never get to be a teacher and coach. Some nonsense about how she couldn't help herself, that she might be in love." Becky pursed her lips in distaste.

"Do they know who Varenka was talking to?"

"They didn't say. They'd already heard way more than they wanted to."

Poor Varenka, believing that her life was over because she liked girls.

"That's not the worst of it." Becky set her dish towel on the counter and edged toward me.

I couldn't imagine what—in her mind—could be worse than lesbianism.

"You're not going to believe this." Becky's compunctions about gossiping were long gone. "When Gina and her friends told a coach, *they* got in trouble."

Please, I thought, don't let it be Bridget. "Coach Carol?" I asked.

"That's who they should have talked to," Becky said. "She's a mother—a grandmother. She would have taken proper action. But they couldn't reach her. So they took who they could get:

Bridget Stokes."

I tried to make sense of what I'd just learned. Bridget had intentionally misled me into thinking that the three freshmen left because of the rape. I wasn't sure whether I was angrier at her for deceiving me or at myself for trusting her. Or for assuming that she trusted me. One lesbian to another. Surely, Bridget could have counted on me to be discreet about her players' sexuality.

"She said they needed to be more open-minded." Becky darted to the sink and plunged her hands into the soapy water. "She said she respects her players' privacy unless their off-court activities compromise their game. What about compromising their morals?" Becky scrubbed a measuring cup. "She's supposed to be a role model. I trusted her with my daughter." Becky tossed the cup in the drainer and tackled a plate. "I bet you good money that Bridget Stokes is a lesbian. I bet you all those assistants are—every last one of them. None of them are married, and they're not bad-looking women. Who knows? Maybe more of the other players are that way too."

I bit my lip. My interviews with the players had been a big waste of time—because Bridget had lied to me.

"Are you okay?" Becky asked. "I know it's a horrible story. Let me make you some coffee, and we can try those brownies."

I shook my head.

"Don't you worry about Gina. She transferred to a nice small school: a Christian one. No official athletic scholarship, but they got her plenty of money just the same." Becky winked at me. "Yep, my girl is just fine now."

If only I could say the same for myself.

SIXTEEN

I twisted the key in my ignition, yanked my gearshift into reverse, and grabbed my cell phone. Halfway out of the Hofmeyers' driveway, I almost collided with an SUV. I honked my horn even though I was clearly in the wrong and whipped into the street. Punching in Bridget's number, I readied myself to pummel her with questions: Was she happy now that she'd made a fool out of me and wasted my time? Was she glad she'd made it nearly impossible for me to help her team? Was she crazy? As I listened to her phone ring, more questions surfaced: Did she really believe that any of her players' parents thought she was straight? Why had she sought me out only to play games with the truth? What the fuck had she been thinking?

My only answer came from Bridget's machine. Fine. I'd deal with her in person soon enough.

I turned onto Highway 6 toward Iowa City and phoned Vince, undaunted when I got yet another recording. He never answers the phone unless it's "worth his while." I knew exactly what would get him to pick up. I told him that I was going to stop by El Ranchero on my way home and that I wondered if he wanted anything.

"Mar-Bar! I'd like a beef burrito with an extra side of rice, pretty please."

"How about a world where people answer the phone and tell the truth?" I snapped.

"This is exactly why I screen—so I don't have to listen to such rage. What has you all aflutter?"

Right in the middle of my tale about Becky Hofmeyer, I heard the theme song to *Xena*. "Are you watching TV?"

"No, my sweet, that's Richard. He has to do something to occupy himself while I listen to your rantings."

"While you order a burrito."

"I'm a man of many needs." I pictured him winking at Richard, and I hurried through the rest of my story.

"Female athletes engaged in Sapphic activity," Vince said. "I'm shocked. Truly shocked."

"I'm looking for some sympathy here."

"You must feel perfectly sullied—having to make nice with that homophobic homemaker."

"Those feelings are buried way, way deep beneath my anger at Bridget."

"Because she lied to you."

"Of course."

"And because you have feelings for her."

"Oh, please," I said. "Get back to Richard."

"Ah," Vince murmured. "You don't deny it. You deem the dyke delicious despite her duplicity."

Richard was probably rolling his eyes if he was paying any attention at all to Vince's strained alliteration.

"At least now," Vince said, "you have one less thing on your to-do list."

As I pondered his comment, I listened to Xena's battle cries and flexed my fingers to keep them warm.

"You're not going to keep playing detective after she lied to you?"

"I'm not doing it for her," I said. "I want to make sure that Anne isn't falsely accused."

No response from Vince.

"I also care about some of the players."

"Let's hope that one of them didn't go all Aileen Wuornos."

"You always know how to cheer a girl up, Vince."

Our call-waiting clicked.

"Get it," I said. "It might be Neale." My heart racing, I drove all the way through West Liberty before Vince got back on.

"Sorry, Mar-Bar. It was the cellist from Richard's quartet."

I sighed.

"Patience," Vince said. "She'll call."

I took a curve and nearly rear-ended a slow-moving pickup. With my luck, I'd be stuck behind it all the way to Bridget's.

✧ ✧ ✧

Her condo was on the far west side of Iowa City, where many of the "single-family dwellings" were larger than entire apartment buildings. When Bridget opened her door, she gave me a tentative smile and said my name—part greeting, part question. I gazed at her fleece shirt and plaid flannel pants. She was all comfy for the evening, but she wasn't going to stay that way unless she had a really good explanation. "Why didn't you tell me the real reason the freshmen left?"

Bridget's mouth dropped open and she froze.

"I thought you wanted me to help you." The wind tore through my hair, and the cold burned my cheeks.

"Come inside." Bridget turned her back to me and padded up the stairs.

I followed her until we stood in her living room, inches apart. "What'd you do?" I asked. "Tell all your players to keep quiet about Varenka and Jessie? Did you really think I wouldn't find out?"

Bridget turned from me again. She collapsed onto her sofa and buried her head in her hands.

"Did you?" I stood over her, my arms folded across my chest.

"You don't understand—"

"You've got *that* right. Why ask me to find the truth and then lie to me?"

The phone bleated, and Bridget practically threw herself at it. Receiver in hand, she strode toward the picture window, her back to me again. She had solid hips, solid legs—a swagger. Ready to conquer the world even in her pj's. Surrounding her were a few orchids and mounds of plants I didn't recognize—all high maintenance, no doubt. Regular plants wouldn't be enough of a challenge.

Whoever was on the phone wasn't giving Bridget a chance to speak. As she made a couple noncommittal murmurs, I checked out her living room: a vaulted ceiling, a state-of-the-art TV, an aquarium, a leather couch with matching chairs. I drifted toward her kitchen. Granite countertops—assistant basketball coaches make a lot more money than lowly DJs. Still, except for the fish tank and the plants, the place had an empty feel.

"I had no idea." Bridget paced back and forth. "Don't worry," she said. "It won't happen again." She glared at me. "I need to go," she said. "I've got company."

Whoever was on the other end gave her another earful; she then made some soothing noises and finally hung up.

"What were you doing harassing the Whites?" Before I could answer, she barreled on. "You asked Varenka's mother for an alibi?" Bridget's face was flushed with indignation. "Did you stop for one minute to think how Varenka would feel if she knew her parents were being treated like murder suspects?" She threw her arms in the air. "I can't believe this."

Call me crazy, but I don't like being chewed out as if I'm some bungling ref. "Did you know that her father's been drinking more than a frat house?" I asked. "He was three seconds from passing out as he gloated over DeVoster's death."

"Do you expect him to be sorry?"

"The cops have questioned him," I said. "Did Mrs. White tell you that?"

Bridget retreated to the couch and started jiggling her leg. She gazed at her phone as if she'd never seen it before.

"He made threatening calls to DeVoster."

"He has an alibi."

"Yeah," I said. "Real iron-clad."

The room was silent except for the aquarium's burble.

"You still haven't answered my question," I said. "Why did you lie to me?"

Her eyes met mine but darted away. "I wanted to protect my players' privacy."

I turned to go.

"They have so little," she said, "especially since the rape."

I headed toward the stairs, and she followed me.

"I didn't keep anything important from you."

I whirled around. "You don't know that," I said. "Jessie had a fine motive for killing DeVoster."

"You don't really suspect her."

I started down the stairs. The sooner I was out of there, the better.

"Wait," she said. "Let me explain. Please."

I wanted to make a dramatic exit, but I also wanted the truth.

"Take your coat off," she said. "I'll get you a drink."

"Just tell me why you lied."

As she headed toward the couch, I wanted to tell her how insulted I felt—how betrayed—but instead I simply trailed after her.

"At least sit down."

I perched on the arm of an easy chair.

"You have no idea what it's like," Bridget said, "the negative recruiting. All another coach has to do is suggest that their team is 'more like a family' than ours, and it's over. Once you get a reputation as a gay program—"

"What does this have to do with me?" I asked. "I'm not going to sabotage you."

Bridget leaned forward and rested her elbows on her knees. "You're not going to tell your housemate or your girlfriend?"

I thought about my phone call to Vince, but that was because I was angry about Bridget's deception. "They're not going to hurt your team."

She shook her head in disgust. "You think they won't tell anybody?"

"Not homophobes." How had she put *me* on the defensive? I was the one who'd been wronged. "You should have told me about it," I said. "I wouldn't have told anyone if you'd asked me not to."

"What happened between Jessie and Varenka has nothing to do with the murder, trust me."

Trust me. That was rich. She sure didn't trust me. And she had no interest in learning the truth about DeVoster's death—not if it would hurt her team's reputation or—God forbid—crack open a closet or two. I was outta there.

SEVENTEEN

I'm no fan of the alarm clock, but it sure beats dog breath. Labrys licked my cheek as Vince said, "Mar-Bar, wake up. There's something you've got to see." He flipped on my lamp.

I tried to push Labrys away, but it was a no-go. Through one barely opened eye, I could see that it was still dark. Vince rustled a newspaper with no consideration for my delicate pre-coffee condition. "Go away," I mumbled.

Vince wrenched the dog off my bed and sat on it himself.

"Both of you." I shut my eyes tight. Since when did he get up earlier than me?

"It's Anne," he said.

I jolted to attention and pushed myself into a sitting position.

"She's in the paper," he said. "It's not good."

I fumbled on my nightstand for my glasses. Vince handed them to me along with the paper. "HE HAD IT COMING," SAYS

DIRECTOR OF WOMEN'S CENTER. That was the headline. I gazed at Vince in disbelief. Anne was usually so careful when she talked to reporters.

"Read the whole thing," he urged.

Then I noticed the byline: "Lexie Roth." Causing trouble for Anne again. "The murder of controversial Hawkeye basketball star Dave DeVoster has prompted mixed reactions in Iowa City." The opening was objective enough. I skimmed until I found Anne's name: "Director of the Women's Center, Anne Golding, has a different take." I went back to the previous paragraph.

"Head basketball coach Eldon Bly said, 'Words can't express how much D (DeVoster) will be missed both on and off the court. His last months were difficult, but he handled them with dignity. I'm proud to have coached him.'"

Can we say bullshit? I returned to Anne and her "different take."

"During the memorial service for DeVoster this evening, Golding has organized an alternative memorial for rape victims. 'If DeVoster was a rapist,' said Golding, 'then he had it coming. It's a perfect example of karma.' "

"The headline is so misleading," I said. "And it's so damning. Is she trying to get Anne thrown in jail?" I shook with rage.

Vince grabbed a comforter from the foot of my bed and draped it around my shoulders.

I pulled it tightly around me. "That so-called reporter is going to be sorry she ever took pen to paper when I'm through with her. She's probably the one who killed DeVoster, and now she's trying to frame Anne because of the whole Women's Center thing." I tossed the paper on my quilt. "Can we say sensationalism? She doesn't deserve to write for a high school paper."

Vince sighed. "Will you stop hyperventilating if I bring you some coffee?"

"I'm not hyperventilating."

He hefted himself off my bed, adjusted the tie on his robe, and exited with Labrys in tow.

My clock said 6:35. Anne was probably up. If she'd already seen the paper, she'd need some moral support. I leaned toward the phone on my nightstand. I'd tell her not to worry, that no one could seriously suspect a pacifist like her of killing someone, that I'd figure out who really did it.

As I began to punch in her number, the phone's beeps pierced the morning quiet. I stopped mid-number. I wanted to help Anne, but I also wanted to show Bridget that I wouldn't be used. If I kept investigating, I'd need her cooperation—I'd have to make nice with Bridget despite her cavalier attitude toward the lies she'd fed me. I gazed out my window. Behind bare tree branches, the sky was a fiery pink scar. What choice did I have? Anne was in trouble.

I finished punching in her number, and as Orchid's voice came on the machine, Vince and Labrys returned with the coffee.

"Hi, Anne," I said. "I just wanted to let you know that I saw the paper and I'm thinking of you." I glanced at Vince. It's hard to leave a message with someone watching. "I hope you're okay. Call me."

Vince held a mug toward me, but I didn't take it. "What if she's already in jail?" I said.

"She's probably still sleeping." He sat on the edge of my bed.

I could feel the coffee's steam on my face. I took a mug and inhaled. Hazelnut. I took a sip.

"That's right," Vince said. "Drink it down. It'll restore your sanity."

"She could be in jail as we speak," I insisted.

"Or she could be doing yoga with the ringer off." Vince waved one hand, fanning the steam that rose from his own mug.

"Anne never turns the ringer off. Only when—" I stopped. If there was one picture I didn't want in my mind, it was Orchid making love with Anne. "Maybe they're fighting," I said. "I bet Orchid took umbrage with Anne's 'if.' 'How could you say *if* he raped her. Of course he raped her.' I can just hear her."

Vince sipped his coffee and rested it in his lap. "Are you going to ride in and save the day?"

I was about to call him on his sarcasm when the doorbell rang.

Labrys started barking, and Vince and I both raised our eyebrows. None of our friends would dream of disturbing us so early on a Monday morning. I twisted around and looked out my front window.

Bridget.

"She can't stay away from you." Vince hovered next to me.

"Do the words *personal space* mean nothing to you?"

Vince jerked back. "Come, Labrys," he said. "We're not wanted here."

"I'm sorry," I said. "Bridget and I had a fight last night."

"Already?"

"About DeVoster."

Bridget rang again.

"Shall I get it while you freshen up?"

"I don't need to freshen up, and I don't want to see her."

"Wrong on both counts," Vince said.

✧ ✧ ✧

When Bridget heard me on the stairs, she eased out of Vince's chair, still in her coat. Her eyes were a listless blue-gray, like the circles beneath them.

For a moment, I felt sorry for her.

"About last night," she said, "you were right. I should have been straight with you."

An odd choice of words, but it was nice to have an apology.

"I made a bad call," she said.

In sashayed Vince with two cups of coffee, his silk robe trailing behind him. He handed them over and batted his eyes.

"Thanks," I said. "See you later."

After he slunk away, Bridget and I stood in silence. She hadn't driven across town at the crack of dawn simply to apologize. "What's up?"

Bridget held her coffee with both hands. "When Varenka sees the paper this morning, she'll blame herself for Anne's troubles."

I wondered if Bridget knew Anne was my ex.

"I know you're angry," Bridget said, "but think of Varenka. She's just a kid. Scared and confused."

I thought of the young woman huddling on her bed, sobbing as I asked her questions, and I pushed the image out of my mind. "Yeah," I said. "All those lies are hard to keep track of."

Bridget set her mug on the coffee table. "I know what you think," she said. "That I'm some closet case, and I'm teaching my lesbian players to be ashamed of themselves. But that's not it. I'm teaching them how to survive, how to stay in the game." Her voice caught, and she unsnapped her coat. "I'm proud of who I am, but I'm also proud of our program. And you need to remember, it's not my team. It's Carol's ..." she trailed off.

I wondered if this was Bridget's first time being in charge of the team—alone, without the woman who'd coached her when she was a player. That would be hard enough during a normal season.

"Please," Bridget said. "Give me another chance. No secrets this time."

Maybe she was willing to be honest with me. But was she ready for me to be honest with her? There was only one way to find out. "Finding DeVoster's killer might not make things better for Varenka," I said, "especially if it was someone she loves."

Bridget pressed her lips together as a city bus droned down the street. Maybe, at this very moment, Anne was opening her front door and reaching for the paper. If I kept helping Bridget, I was bound to learn something that would help Anne. I extended my hand for Bridget's coat and invited her into the kitchen.

✧ ✧ ✧

There's something intimate about making breakfast for someone, and as I handed the box of Rice Krispies to Bridget, some of my anger melted away. But my wariness remained firmly intact. Whatever she told me, you could bet I'd double-check it. "The team's hostility toward Jessie," I said. "That's all because of her lesbianism?"

Bridget shook her head and doused her cereal with milk. "It's how she handles it. She refuses to put the team first. During one of our camps, she was holding hands with a soccer player right in front of the campers—middle-school girls."

God forbid they should see a happy and uninhibited lesbian. That's what I wanted to say. But I slurped my Rice Krispies instead.

"She goes to all the GLBTU meetings," Bridget said, "even after I asked one of our veteran players—another lesbian—to talk with her about keeping a low profile."

I wondered who this player was, but it didn't seem relevant

to the DeVoster situation. And Bridget wouldn't respond well to idle curiosity about her players.

"And sleeping with Varenka—" Bridget snapped her toast in half. "She should have known better. She didn't think about how it would affect them on the court—how it would hurt our team's chemistry."

I could see Bridget's point, but I admired Jessie's refusal to sacrifice her freedom and her identity.

"Jessie's a heck of a player, but I'm sorry we signed her. Carol said she'd be trouble, but I talked her into it ..." Bridget trailed off and stirred her cereal.

She was so concerned about Varenka's self-blame and so absolutely unaware of her own. I resisted the impulse to reach across the table and quiet her hands. "How serious are they?"

"I don't know." Her spoon clanked against the edge of her bowl. "But Jessie's no murderer."

Upstairs, the shower groaned as Vince commenced his morning ablutions. "I'm going to need to talk with Varenka again."

Bridget frowned and rested her spoon on her plate.

"What was your impression of her relationship with Tyler Bennet?" I asked.

"I can't imagine that he killed DeVoster. You couldn't ask for a nicer—"

Before Bridget could continue singing Tyler's praises, the phone rang. I thought about letting the machine pick up, but then I remembered that I'd asked Anne to call. On the next ring, I spotted the receiver on the counter next to Vince's Betty Boop cookie jar and several telltale crumbs. He'd moved in with me after Anne moved out, and he still hadn't gotten the hang of cleaning up after himself.

I answered in the middle of the next ring.

"Mara, I'm so glad I caught you."

It was Neale. She never called me in the morning.

"Listen, I'm sorry about how we left things."

We? She was the one who left. And if she was so sorry, why hadn't she called yesterday?

"I wished I'd stayed," she said. "I miss you."

That was more like it. "Me too." I imagined that she'd already gone running, that she was sitting flush-faced in front of a huge glass of orange juice. "How was the party?"

"A schmooze-fest."

In other words, exactly what she wanted. I wondered if she was really sorry about her early departure.

"How was your time with the team?" Neale asked. "Did you learn anything interesting?"

I watched Bridget eat her cereal, and I thought about my promise to keep mum about her players. "Not really."

"Oh, come on, you must have discovered something."

"Sweetheart," I said, "I'm really glad you called, but this isn't the best time."

Silence from her end.

I'd never put her off before. Even though I hadn't meant to, I'd given Neale a taste of her own medicine, and to be perfectly honest, I'd enjoyed it.

Before either of us could speak, Bridget's cell phone began playing "Funky Town," and she answered it. She's used to making herself heard over the roar of Carver-Hawkeye Arena, so let's just say that *sotto voce* is not her strong suit.

"Who's that?" Neale asked.

I saw no reason to lie, so I told her that Bridget and I were working on the case.

"The case?" Neale's voice was equal parts ice and sarcasm. "I won't keep you then. Call me when you can spare the time."

She hung up on me just as Bridget finished with her caller.

I was feeling less than grateful to Alexander Graham Bell.

"Coach's brother died. She'll be back for Thursday's game."

Death, anguish, love. If it wasn't basketball, it was an interruption.

As Bridget gazed at her half-eaten breakfast, Vince's hair dryer started its steady whine. Our privacy would soon be over. "Have you been in close communication with Varenka's parents?"

Bridget picked up her dishes and took them to the sink. "Do me a favor. Please. When you talk to Varenka, don't mention her father's drinking—or your visit. Try not to upset her any more than she already is."

The phone rang again.

"I should go." Bridget headed toward the living room.

"Wait." I headed after her. "The machine can get it. I need to ask you something else—just one more thing."

We eyed each other as the phone kept ringing. Her long-sleeve T-shirt bore a faded picture of Rosie the Riveter. I imagined Bridget flexing her arm like Rosie.

Vince's hair dryer fell silent, and the phone stopped ringing. I tried to focus on my question. "About Kate," I said. "Why would she—"

"Mara! Are you there?" Anne's voice squawked on the machine.

Why hadn't I noticed that the volume was cranked?

"I'd rather say this in person, but ..."

Right then, I should have flung myself at the machine and turned the volume down. But I froze.

"I totally appreciate your concern," Anne said. "It's really sweet, but maybe you could phone just a little less often? Sometimes your calls create bad energy between Orchid and me. I hope you understand. And I'm fine—really. Don't worry."

A dial tone filled the room. Could I be more completely humiliated? I couldn't bring myself to look at Bridget, but I saw her feet move toward mine, and, for a moment, I felt her hand on my shoulder.

"You wanted to ask me something?" she said quietly.

I wanted to hug her for ignoring what just happened.

"Something about Kate?" she prompted.

But she hadn't really ignored it. That touch on my shoulder. What was that about?

"You said 'why would she?' and then the phone—"

"She practically accused Jessie of killing DeVoster," I blurted. But I regretted my words as soon as they were out. Bridget glowered and scratched her eyebrow. I could see her giving Kate a lecture on the importance of presenting a unified front as the poor girl struggled to complete yet another pushup.

Bridget sighed. "I'm guessing that Kate has it really bad for Varenka."

I thought about Kate's eagerness to protect her teammate.

"I don't know it for a fact," Bridget said.

But if it were true, her team had more lesbian drama than *The L Word*. And I had more angles to investigate: Kate and Varenka. Perhaps DeVoster's murder had been a team effort.

EIGHTEEN

As I entered the radio station, I said a silent prayer of thanks that Orchid's door was shut. Our offices are right across from each other in a narrow hallway, and when both our doors are open, I hear every stroke on her keyboard, every squeak of her chair, every tirade against patriarchy and hegemony. Anne says our office arrangement is an example of bad feng shui. Talk about an understatement.

I shut my door, determined to avoid Orchid before I went on the air. I had no idea whether she knew about the message Anne had left for me, and I didn't want to find out. No, scratch that. I wanted to know whether Orchid insisted that Anne make the call, but Orchid wasn't about to share that with me. Mostly, I just didn't want to see her. I was already running behind, thanks to a fruitless detour past Varenka's apartment building. After two canvasses—first Vince's and now mine—we had yet to talk with the other tenants.

Peeling off my coat, I slumped into my chair and clicked on my e-mail. My screen saver, a caricature of the immortal Shakespeare, gave way to a page full of new messages—half of them marked "urgent." Right. I opened the day's program guide and realized that after the noon news, I was scheduled to interview the coordinator of Herky on Parade. I imagined asking fun-filled questions like, "How will your project continue 'taking the Hawkeye spirit to the streets' now that one of the birds has been used as a murder weapon?"

Exhaust spewed out of the parking garage across the street. I didn't exactly have a room with a view. Nor did I have much space on my desk. On one side of my computer was a stack of evaluation forms for the interns I supervise and, on the other side, a tower of books I needed to read—or at least skim—before interviewing their authors. There's only one thing you can do when you're woefully crunched for time. Get thee to a coffeemaker. Even if it means risking a run-in with your boss.

✧ ✧ ✧

My mug was half full when Orchid stormed into the mail room, her peace sign earrings belying her true nature. She dropped her hemp book bag to the floor and yanked at the envelopes in her mailbox. "We need to talk."

I braced myself for a rant about boundaries, about my need to let go of Anne and move on. Psychobabble 101. I was utterly unprepared for what came out of her mouth.

"Eldon Bly called." She squeezed an armload of mail against her ample chest. "He said you've been harassing his players."

"I've only talked to one—"

"He said that the university shouldn't support such insensitive journalism." She dropped her mail on the counter next to Mr. Coffee. "Do you have any idea how tight our budget is? We can't afford an enemy like him." She started tossing unopened envelopes into the recycle bin.

Tyler Bennet must have complained about me to his coach. Either he was a big baby, or I was close to the truth.

Orchid tore up a flier before it too went into the bin. She was furious with me—there was no doubt about that—but she was probably even angrier at Bly. She'd never let some good old boy tell her how to run her station. At least I hoped not. Otherwise, she could use Bly's wrath as an excuse to fire me without being the heavy, without upsetting Anne.

"Bridget asked me to see what I could find out about the murder," I said. "She's afraid that some of her players might be suspects."

Orchid ripped open a package and pulled out a tiny cassette tape. Barely looking at it, she shoved it in her bag. For once, she had nothing to say about the women's basketball team.

"Since some of the evidence points toward Anne, I thought I could help—"

"Anne doesn't need you," she snapped.

Behind her, wide-eyed, stood Roshaun and Shelly. So much for teaching our interns about office courtesy and professional demeanor.

For a moment, we all stood silent, Shelly with her head peeking around the doorframe and Roshaun just inside the doorway.

"Sorry to interrupt," he said, "but I was wondering if you all had decided about the Waddell Jones interview. I need his book if I'm going to do it."

Orchid and I exchanged tense glances.

"You know," Roshaun said, "the one about Kobe Bryant."

"We decided that it wouldn't be right for you because of the parallels—"

Orchid cut me off. "I've changed my mind." She shot me a nasty smile. "The interview is yours. I believe Mara has the book in her office."

Could we say passive-aggressive? And selfish? She was letting Roshaun put himself in a bad situation just to piss me off. But I kept my anger under wraps. Once Orchid returned to her lair, I'd send Roshaun on his merry way, book in tow, and I'd grill Shelly about the Sapphic proclivities of the Hawkeye hoopsters. This round of sleuthing would be on the station's dime.

✧ ✧ ✧

"I can only stay a minute," Shelly said. "I've got class." She stood next to my file cabinet, a backpack slung over one shoulder, a bottle of apple juice in one hand and a violin case in the other. Her Doc Martens added a couple inches to her height, and her down coat enhanced her broad shoulders. I felt positively Lilliputian.

But what I lacked in size I made up for in persistence. "Coach Stokes told me about Varenka and Jessie."

"What about them?"

"Their relationship," I said, "the real reason the freshmen left."

Shelly bit her lip and narrowed her eyes at me. She glanced toward my closed door. In the hall, someone groused about the copy machine.

"If you think I'm trying to trick you, call your coach." I nodded at the phone on the corner of my desk.

Shelly set her drink and violin on the floor. Before she punched in the number, she turned her back on me. I hoped that Bridget would urge her to tell the truth and that she'd actually do so before Orchid caught me in the act of sleuthing. When Shelly hung up, I invited her to sit, but she remained standing.

"It's not like they're in love," she said.

Was this simply the interpretation of a straight girl who didn't want to believe that her roomie was a lesbian?

"It was a one-time thing. Varenka got all freaked out, so Jessie moved on."

I thought about the shortstop Orchid had mentioned. "To a softball player?"

Shelly shrugged.

"I heard Kate has a crush on Varenka."

Shelly's glare was on high beam. "Who told you that?"

Now it was my turn to shrug.

"Kate is a really gentle person. She'd never kill any—"

"Is she in love with Varenka?"

"How should I know?" Shelly leaned over to pick up her stuff.

"I guess I'll ask them."

"No!" She returned to her full height empty-handed. "Varenka's in enough pain already. It would hurt her to know that Kate is pining away after her."

"She doesn't already know?"

Shelly sighed. "She can be kind of naïve."

So can we all, I thought, when it comes to love.

"If you ask her about it," Shelly said, "you'll just make their friendship weird. Varenka needs all the friends she can get right now."

"How long has Kate been pining?"

"She didn't attack DeVoster."

Since high school, I guessed. Poor unlovely, stuttering Kate longing for beautiful Varenka.

Shelly shifted her backpack to her other shoulder and stared at the postcards on my bulletin board. They were from all over the world, part of my late Aunt Glad's collection. "What's the longest you've ever been in another country?" Shelley asked.

Talk about changing the subject. I decided to play along. Maybe she'd let her guard down and answer some more of my questions. "A couple months," I said. "I was an exchange student in Tokyo one summer."

"Were you homesick?"

"A little," I said, "but it was worth it."

Shelly picked up her stuff. "Just to set the record straight," she said, "Kate's crush, or whatever, is history. After Win had a talk with her, Kate got things under control." I started to ask a question, but Shelly cut me off. "Before the rape, Kate stopped coming by our apartment so often. She'd gotten rid of her crush."

I'd learned the hard way that crushes don't go away that easily. But I thought about Win with her mother and sister back in West Virginia—Win who desperately wanted to go pro, Win with no alibi. Maybe she'd figured her team would have a better chance at a championship with DeVoster out of the picture.

NINETEEN

The sleet didn't keep anybody away from DeVoster's memorial service Monday night. Vince and I dodged several clumps of humanity—sorority girls, older couples, entire families—as we made our way through the parking lot toward Carver-Hawkeye Arena. Vince stepped in a puddle and moaned. "My one night without rehearsal, and you drag me into this inclemency. Lexie and her entourage might not even show."

"They'll be here," I said. "People like her are as predictable as hummus at a lesbian potluck."

"Why not grill her tomorrow?" Vince tightened the belt on his trench coat. "Indoors. Somewhere nice and toasty."

"Don't you get it?" I said. "The police have taken Anne in for questioning. She's an official suspect."

"It could have been a formality. Wasn't that what Anne said?"

I picked up my pace and decided to let Vince think that

Anne had actually told me about the interrogation herself. The truth was, I'd learned about it during an eavesdropping stint outside Orchid's office door. It's not as bad as it sounds. I was leaving work. I heard voices. I listened.

As Vince and I crossed the street, I peered through the darkness. There was a tiny group of people with a banner near the west entrance. One of them was tall enough to be Lexie, but with my sleet-spattered glasses, I couldn't tell. We strode past a couple guys with cigarettes, and I took a deep breath. Even though I quit smoking years ago, I never pass up an opportunity for some secondhand smoke. To my left, a man grumbled, "There should be laws against that." He was staring at a banner that said JUST DESSERTS. Holding one end of it was Lexie Roth, her spirally hair spilling out of her stocking cap.

I'm an ardent supporter of free speech, but I also know tacky when I see it. Lexie's banner wasn't going to win her any new allies. In fact, it was garnering so much hostility that I was tempted to take Vince's advice. I had no desire to stand next to a woman who was inspiring a riff on the *b* word. Vince dashed into the arena, abandoning me to the expletives.

Sleet stung my face as I greeted Lexie. She was familiar with my radio shows and happy to meet me, all smiles until I explained that I was trying to find DeVoster's killer. "Why bother?"

"To protect the innocent." Cheesy allusions to *Dragnet*—that was no way to get her to open up. "The police are going to arrest somebody," I said. "Maybe one of the female players. Or Anne Golding." I wanted to say, *Thanks to your reporting*.

Lexie frowned, her brow furrowed. "Which players do they suspect?"

"They're considering several possibilities." I wasn't about to give her any information.

"How awful." Lexie's frown deepened.

"Since you've been covering the story and"—I didn't want to use the word *stalking*—"keeping a close eye on DeVoster, I thought you might know something."

Lexie nodded, oblivious to the woman who'd just told her that she should be ashamed of herself and the man who informed her that she could rot in hell.

"Is there anybody in your group who's particularly angry with DeVoster?" I asked. "Somebody with a history of violence?"

"We all took an oath of nonviolence."

I should have guessed. There were several peace signs among the many buttons that riddled Lexie's parka (BI PRIDE, GO VEGAN, THE ONLY BUSH I TRUST IS MY OWN). "What about your banner?" I asked. "The one that said 'Castrate DeVoster'?"

Lexie shrugged. "Just words."

An odd sentiment for a writer. Maybe it explained her penchant for exaggeration and bias. "When you were following him, did you see anyone confront him directly or threaten him?"

She shook her head.

"You interviewed several members of the women's team—"

She cut me off. "None of them did it. They were scared of him. Most of them wouldn't even say the guy's name."

"Most?"

"Jessie March had plenty of ugly things to say, but talk is cheap. She wouldn't join my group."

Probably because she didn't want to get kicked off the team, I thought. The girl had more discretion than Bridget gave her credit for. "Did you ever have a chance to observe DeVoster with his teammates?"

"Why do you ask?" Lexie nudged up the sleeve of her parka and checked her watch.

At least that's what I thought she did. My glasses were

completely coated. "Some people suspect DeVoster's backup, Tyler Bennet."

A group of high school girls flipped Lexie off and told her that she sucked.

Lexie gazed at me, holding her banner with both hands. "Do you honestly think that one of DeVoster's teammates killed him? After the way they circled their wagons?"

I recalled the team's avalanche of support: "D is a real decent guy," "I can't believe it," "The girl must be confused," "D would never do a thing like that." I couldn't remember Bennet adding his two cents' worth. Nor could I think of a graceful way to ask Lexie for an alibi, so I opted for the direct approach.

She didn't seem to mind. "I was in bed—just like I told the cops."

I was happy the police had questioned her, but my happiness didn't last long.

"You need to cast your net wider," Lexie said. "Varenka White isn't the first woman DeVoster raped."

My stomach lurched. "You know that for a fact?"

She nodded. "But I can't reveal my sources."

Now she developed journalistic ethics? I struggled to keep my voice calm. "How many?"

Lexie started to say something but stopped.

Just what I needed—a stubborn journalist and a vast network of anonymous suspects.

✧ ✧ ✧

Vince and I didn't need to worry about our binoculars attracting attention during the memorial service. Carver-Hawkeye Arena looked like a birders' convention. Most eyes were riveted to the stage at one end of the floor, where a row of men in suits flanked a podium and the world's largest black-and-gold bouquet.

"That florist had to be straight," Vince mumbled.

A sharp-nosed woman next to him told him to "can it." Like us, she stood at the railing that lined the arena's top floor, pinned there by the many fans who'd arrived too late to get a seat.

Down on the floor, the athletic director leaned over the podium and praised the university's long and venerable tradition of scholar-athletes. The service wasn't about DeVoster. It was about damage control and image.

I focused my binoculars on the media section, where Lexie was scribbling, and saw that a burly security guard was also watching her. If only she had been on the list of people who'd received a pair of incriminating sweats. If only she were close to someone on that list.

Lexie pulled her hair away from her face and looked up from her notebook. The crowd watched DeVoster highlights on gigantic screens, but Lexie scrutinized the arena's floor. It was filled with rows of folding chairs, which were in turn filled with hoards of student athletes supposedly mourning the loss of a fallen brother. There were a lot more men than women.

Bridget and a remnant of her team were wedged in between the football players and the male gymnasts. Bridget herself was on the end of a row, clad in a silvery silk shirt and a handsome black jacket and pants. She glanced into the stands as if she'd felt me watching her through my binoculars. I wondered what it was like for her to sit there on display in front of all the DeVoster supporters. Probably the athletic director—or even the university president—had demanded the presence of all the coaches and teams. If so, then Bridget had followed orders only part way. To her left were the other two assistant coaches and

Shelly. In front of them were Win, Jessie, and three other players. Varenka and Kate were not among them. Maybe Bridget had brought half her team so Varenka could stay away without being noticeably absent. I would have boycotted the whole charade, but I admired the way that Bridget worked the system. I also admired her control. Except for her hands, which were clasped on her knees, she didn't betray a trace of emotion.

You couldn't say the same for the folks blowing their noses around me—a veritable flock of Canadian geese. They were generating a lot of heat too. I removed my coat and tied it around my waist. Vince was grinning, his binoculars trained on the middle of the floor—on the wrestlers. "You're supposed to be watching the men's basketball team," I hissed.

Vince turned and peered at me. "Don't tell me you weren't checking out Bridget Stokes."

I scowled at him.

"What?" he said. "Didn't get enough of her at breakfast?"

Vince is incapable of anything softer than a stage whisper, so his comment prompted several glares and shushes.

On stage, a university bureaucrat pontificated about respect and safety and the campus climate committee.

"Sounds like a gathering of meteorologists," Vince said.

I returned to my binoculars, meaning to watch the men's team myself, but my gaze fell upon the DeVoster clan. Ultrablond, every last one of them, they filled three rows in front of the stage across the aisle from the men's team. There were plenty of children—Dave's nieces and nephews, I guessed. One boy, around ten years old, was so lost in his own sadness that when his mother put her arm around his shoulders, he crawled right into her lap. I could guess how the boy felt. Even though I'd been thirty-five when Glad was murdered, I needed solace, sanctuary—a safe, quiet space where I could work through the layers of shock. Someone I knew and loved was gone forever—that was hard enough to grasp. But harder still was the fact that another human being had purposefully ended my aunt's life.

I adjusted my binoculars and forced myself to focus on the present. Darren DeVoster stroked his wife's hair as she cried into his shoulder. His lips were pressed so tightly together that they nearly disappeared. He refused, I imagined, to lose more control than he already had. He may have lost his son, but by God, he would not lose faith in his own power, his own clout, his belief that other people were at his beck and call. In interview after interview, Darren DeVoster made it clear that he expected the police and the university to act swiftly. A big "or else" lingered behind his words. He was wealthy; he was powerful. He would get his way. From this man, Dave had learned that the world was his for the taking, and from the crowd in the arena, he had learned that he was the world—a twenty-year-old hero who could do no wrong as long as he put the ball through the hoop.

Raging against society was Orchid's thing. Taking action, that was mine. I focused on the men's basketball team, searching for something—anything—that would help me keep Anne out of jail, but all I saw were game faces and tailor-made suits. With his red hair, Tyler Bennet was easy to spot, sitting in the second row next to Roshaun. If Bennet felt any glee over DeVoster's death, he wasn't showing it. As he listened to a university choir, his pale face was expressionless except for an occasional twitch when the sopranos hit an extra-high note.

Looking through my binoculars was starting to give me a headache, so I let them hang around my neck. Vince pulled out his phone and started text-messaging. I thought about Neale hanging up on me. It wasn't like her to be a drama queen, or to be jealous. Maybe something was wrong. I should have called her back right away even though I was angry.

As the choir's final chords evaporated, I started to reach for my own phone, but then Tyler Bennet headed toward the podium. Surely he hadn't volunteered to give a eulogy. Coach Bly must have drafted him. It was a clever move, one that would allay any suspicions about the new starter.

Bennet stood in front of a microphone that was a good two feet below his mouth. He leaned over and tried to raise it, but it whined and dropped closer toward the floor.

A tiny man dressed all in black sped to his rescue and wrestled with the recalcitrant mike. As it continued to hum and whine, two more techies dashed on stage and finally got the mike within range of Bennet's mouth.

He laced his fingers together and twisted his palms outward, no doubt ready to crack his knuckles, but he stopped himself and cleared his throat. His speech, which gave new meaning to the word *monotone*, praised DeVoster the team player. Dave not only helped his teammates with their game, but also with their academics and their personal lives. He helped Bennet through Calculus II and loaned him money when he couldn't afford to fly to his grandfather's funeral.

If these stories were true, they must have taken place before DeVoster raped Varenka. I couldn't imagine Bennet accepting DeVoster's help afterward. Of course, a few short minutes ago, I couldn't have imagined Bennet eulogizing his teammate.

But what happened after the speech didn't surprise me in the least. As Bennet left the podium, Coach Eldon Bly met him at the edge of the stage and patted his back. Cameras flashed madly, lighting up the floor of the arena.

"Front page, above the fold," I whispered.

"We'll be seeing a lot of that shot," Vince agreed.

When Coach Bly reached the podium, a few people clapped before remembering they were at a memorial service, not a pep rally. Not that Bly himself remembered. The opening of his speech sounded like a thesaurus entry for the word *victory.*

Seeking refuge from his rhetoric, I scanned the media section with my binoculars. Lexie was no longer taking notes. Instead, she seemed to be studying someone, her gaze fixed, her brow furrowed. She sure wasn't paying attention to Bly's platitudes about the heart of a champion, but she was watching someone near the stage—someone on the men's basketball team. Tyler Bennet? If only she'd start investigating him and leave Anne alone.

At the podium, Eldon Bly praised his dead player's triumph over adversity, referring to the rape charge as "a rough start to DeVoster's senior season."

I aimed my binoculars at the women's team. Bridget jiggled her leg and tensed her jaw. Shelly frowned at Jessie, who was leaning over to pick something up. I adjusted my focus. At first, I couldn't tell what the freshman held, but then she set it on her lap. A miniature cassette tape and a small recording device. Jessie was taping DeVoster's service. Win watched, smiling, as Jessie changed the tapes. Their eyes seemed filled with the cold desire for Eldon Bly and his team to suffer as Varenka had.

TWENTY

Two heads are not always better than one. The next morning, when I dragged myself into the kitchen for my first cup of coffee, Vince was at the kitchen table, combing a blond wig that perched atop a Styrofoam head.

"Pardon my brutal honesty," I said, "but that I-Dream-of-Jeannie look is definitely not you."

"I couldn't agree more." Vince set his comb next to a box of Pop-Tarts. "It's for you." He slid *The Daily Iowan* across the table and pointed to a color photo of me and Lexie. It looked like I was helping her hold the banner that said JUST DESSERTS.

"Read the caption," Vince said.

I picked up the paper and held it close to my face. "Iowa City journalists, Lexie Roth and Mara Gilgannon, protest in front of Carver-Hawkeye Arena minutes before the memorial service for slain Hawkeye basketball star, Dave DeVoster."

I tossed the paper back on the table, speechless.

Vince glided to the coffeemaker and poured me a cup.

As I began sipping it, I made mental notes about the letter I'd send to the editor of *The Daily Iowan.* I'd demand that the paper apologize for its misrepresentation and gross journalistic negligence. Better yet, I'd ask for Lexie's resignation.

"That photo might make you the target of a distraught DeVoster fan," Vince said.

I hadn't thought about that. My stomach clenched.

"I'm not going to be able to accompany you on your sleuthing adventures today," he said, "but you should be safe with a proper disguise." He patted the wig and winked.

I laughed so hard I nearly spit my coffee on him.

"Careful," he said, glancing down at his shirt. "These are my work clothes."

I managed to swallow my coffee, but I couldn't quit laughing.

He prattled on about sunglasses and a foundation that would hide my freckles.

"Vince," I said, "I can't go around looking like CIA Barbie."

"Would you prefer a brunette wig? I think Richard has—"

"I'd prefer that you quit worrying about me," I said. "I'm a big girl. I'll be fine."

"Very well, then," he said. "If I can't talk any sense into you, I'm off to work. It's going to be a busy day at the shelter. We have an inspection tomorrow." He grabbed his wig and strode out of the kitchen.

I was sorry I'd hurt his feelings, but I didn't have the energy to make nice. Truth be told, I was a little worried myself. DeVoster had a lot of fans.

I reached for the paper to see what else it had to say about his death. POLICE AND PAPER RECEIVE MYSTERY TAPE, the top headline read. Yesterday's mail had brought them a miniature cassette tape with a recording of Dave DeVoster saying, "I don't take no for an answer, not from some c-nt."

Quoth a police department representative: "It's too early to tell whether the tape has any connection with DeVoster's death."

I saw connections aplenty. Whoever sent the tape wanted to damage DeVoster's reputation—that was clear. If the sender had captured the damning words before DeVoster's plea bargain, the police and the prosecution would have received them then. But because the words surfaced only after his death, they were no doubt among the player's last.

I took Vince's mug to the sink and gazed out the window. A small bird pecked at an empty feeder. As it flew off, I thought about Jessie and Win taping the memorial service. I didn't want to believe that either girl had killed DeVoster, for their sakes as well as the team's. And Bridget's.

"See you later," Vince said, ducking his head back into the kitchen. "Be careful."

As the front door banged shut, Labrys strolled into the kitchen and began lapping at her water bowl. I poured myself some more coffee and returned to the paper. When I opened it to finish reading the story about Lexie's protest, I discovered that she had once again linked herself with Anne and the Women's Center. There, on page three, under the headline DEVOSTER SERVICE PROMPTS PROTEST, was a photo of Anne at the center's alternative memorial for rape victims. Before I could skim the article for further misrepresentations, the doorbell rang.

Labrys barked furiously and dashed to the door. I was less eager, given my morning breath and my seen-better-days flannel jammies.

I was even less eager when I saw Orchid.

As I opened the door, Labrys nearly knocked her over, whining and licking her face. It was then that I noticed her tears.

I pulled the dog off her, filled with panic. Where was Anne? What had happened?

Orchid stood there in the freezing cold, trying to speak, but whatever she needed to tell me, she couldn't bring herself to say.

I invited her in, but she didn't budge. Finally, I reached for her shoulder and propelled her into the living room.

"The police have taken Anne in for questioning," Orchid said, "for the second time. Cecile Lodge thinks she's going to be charged."

I tried to make sense of Orchid's words. Cecile Lodge was a high-profile defense attorney. Surely, it hadn't come to that? Anne arrested and on trial?

"Cecile is the only one who can see her," Orchid said.

I snapped out of my shock. "I'll get you some coffee, and you can tell me what happened." Orchid doesn't drink caffeine, but I needed to *do* something. I needed to steel myself before I heard more. My hands shook when I poured the coffee, and they were still shaking as I returned to the living room with two steaming mugs.

Orchid sat in Vince's chair, her tears under control, her eyes vacant. She seemed unaware of the dog's chin on her knee.

I held a mug in front of her until she took it with both hands.

"What I said to you yesterday," Orchid said, "I didn't mean it."

"I know. Just tell me about Anne."

"You didn't take me seriously," she said. "You're still going to find out who killed DeVoster, right?"

My fear rose with Orchid's desperation. She often ordered me around, but never once had she asked me for anything—not so much as a piece of advice. And now she wanted reassurance? What kind of case had the cops built against Anne?

"They searched our place." A tear rolled down Orchid's cheek.

"When?"

"This morning."

I glanced at the clock on my end table: 8:56.

"It was early," Orchid said. "They woke us up."

"They didn't find anything," I said stupidly. Of course, they had. Or why would Anne be in jail?

"There were the sweats—the kind like the murderer wore. Anne had just washed the pair that the team had given her." Orchid set her coffee atop the magazines that covered Vince's end table. "There was also lots of pepper spray," Orchid continued. "Opened and unopened."

"But that's circumstantial." I knew my protest was pointless, but I couldn't help it.

"They found her fingerprints at the crime scene. On the bird." Orchid's voice was swollen with tears. "I told the police that I took her photo there with her nieces, that hundreds of people must have touched that bird, but they wouldn't listen."

Orchid looked around for a Kleenex, so I handed her a box. She set it on her lap as if she wasn't sure what to do with it.

I felt sick and dizzy.

"They also found a small cassette at our place," Orchid said. "It had DeVoster's voice just like the one they'd received. I told them I got it at work, but they wouldn't believe me about that either."

"I'll tell them," I said. "I remember exactly how it happened. We were arguing and you threw it in your bag."

Orchid met my eyes and shook her head. "Anne took it out and set it on our kitchen table. She was looking for something."

The tape would have Anne's prints. I tried to get my mind around that fact, but I was besieged with *if-onlys*. If only the police weren't so eager to make an arrest. If only the team hadn't given Anne those sweats. If only I hadn't been fighting with Orchid when she received that cassette.

Sunlight spilled through the window, illuminating the tip of Labrys's tail. I wondered if Anne could see the sun from her interrogation room. A lump formed in my throat, and I swallowed hard.

"Cecile says that once the police identify Anne's prints on the tape, they'll charge her." Orchid's lips trembled. "It's just a matter of time."

✧ ✧ ✧

I kept myself calm by visualizing a to-do list. Convince Orchid to eat something. Check. Arrange for someone to take my shift at the station. Check. Decide who to question next. I was tackling that item when my phone rang. It was Neale, saying we needed to talk.

She'd picked a heck of a time to finally see things my way.

Orchid nibbled her toast and gazed at the cell phone in her lap. I left the kitchen and headed upstairs.

"I've managed to clear my schedule," Neale said. "I could come see you this weekend."

This weekend seemed years away. I sat in the middle of my unmade bed and pulled a flannel sheet over my legs.

"Mara?"

"The police are questioning Anne for the second time," I said. "Her lawyer says she's going to be charged."

Silence on Neale's end.

"With the murder of that basketball player." I pulled the sheet around my shoulders. The penguins on it looked carefree and happy—downright jaunty. "I just found out." If only Neale would say something comforting. "I'm still trying to figure out what to do."

"Let me guess," she said. "You're going to be busy finding the real killer, so next weekend isn't a good time."

What was up with the anger? "I'd love to have you visit but—"

She cut me off. "But Anne is more important."

"She's about to be falsely accused of murder," I said. "Didn't you hear me?"

Outside, an engine rattled like a sickly machine gun.

"I didn't want to say this over the phone," Neale said, "but you and me—it's just not working."

A car door slammed shut.

Was Neale actually dumping me? "You haven't given us a chance," I said. "We've hardly seen each other since you moved to St. Louis."

"I know. You deserve a lot more time and attention than I can give you."

Her voice was annoyingly calm. How dare she make me sound so needy—so high maintenance?

"I need more space than you can give me."

She sounded like she was reading from an outline she'd made, a list of reasons why we needed to break up, an itemized account of our incompatibilities.

"You're settled in Iowa City," she said, "but there's nothing for me there."

She wasn't telling me anything I didn't already know, but I wanted to scream at her.

"Besides you, I mean."

That bit of tenderness hurt most of all. I thought about Neale's eyes in the moonlight, the way she clasped her fingers around the back of my head, pulling me toward her waiting lips.

"Mara?"

Nothing good ever comes of arguing with someone who wants to break up with you, but I couldn't help myself. "We could make a long-distance relationship work if we both really wanted it."

"But we don't," Neale said. "You want what you had with Anne."

Did I? I recalled my ex's most frequent complaint: "You never want to stay home and just *be*." My throat ached with the tears.

"Let's face it," Neale said gently. "You're still not over her."

I started crying.

"I'm sorry," she said.

I walked over to my dresser to get a tissue. Next to the box was Neale's hairbrush, a few strands of her bright wavy locks caught in its bristles. "I need to go," I said.

"I had fun with you," she said, "I want you to know that. I care about you, and I want us to stay friends."

I closed my eyes. Was she going to tote out all the other end-of-relationship clichés?

"I mean it," she said.

Maybe she did. I dug deep within myself, trying to find some part that wasn't bruised, but all I could see was Anne behind bars—way beyond my reach.

TWENTY-ONE

Despite a week's worth of newspapers at my feet, I kept knocking on the door of Apartment 1. I'd already struck out with the other tenants in Varenka's building, and my knuckles were killing me. I gave them a break and started pounding with my fist. If I tried long enough and hard enough, someone would have to answer the damn door.

They would.

Answer.

The door.

I paused and listened. Nothing. Not so much as a footstep or a murmur. The hallway's only light came from an exit sign. Then I heard it.

A toilet flushing. From inside number 1.

I pummeled the door with such abandon that when it finally opened, I almost fell onto the tenant, a tiny woman with a black sleeping mask atop her white hair and half an unlit cigarette dangling from her wrinkled lips. "Didn't anybody ever teach you how to knock like a decent person?" Her voice was a cross between a croak and a bark, smoke-ravaged but loud. "I ain't buying anything."

When I explained that I wasn't selling, she screwed up her face and asked me if I was one of them Jehovah's Witnesses. I assured her that I wasn't, that I just wanted to ask her questions about the night Dave DeVoster was killed.

"I already talked to your people last night. Hadn't been home two minutes and I get the third degree—what had I heard? what had I seen?—never mind that I was bone tired from eight hours in the car with my second-cousin Eddie. Talks about nothing but his blood pressure and his bowels, that one does."

At least I wouldn't have trouble getting this woman to open up. "You talked to the police last night?"

"That's what I said. In my day, folks listened when people talked." She pulled a lighter out of her robe pocket and lit up—all without removing the cigarette from her mouth.

"And you were out of town before?" I prompted.

"Wasn't no vacation. My uncle keeled over from a stroke, and me and Eddie had to make arrangements and take care of his things in Indiana. Talk about an ugly drive."

"Were you here the night DeVoster died?"

She puffed on her cigarette and screwed up her face again. "How come you don't got a uniform?"

I explained that I was simply a concerned citizen whose close friend was being scapegoated for the murder.

"You trying to find the real killer?" she asked.

I nodded and smiled weakly, hoping she wasn't a devoted DeVoster fan.

"I like a girl with gumption." She stepped away from the door and ushered me in.

Her walls and ceiling were stained from decades of cigarette smoke, but the rest of her place was cheery enough. A bright afghan covered her couch, and photos of smiling children dotted her walls. "Have a seat," she said, "and I'll tell you exactly what I told the cops."

She pulled a pack of Camels out of her robe and offered me one. When I declined, she offered me some coffee. And then some toaster strudel.

"I'd just like to hear about the night of the murder."

"Frozen waffle?"

I shook my head. What I really needed was some Visine.

She plopped next to me on the couch and leaned in close. "I didn't know it was the night of the murder when it happened," she said. "Me and Eddie were up practically the whole night. First, he had to do his laundry—two weeks worth, I swear to God, and the dryers here take forever. Then he had to pack." She paused for a puff.

I knew better than to interrupt.

"Then he had to study the map and mark our route. Then he needed a snack. You get the picture?" She barely waited for me to nod. "It was close to two when we finally got to bed, but I couldn't sleep on account of them girls upstairs."

My heart quickened. The apartment directly above belonged to Varenka and Shelly. And Shelly had been with Roshaun.

"They weren't blaring their music—not like most young people these days—just walking around." She leaned forward and flicked her cigarette over a pristine ashtray. "But they're big girls, so they're loud—and I mean loud. Tromp, tromp, tromp—like elephants above my head. So I said to myself, just this once, I'll go up there and ask them to quit their pacing."

"Did you?"

She held up one hand, and with the other, took a long drag.

"I was putting on my robe, when—wouldn't you know it—I knocked a jar of face cream off my dresser and woke Eddie up even though he was out here on the couch. So he tagged along after me for protection." She rolled her eyes. "I told him these girls are real nice, but he said you never know. And I said, maybe you don't, but I do. Then—"

"You both went up there?"

She narrowed her eyes at me.

I shouldn't have interrupted. "Please," I said, "go on."

She put out her cigarette and folded her hands in her lap. I was just about to ask her again when she spoke. "The one who answered the door was real apologetic. She has a stutter, poor thing."

Kate Timmens. Who was supposedly in Independence with Varenka's parents watching *To Kill a Mockingbird.* "A brunette?" I asked. "Kind of moosey?"

"That's the one. Eddie asked her if she was a basketball player, and I said of course she is—weren't you listening when I told you about all the Iowa players in my building. He ignored me—just like always—and then he asked the girl for an autograph. For his granddaughter, he told her. I said not to bother—just to please quit pacing—but she was a real sweetheart. Invited us in and everything."

"Was anyone else there?"

"A pretty blond lying on the couch—real out of it. And a dark-haired girl."

The blond had to be Varenka. "Did the dark-haired one have a Southern accent?"

"Straight outta Dixie."

Maybe I shouldn't assume that the blond was Varenka.

"Did you happen to see their signatures?" I asked.

"See them? I got them. Eddie's not the only one with grandkids. I'm saving my autographs for Christmas." She headed to her dining room table and retrieved a poster of the women's basketball team. There were John Hancocks scrawled across the jerseys of three players: Varenka, Win, and Kate.

They had airtight alibis for DeVoster's murder, yet they'd lied about their whereabouts. I had a pretty good idea why.

✧ ✧ ✧

"I know where you really were that night," I said, "so you can quit trying to protect your parents." Varenka started to protest, but I cut her off. "I had a very enlightening chat with your downstairs neighbor. She loves the poster that you and Kate and Win signed for her." I pulled out a chair and seated myself at the table. "At the exact same time that someone else was murdering DeVoster." Varenka looked so young in her waffle-weave pajamas. Her lip trembled as she gazed at the eggs she'd barely touched, and her eyes filled with tears, but I didn't care. She and her friends had lied, and Anne was in trouble. "I can see only one reason why you made up a story about being at your parents. You think one of them did it."

"No!" Varenka leaped to her feet. "It was my mom's idea. She was afraid *I'd* be a suspect."

I stood too, trying to decide if this was yet another lie.

"She said I didn't need any more trouble." Varenka spoke quickly. "She's the one who made up the story. She even checked the *TV Guide* to see what movies were playing."

"Your mom asked you to lie."

"To protect me." Varenka's voice was defiant, but her brow furrowed.

I didn't want to cause this young woman any more pain, but I needed the truth. "What did she want to protect you from?"

"The cops."

"But didn't she know that you have a good alibi?"

Varenka studied me, biting the inside of her lip. Then she darted past me to the door and pulled it open. Her message was clear, but I didn't budge.

"Do you know that Anne Golding is at the police station about to be charged with DeVoster's murder?"

At one of Varenka's temples, a vein pulsed manically.

"A woman who helped you is in big trouble," I said. "Now it's your turn to help her."

"Maybe she did it. How should I know?"

"You don't believe that," I said quietly.

"She convinced me to press charges." Varenka's eyes darted around, and she shut the door. "I said it wasn't really rape—just a horrible mistake. But she kept saying it was. She said he deserved to be punished. She said I could stop him from hurting other women."

Varenka's words sounded like testimony against Anne. That thought hardened me against her.

"But she was wrong," Varenka said. "I couldn't stop him, and now my dad—" She stopped herself.

"What?" I said. "Your dad is what?"

"Worried about me." She gazed at her stocking feet and blinked back tears.

I decided to take a risk. "I already know about his drinking."

She met my eyes, briefly, and started crying. If only I hadn't started drinking that night. I promised him I'd never drink, but I broke my promise, and look what happened." Varenka's breath was jerky, her shoulders heaving.

Dave DeVoster had found himself a girl who was drunk for

the very first time. I wanted to tell Varenka it wasn't her fault, but I knew she wouldn't believe me. And I needed to help Anne. "Why were you drinking?" I asked gently. I handed her a napkin in lieu of a Kleenex, and she blew her nose.

"I was upset. Confused. After me and Jess ..." Varenka leaned against the door. "That was so stupid." She tried to catch her breath, but started sobbing again.

She didn't seem to notice when I went to the kitchen and poured us both a glass of water. Adding some ice just to give her some space, some time to cry, I wondered how Varenka really felt about Jessie—and more important, how Jessie felt about her.

When I placed the glasses on the table, Varenka just stared at them. I sat and took a long drink, but she remained at the door. "Your roommate said you were freaked out about being with Jessie."

No response.

"She said it was a one-time thing."

Varenka's lip spasmed.

"Jessie wanted more, and you didn't?"

She shrugged, and a tear rolled down her face. "She didn't understand. I want to be a coach. Have a family."

So they both wanted more, but Varenka was scared. I felt like crying myself, but that wouldn't have done either one of us any good. "Do you think Jessie is in love with you?"

Varenka brushed her tear away. "Everybody's seen how she is with that softball player."

"When did she enter the picture?"

"I don't know." Varenka leaned over, her hair completely hiding her face.

I wondered if she'd found out about the softball player the night she'd decided to try drinking. If that were true and

Jessie knew it, the freshman might have blamed herself for what happened with DeVoster. A go-to girl like Jessie March might have decided to make things right. "Is that why you were drinking?"

Varenka remained motionless.

I didn't want to keep pushing her—I didn't want to make her relive that horrible night—but maybe there was some detail within it that would help me discover the truth, that would enable me to establish Anne's innocence. "Was DeVoster giving you drinks?"

She nodded, leaning over further and clasping her hands behind her neck. When she finally spoke, her voice was barely audible. "He was grabbing at me, and when I pulled away, he said I was a dyke. He said it over and over." Varenka took a deep breath. "I wanted to show him …"

Not as much as she'd wanted to show herself, I suspected.

"He hurt me, but I didn't say anything." Varenka lifted her head for a moment. "I didn't want him to think that I—" She tried to meet my eyes and started crying again. "I never said no—not even once—so no matter what Anne says, it couldn't have been rape."

If DeVoster weren't already dead, I would have killed him myself. "Did you tell Jessie about how it happened—what he said to you?"

"No!"

It was possible, I thought, that DeVoster himself had told someone—had bragged about his methods—and that eventually Jessie had heard about how he'd manipulated Varenka.

"I never told anyone," she insisted.

"Not even Anne?" I asked.

She shook her head. "Not about what he called me. I didn't want anyone to know."

✧ ✧ ✧

Blinking back tears, I gripped my steering wheel and gazed at Varenka's apartment building. Just as I was ready to go back inside and insist that she let me sit with her, my phone rang. I snatched it right up. What if it was Anne calling to say the cops had made a horrible mistake? Or Neale saying she had?

"She's been charged."

Even through the static, Orchid's words were unmistakable, but I couldn't make sense of them. I felt sluggish and terrified, like I couldn't wake myself from a long nightmare.

"Cecile says she's holding up okay."

I squeezed the steering wheel harder and tried to summon some words. "What about bail?" I asked.

"The hearing is tomorrow, but ..." Orchid started crying.

I wanted to say something comforting, but all I could think about was the day of the week. What was it? Yesterday I'd gone to work. That was Monday. This was Tuesday. When had I first learned about DeVoster's death? During the weekend: Saturday. Everything was moving too fast.

"Cecile thinks bail will probably be denied." Orchid took a deep breath. "Because of the violent nature of the crime."

I was already feeling so numb that this last horrible fact barely registered.

"Anne will be in jail until her trial," Orchid said.

The despair and panic in her voice frightened me.

"Cecile says it could be months," she moaned.

"Are you sure she knows what she's talking about?"

"Of course," Orchid snapped. "I hired the best."

My nose tingled, and my eyes burned with tears.

When Orchid asked if I'd learned anything helpful, I wasn't sure what to say. I'd eliminated three suspects, but I had no idea whether that would encourage her or help Anne. I wondered if Cecile had her own private investigator, but that question, I knew, would not hearten anybody. "I've made some discoveries," I said, "but I don't know what they mean yet." My throat was so tight I could barely mumble a goodbye and a promise to check in.

After hanging up, I rested my head on the cold steering wheel and cried, quietly at first but then louder as I struggled against wild, merciless sobs.

TWENTY-TWO

When I awoke on my couch, my eyes were swollen and my nose was stuffy. Vince still hadn't called me back, but Labrys stood guard over me. Firmly stationed in between the couch and the coffee table, she edged her face closer to mine until they were inches apart. My one loyal friend was a dog that belonged to my ex—my ex who was in jail on a murder charge.

I eased myself into a sitting position and patted the coffee table until I found my glasses. Labrys sniffed at the wadded Kleenexes surrounding the base of the sofa. As I began picking them up, she charged to the door, barking. A second later the bell rang. I shoved some of the tissues in my pocket and rushed to the entryway.

It was Shelly, the girl who'd wanted to bolt out of my office just the day before. She kept her eyes on Labrys, who was pulling out all the stops—joyous yelps punctuated with a few crotch sniffs. No guard dog, Labrys. As Vince says, she's a lover, not a fighter. After Shelly refused my offer to take her coat or get her something to drink, I suggested that she pet Labrys. This soothed the canine, but it didn't do much for Shelly. Still avoiding my gaze, she shifted her weight from side to side until I felt like I was on the deck of a lurching ship. When I suggested we sit, she nodded and squared her shoulders as if she were about to face a firing squad. Once settled in Vince's chair, she eyed the Kleenex strewn on the floor.

"You have something you want to tell me?" I asked.

"No, but I don't see any other way." Her face was tight with worry.

My curiosity was on level-orange, but I managed to keep quiet and let her follow her own pace.

She wriggled out of her coat and rested it on her lap. She was clad in sweats and, given that it was a little after two, probably on her way to practice. "You can't tell anyone this," she said.

Labrys wandered over and placed his front paws on her lap.

"The only reason I'm telling you is so you'll leave Varenka alone." Shelly's scowl told me that she knew about my latest interview with her roommate.

Part of me wanted to justify it—I hadn't wanted to hurt Varenka; I'd only wanted to help Anne. But another part of me knew that my desire to save Anne was so strong that I no longer cared about anyone else. Shame kept me quiet.

"I know where her parents were that night," Shelly said. "My mom told me. Varenka's dad woke her and my dad up in the middle of the night, yelling and banging on their door."

"What time?"

Shelly pressed her lips together and stroked Labrys. "After two—a little after."

Right after the bars closed, I thought. "Drunk?"

Almost imperceptibly, Shelly nodded. "He said it was my dad's fault, what happened. He said my dad pushed Varenka into going to Iowa. But that's not true." Shelly raised her voice and looked at me. "Varenka always wanted to be a Hawkeye. My dad helped her. I can't believe Mr. White ..." She trailed off, shaking her head. "My dad tried to calm him down, but he just kept yelling and then he—" Shelly dropped her eyes. "Then he punched my dad."

I thought about Varenka's father seething at the season opener and later at his own home, wanting to toast DeVoster's death. It was easy to imagine Mr. White hitting someone. Not surprising that it had been Shelly's father—Varenka's high school coach, the man who had stolen away some of her admiration, the man who was like a father but couldn't protect her after all.

"My mom said my dad's nose was bleeding. She said she never wanted me around Mr. White again. But later, when I talked to Dad, he said it was no big deal, that she was overreacting." Shelly sighed.

I wondered if she'd tried to patch together her own version of the fight, or if she'd realized that it would be a losing game—trying to decide which parent was withholding the most truth.

"After my dad got Varenka's dad in some kind of hold, Mom wanted to call the police, but Dad talked her out of it. He said it would only hurt Varenka and her family if people knew. He didn't even want Varenka's mom to know, but my mom said she'd be worried. So they called her—Varenka's mom—and she came over."

That left only three suspects: Jessie March, Tyler Bennet, and Lexie Roth.

"When she got there, Mr. White was still talking trash to my dad, but Paulette—Varenka's mom—eventually managed to calm him down."

Labrys barked and leaned toward Shelly. She hadn't met my gaze once during the last part of her story, and her face was slightly flushed. Was she embarrassed and pained on Varenka's behalf? Or Mrs.White's? I wondered about her use of the woman's first name. "Were you and Paulette close?"

Shelly tried to push Labrys away, but the dog would not be moved.

I tried throwing Uggles, her eviscerated stuffed bunny, across the room, but it had no effect. "Sorry," I said, "she's one codependent canine. If she senses emotional turmoil, she's off to the rescue."

"I'm not in emotional turmoil," Shelly said evenly.

I wanted to touch her shoulder—comfort her—but I didn't. "About you and Paulette," I prompted.

Shelly rested a hand on Labrys's back. "She always had something nice to say about my game even when no one else did."

In other words, even when the coach—Shelly's own father—lavished all his praise on other players.

"She'd be humiliated if she knew that I knew about what her husband did."

I was stuck in one hell of a tangled web—people "protecting" each other against the truth until its thread was completely unraveled. "When Paulette concocted her false alibi, you think she was trying to keep Varenka from discovering what her father did to yours?"

Shelly nodded.

"What about Kate and Win?" I asked. "Do they know what happened between Varenka's dad and yours?"

"None of the girls do."

"Then why'd they go along with the fake alibi?"

"They could tell Varenka wanted them to. We've all been wanting to do something for her. You know, help her get back to normal."

"Did any of you think about why Varenka would want such a thing?"

Shelly squirmed, her eyes on Labrys. "She just wanted to make things easier for her parents. She didn't want them treated like suspects. They'd been through enough."

"And why wasn't Win included in the alibi? Why leave her with none at all?"

"That was her idea," Shelly said. "She said she wanted a simpler story to tell the police."

She may have also had her doubts about the Whites. If they had been involved with DeVoster's death, anyone who'd lied on their behalf would be an accessory. Win had her own family to think of. I could sort of understand her actions. And Kate's and Shelly's too. Young and naïve—and in Kate's case, in love—they were trying to help their friend. But Varenka's mother? I stared at Shelly until she met my eyes. "Paulette asked her own daughter to needlessly cast suspicion on herself?"

"No! It wasn't like that." Shelly scooted to the edge of her chair. "Varenka told her mom that she and Kate didn't have alibis."

A daughter protecting a mother who thought she was protecting the daughter. My head hurt. "Varenka knows about her father's drinking," I said.

"She's never said anything about it." Shelly's voice was defiant, but her brow furrowed.

I thought about Varenka's mom—her pride and dignity, her desire to hide her husband's problem. I thought about Varenka hiding her own desires, hiding from the truth of what DeVoster had done to her. "Maybe she didn't want you to know about it,"

I said, "or maybe she didn't want you and her teammates worrying about her any more than you already were."

Shelly started to protest, but I cut her off. "She knows," I said, "and now you know she knows. Why not tell her the rest?"

"I promised I wouldn't." Shelly stood. "I promised my dad."

I rose too, although I might as well have remained seated for all the good it did me. Shelly still towered over me, glaring.

Labrys whimpered, perhaps uncertain about which of us was most in need of her comfort. I knelt next to her and stroked her side. "These lies aren't helping anyone." I waited until Shelly met my eyes. "Don't you see? Varenka is afraid that her dad killed DeVoster."

Shelly's face was a kaleidoscope of emotions. Pain? Worry? Defeat?

"A drunken fight is nothing compared to that," I said. "You'd be doing Varenka a favor if you told her the truth."

"Some favor." Shelly scoffed and struggled with her coat. "If you tell her, I'll deny it." She was out the door before I could ask a single question about my other suspects.

But I didn't rule out Varenka's parents strictly on the basis of Shelly's tale. After she left, I did an online search and got the names and numbers of all five bars in Independence, Iowa. I was on the phone with the last of them when Vince barged in the front door and dashed up the stairs, with Labrys barking at his heels.

"You gotta loud office there, Miss," said the scratchy voice on the other end of the line. "What kinda survey didja say this was?"

I wanted to follow Vince up the stairs and tell him about Anne and Neale, but I couldn't put Jodine Tallman on hold. "I'm with the American Wellness and Leisure Institute." I honeyed my voice until it oozed with good will and professionalism.

"We're conducting a study on the drinking habits of rural men."

"What for?"

No dupe, this Jodine. I needed something that would get her talking. "Our hypothesis is that men who consume alcohol in bars are less prone to health problems than men who drink in their own homes."

"Say what?" Jodine yelled at someone to turn down the damn jukebox.

I repeated my "hypothesis," and Vince thudded around upstairs. What was he doing home in the middle of the afternoon?

"That sounds about right," Jodine said. "How many questions you got?"

"Just a few," I answered. "How many patrons do you usually serve on a weeknight?"

"That depends on the special. We got Monday Millers, Tuesday tonics, Wednesday …"

I like alliteration as much as the next girl, but what I like even more is when an interviewee gives me a smooth segue to a question I really want to ask. "What about Fridays?" I asked. "How many patrons do you usually serve then?"

"Friday is our best night on account of Friday Freebies. Five to six, everybody gets a free draw, and then most folks stay put."

"Until close?"

"Nah, only a few stay till then. Kids mostly. But legal. I don't serve them underage."

"Of course not. Were you there at close this Friday?"

"Me and my granddaughter, Leona."

"What about patrons?"

"This past Friday was a bit unusual. We had a problem."

I felt a prickle of excitement. "What kind of problem?"

"It ain't gonna matter for your study."

This woman was really putting my bullshitting abilities to the test. "It might," I said. "Part of our hypothesis is that bartenders are better than regular citizens at knowing how to handle problem drinkers."

"Amen to that," Jodine said.

"So what was the problem?"

"A man who'd recently fallen off the wagon got sloppy drunk."

So far her description fit Mr. White.

"I woulda never served him, but Leona, she didn't know his story."

"An honest mistake," I said.

"That's right, and we didn't want to make any more, if you get my meaning. We don't want no accidents coming out of our place. I took his keys—he'd left them right on the bar—and offered to drive him home, but he was stubborn as a mule. Kept saying I'd stolen his car and he was calling the police. I told him to go ahead so they could lock him up for public intox. Then he just grunted and stumbled off."

"Did you call the police?"

Labrys and Vince thundered down the steps. Vince held a few hangered suits in front of him as if they were a battle-shield. I silently motioned him over. He paused and signaled me to wind it up.

"Ordinarily I woulda," Jodine said, "but I knew this man and his wife, and I didn't want to add to their troubles."

Vince pantomimed impatience, tapping his foot and checking his watch. Labrys wagged her tail.

"You say they were having trouble?" Vince headed to the door, and I went after him. "What kind of trouble?"

"You don't really need to know that for your survey, do you?"

Vince held his watch up and mouthed that he was late.

I held up a finger: *One minute.* "It might help create a context for his excessive drinking."

Sorry, Vince mouthed, and he was out the door.

I peered through its window, and Labrys pawed at its bottom. I hoped she had no urgent need to go out.

"I gotta get back to work," Jodine said.

Vince carefully placed his suits in the backseat of Richard's car.

"How old was the man?"

"Forty, forty-five."

"What about his height?"

"Tall as they come. Used to be quite a cager back in the day."

Richard's car pulled out of the driveway.

I'd verified Shelly's story and eliminated Varenka's parents as suspects, but my triumph felt small. There was no one to share it with.

TWENTY-THREE

Varenka trailed the other players as they rumbled down the floor on a fast break. Given her tearful admission earlier that morning, I was impressed that she'd even shown up for practice. But Bridget had higher expectations. "Come on, V! Quit standing around. Make a cut!"

Jessie caught the ball near the lane and, despite a hand in her face, sank a fadeaway jumper, hanging in midair, tantalizing her defender, before releasing the ball—such power and strength, such controlled physicality. I shivered as DeVoster's injuries pressed themselves upon my consciousness.

"Varenka!" Bridget shouted. "You gonna play defense today?"

The poor girl glanced over at her coach and wiped her face with her shirt.

I have no idea how athletes endure their coaches' yelling and jibes. But Bridget's antics didn't seem to bother anyone but me. The other two assistants were doing their own share of shouting while Shelly and a male manager leaned calmly over clipboards. Shelly sighed as Varenka missed yet another chippie.

"How many is that?" Bridget asked.

"Five."

Bridget sighed too and took off her jacket, revealing a T-shirt that touted the team's Big Ten championship last year.

I wanted to reassure her that they could win again, that Varenka would get her game back once she knew that her parents were off the hook. But truth be told, the young woman would have a full plate for a good long time—especially if someone else she loved turned out to be DeVoster's murderer.

Varenka got beat on defense, and Bridget wrote something on a clipboard. Her hand moved across the paper, fiercely and purposefully.

Jessie sank a three. If the rookie had a guilty conscience, it wasn't affecting her game. I hoped I wasn't wasting my time, waiting for practice to end so I could ask her about taping DeVoster's funeral. Then again, the alternative had been staying home and throwing myself the mother of all pity parties.

What was wrong with me? I couldn't get over one ex before I acquired another. If lugging emotional baggage were an Olympic event, I'd be a gold medalist.

The players on offense—Varenka's team—were really struggling against their teammates' zone, tossing the ball around the perimeter, wasting clock. After Varenka launched a wild jump shot, Bridget blew her whistle and barked the name of a drill. Varenka started to line up behind her teammates, but Bridget waved her over. Me, I would have been far from eager for a private chat with the woman who'd been verbally assaulting me, but Varenka sprinted right over. "Pass," Bridget said.

"You don't have to do it all." Varenka nodded. I expected Bridget to rail about poor shot selection, but instead, she rested a hand on Varenka's waist. "You're showing a lot of heart this practice. Keep it up."

Here was a side of Bridget I hadn't noticed before. Gruffly maternal. Sure, she'd been doggedly protective of her team all along, but that, I'd assumed, had been all about wins. Now, it seemed, she cared about her players as people. That made her hush-hush homosexuality all the more puzzling. She seemed to understand her own power: one kind word from Coach and all was right with the world. How dare she encourage her lesbian players to closet themselves! How dare she leave Varenka defenseless against the DeVosters of the world!

I shifted in my hard plastic chair, growing angrier and angrier. If older lesbians didn't look out for younger ones, who would? Bridget, of course, believed that she was doing what was best. What a closet case. Just like Neale.

As the team started a suicide drill, the arena echoed with the squeaks of shoes against the floor. I was close enough to hear the players' grunting and ragged breathing, but I was an observer, nothing more.

✧ ✧ ✧

Practice ended, and I stopped Jessie March just as she was about to enter the tunnel to the locker room. She was glazed with sweat and noisily sucking a water bottle. When I said that I needed to ask her a couple more questions, she smiled and faced the court again. Bridget conferred with the other coaches, Varenka practiced her midrange jumper, and Shelly rebounded for her.

"Can we make this quick?" Jessie said. "I got class tonight."

Her eyes were on Varenka.

"I noticed you were taping DeVoster's memorial service."

She nodded, her gaze still on her teammate.

"Why?"

"A class project."

She wasn't as chatty as the first time we'd talked. "A project," I repeated.

Varenka made two shots in a row, and finally, Jessie focused on me. "I'm making an audio collage for Intro to Women's Studies. A critique of all the support DeVoster's received—lots of material, unfortunately." Jessie tugged at the towel that was draped around her neck and mopped her face. "But I didn't send that cassette to the paper."

She turned her attention back to Varenka, who started shooting from the other side of the basket. Shelly shifted sides as well. Staring at me, her face tight, she missed a rebound. As she chased after it, I tried to think of a way to discover what Jessie knew about the rape without betraying Varenka's confidence.

"Jess," Bridget said, "I'd like a moment with Mara."

The freshman all but sprinted to the locker room, the other two coaches trailing behind her.

I wondered if Bridget really wanted to talk with me or if she simply wanted to prevent me from questioning Jessie.

"You look beat." She put her hand on my shoulder as if I were a player who needed a pep talk. "How about you let me make you dinner?" The offer seemed guileless enough. Faint laugh lines sprouted from her eyes as she smiled, and a beauty mark nestled in the curve of a dimple.

But Anne was in jail. "I can't," I said, "not while—"

She squeezed my shoulder and released me. "Orchid told me about Anne." Bridget's face clouded. "I'm really sorry. The whole team is."

She seemed sorry, but I had my doubts. Anne's arrest took the heat off the Hawkeyes. "You can see why I can't—"

"You gotta eat sometime," Bridget said. "Besides, Shelly and Orchid have organized the team on Anne's behalf."

A lump formed in my throat. I wasn't the only one trying to help Anne.

"They've created a legal defense fund," Bridget continued. "They're calling our season ticket holders, Women's Center donors, your station's donors, and anybody else they can think of who'll contribute."

I'd always considered Orchid so flush I hadn't realized she'd have trouble with the lawyer's fee. I wondered how much cash I could spare and kicked myself for not keeping better track of my finances.

"Yo, Shell," Roshaun called as he walked past us, cornrows jutting out of a Hawkeye stocking cap.

Shelly grinned at him and snagged a long rebound. Organizing all those phone calls—she was a lot more together than I'd thought.

Roshaun gestured for the ball and nodded at Varenka. "Me and Shell are grabbing some pizza. You wanna come?"

Varenka hesitated.

Shelly pitched the ball to her boyfriend, who made an up-and-under shot that was nothing but net. "Shell's buying," Roshaun said.

"You wish." Shelly swiped at the ball and tossed it to Varenka, who rewarded her with a small smile.

"Come on," Bridget said to me, "you deserve a break too."

✧ ✧ ✧

Bridget's breath rose like smoke signals in the darkness as

she prodded the steaks on the grill. I had no idea why she insisted on braving the cold, but I felt deliciously pampered at her dining room table, watching her through the sliding glass doors to her deck. In my hand was a Killian's Irish Red and spread before me were the makings of a feast: a loaf of sourdough, a bunch of grapes, and a colorful vegetable salad. I smiled when Bridget came back inside, her face pink with the cold, the steaks sizzling on a plate. She set them on the table and eased out of her coat.

"I can't remember the last time I had steak," I said. It was true. Anne and Orchid served strictly vegan fare; Neale favored complicated pasta dishes; and my own repertoire hinged upon the sale items in my grocer's freezer section.

"It's the least I can do," Bridget said. "You've been more than generous with your time."

The clock in her kitchen said 7:30. I couldn't linger too long if I wanted to track down some more answers before the evening was over.

"Just relax and enjoy." Bridget nodded toward the steaks, and I speared one onto my plate.

For a moment, I closed my eyes and simply savored the scent of charcoal. When I opened them, Bridget was watching me. I sliced through my steak and tried to think of something to say. Her aquarium gurgled as she ripped a piece of bread from the loaf. Then her phone rang.

"I need to get that," she said. "It's probably Carol." She motioned for me to eat as she headed to an end table a few paces away and picked up the phone.

Whatever Coach Carol had to say, it wasn't good.

"I'm so sorry," Bridget said. "I bet she really wishes she could be there."

The bread warmed my hands as I broke it.

"Don't worry," Bridget said. "Our girls are off the hook. There's been an arrest—Anne Golding."

I turned from my plate.

Bridget met my eyes and started pacing. "Varenka was upset, but she practiced today. She'll be good to go on Thursday."

I assumed that Bridget meant the upcoming game against Creighton. I wondered if she was really as confident as she sounded, or if she was simply trying to lighten Coach Carol's load.

"I'll finish breaking down the film," Bridget said. "Please, just take care of yourself." She hung up, frowning, and returned to the table. "Carol's only daughter isn't coming to the funeral. Her own uncle, her mother's brother—and she can't make the time. She never can. Carol hasn't seen her granddaughters in over a year."

It had been nearly that long since I'd seen my parents, and I wasn't planning to visit them anytime soon. Bridget's family must actually enjoy each other's company.

"I wish I could be there. She's always been there for me." Bridget shot me a glance and then stared at her plate as if there was something she wanted to say.

I picked up my silverware and carved a piece of steak, but it seemed rude to eat when Bridget still hadn't touched her meal.

"I was in the first class she recruited at Iowa," Bridget said. "We were juniors when her husband died."

"I remember him." How could I not? He had been featured in each year's program—his greenhouses and the bouquets he brought to the locker room before every game. "A heart attack, right?"

Bridget nodded. "Things really changed after his death. It was like Carol's whole world vanished except for basketball. Garnet—that's her daughter—she was about sixteen. Never came to another one of our games."

I wondered where Bridget was going with all this.

"Carol loves her players. She'd do anything for them, but she doesn't get what it's like—the closet." Bridget met my eyes again. "She doesn't remember what it's like to have a life outside basketball."

And she's straight, I thought.

"She's not homophobic. She just wants everybody to keep their personal lives off the court."

"Then why does she flaunt her heterosexuality?" The way I saw it, Coach Carol was partly to blame for what happened to Varenka. "Why is she always pictured with the granddaughters she never sees? Why is there a halftime story about her dead husband nearly every time you guys play on TV?"

Bridget was staring at me now. "Carol's not in control of the networks."

"No, but she has a lot of power over her players. So do you."

"What's that supposed to mean?"

I didn't want to pick a fight, but I couldn't get Varenka out of my head. "You could help your lesbian players feel good about themselves."

"What should I do? Take them to a pride parade?" Bridget pushed her chair away from the table. "In your world it's cool to be openly gay, but in mine it's career suicide." She took a deep breath and stared at the floor. "Do you know what's going to happen if I'm named head coach when Carol retires?" Her voice was soft, her anger seemingly spent. "We're going to have trouble recruiting because a lot of parents won't want to surrender their daughters to a big, bad lesbian."

"But your record. Your experience—"

"Mara," Bridget said, "even Pat Summitt worries about the lesbian issue."

The winningest basketball coach ever. A married woman with a son. Maybe Bridget was right. She and I lived in two different worlds. I couldn't imagine my talents and accomplishments counting for so little, and my identity—or ignorant ideas about it—counting for so much. "I'm sorry." I wanted to offer Bridget something more than an apology, but if I told her I no longer suspected Varenka's parents, she'd fume because I'd suspected them in the first place. And if I told her I'd established solid alibis for all but one of her players, she'd stew about my suspicion of Jessie and scramble to protect the rookie.

Bridget pulled her chair back to the table. "I didn't invite you over to argue," she said. "Eat."

A bit of blood had gathered where I'd cut my steak. My appetite was gone, but I needed to keep up my sleuthing strength and wanted to show Bridget that I appreciated her efforts. I sipped my beer. It had been such a pleasant evening. Then Coach Carol had to call, and Bridget had to take a bullet train down memory lane.

She sawed her steak into tiny pieces, her jaw tight. Her silverware clattered as she set it on her plate, and her aquarium bubbled louder in our silence. "I'll put some music on." She dashed to her CD collection, which was housed in a curvy kind of sculpture next to her TV and stereo. Leaning over, she studied a few titles, pulled one out, and shoved it back in. "What do you feel like?"

I felt like going home, forgetting all about the fact that Anne was in jail and that Neale was out of my life, and sleeping for days. "Surprise me," I said, popping a piece of steak into my mouth.

As Bridget returned to the table, a Debussy arpeggio washed over me. I was about to praise her choice when I felt her eyes on me, her gaze growing more intense with each rise and fall of the music.

"It was Carol's idea to lie to you about why the freshmen left. Not mine."

I put my fork down. Bridget's admission didn't exactly surprise me, but it took me off-guard.

"We don't usually disagree," she said.

My guess was that she didn't usually share their disagreements either.

"I never wanted to deceive you." Bridget's eyes continued to hold mine. "It's just that being second-in-command ..." she trailed off.

Was she defending herself or apologizing? "It must be tricky," I said.

"Tricky." She repeated the word as if she'd never heard it before. "I shouldn't have gotten you involved."

"I'd have been in the thick of things anyway because of Anne." *Anne:* I needed to eat and run if I was going to do anything more on her behalf before the day was through. I picked up my fork and took another bite of steak.

Debussy's notes surged and receded. Bridget and I locked eyes again and found ourselves in an uncomfortable silence.

"So what's next with your investigation?" Bridget asked.

"I need to talk to Lexie and Tyler again." No need to mention that I also planned to talk with Jessie.

"Lexie will do anything to get a good scoop."

Just like some people, I thought, who would do anything for their team. But Bridget didn't seem to make the connection.

"Did you know that after the rape first happened, Carol had to call Lexie's editor to get her to back off our girls? Lexie kept pestering them about their teammates and other athletes—drinking habits, drug habits, sex habits. Did they cheat in class? Did they have eating disorders? Were they gay? Were they homophobic? Racist? The whole laundry list."

I could see why the questions had upset Coach Carol, but I wished that Lexie had pursued them instead of generating columns and columns of print about Anne.

"She wanted to do some huge exposé about what she called the underside of college sports," Bridget said. "She has zero respect for people's privacy."

At last, for the first time that evening, I knew where Bridget was headed next. "I'm not going to out your players to Lexie Roth."

"I wasn't implying—" Bridget sputtered. "It's just that—"

I cut her off. "I wish I knew more about the case that the cops are building against Anne."

"Ask your girlfriend to find out for you."

I struggled to swallow a piece of steak and dropped my eyes to my plate.

"Cops," Bridget said, "they're always helping each other."

I poked my salad and tried to think of an excuse to leave.

"You're girlfriend's a cop, isn't she?" Bridget asked. "The woman I met—"

"We broke up." Who was I to take Bridget to task for lying? I was becoming quite the dealer in half-truths myself. "She broke up with me."

A new piano piece rippled through the room as Bridget's eyes softened. "Oh, Mara, that's rotten. What happened?"

What had happened? I took a huge bite of bread and gazed at the tabletop. The lines in the wood grain reminded me of Neale's subtle curves and the almost certain truth that I'd never touch her again.

"If you ever need to talk," Bridget said, "I have lots of experience being dumped."

"I'm no novice myself."

"Bet you never experienced this." She waited until I met her eyes. "After my most recent ex failed to get tenure, she went to a queer theory conference and never returned. She sent her new girlfriend—one of her own students—to get her things."

I tilted my head to Bridget. Her story did indeed top mine.

"Wait," she said. "It gets better—or worse. The new girlfriend actually wanted toward interview me for her dissertation. She wanted to know how the recent shift in my relationship status had impacted my lesbian identity paradigm."

Bridget's laugh was as easy on the ears as Debussy. I couldn't help but join in. And later, after we'd downed several scoops of chocolate ice cream, I sure didn't feel like leaving.

TWENTY-FOUR

Kate's cell phone all but disappeared as she cradled it in her hands. "W-w-in is using the phone in her b-bedroom." She glanced across her living room at the closed door and then at the Iowa Hawkeye quilt behind her. For once, Kate's dark hair fell loosely about her shoulders, but the rest of her was wound tight. "There's n-not much t-time before we'll have to call it a n-night."

"I'll make my questions quick, then."

"Varenka wanted to help, but she was upset w-with her p-play in practice. She went to b-bed early."

"I know," I said. "I saw the sign on her door." After leaving Bridget's, I'd gone to Varenka's to check in on her—to tell her that her parents were off the hook and to see what more I could learn about Jessie—but that talk would have to wait, as would the talk with Jessie herself.

"Shelly did a great j-job s-starting this phone-athon," Kate said. "Once she p-puts her m-mind to something, it's a d-done deal."

Could we say avoidance? "I know you don't want to talk about it, but I need to ask about the rumors circulating about Varenka's rape."

Win's low drawl emanated from the other room, and below us a bass thumped relentlessly.

"I've gotten p-pledges for a thousand d-dollars." Kate rested her phone on the sofa between us. "Do you know how much the lawyer will c-cost?"

I didn't. Orchid's line had been busy every time I'd tried it. I was pretty sure, however, that a thousand dollars was a drop in the bucket. "About the rumors," I said.

"I never heard any." She stretched toward the coffee table and flipped through her pages of phone numbers.

"Do you know who Varenka discussed the evening with?"

Kate raked her eyes over me. "Not her parents."

So that's what she was about. Protecting Varenka's parents. "I've already ruled them out."

"B-but Varenka said—"

"I got some new information after I talked to her. When she wakes up, will you tell her?"

"What n-new—"

I cut her off. "Did she ever talk to you about what happened?"

Kate shook her head and frowned.

I wondered if she was lying or disappointed that Varenka hadn't confided in her.

"She m-might have said something to J-Jessie."

Exactly what I'd been hoping to hear, yet I had to consider my source. Who knew how long Kate had carried a torch for

Varenka before Jessie stepped in and stole her heart. "Did Jessie ever say anything about it?"

"W-we don't talk."

A beep issued from Win's room, and the door opened. "Man, I could never be a telemarketer. I'm 0–5 on my last calls." *Caw-alls.* Her long, lazy vowels ground to a halt when she saw me. "Miss Gilgannon." She made my name sound like an accusation.

"Kate and I were discussing what Jessie might have known about the rape."

As Win studied us, she placed her hands on her hips; the worry lines on her forehead began to deepen. "That's hard to say. But I do know that Varenka tried real hard not to discuss it with her folks."

"Her parents are already in the clear," I said.

Win let her hands relax at her side.

"But Jessie's not," I added.

Win's freckled face tightened, and Kate dropped her gaze to the floor.

Win stepped toward her teammate. "Did you know Varenka's mom and dad were off the hook?"

Kate glanced at me. "J-just n-now," she said, "I found out just n-now."

"And you never told her about Jessie?" Win's voice shot up nearly an octave. "What were you thinking?"

Kate's face grew pink as Win gave her a withering look.

I was completely lost.

Win whirled toward me and pushed up the sleeves of her flannel shirt. "Jessie was with us that night. She stopped by right after the folks who wanted our autographs."

If this were true, then the rookie had an alibi. "How long after?" I asked.

"Like, a minute."

I checked to see if Win's eyes darted around the room, but they bore right into mine.

Then she turned to Kate. "Tell her."

Kate's face soured.

"Tell her," Win said.

The downstairs bass pounded to a stop.

Kate sighed, her shoulders caving. "J-Jessie was there. L-like Win said."

Win glared at her teammate. "What were you thinking—trying to get Jessie in trouble?"

Kate refused to look at either of us.

"Let me get this straight," I said. "You two *and* Jessie all willingly sacrificed perfectly good alibis in order to shield Varenka's parents?"

"She was real worried about them," Win said, "and we agreed we'd tell the truth if any of us became serious suspects." She shot Kate another scorching look.

Unless I'd just been treated to an elaborately staged scene, Jessie March had a fairly solid alibi, compliments of a woman who wanted to hurt her. That left Lexie, the Machiavellian reporter, or Tyler, the world's most sensitive male athlete, to take Anne's place in jail. I tried to tell myself that narrowing my list of suspects was a good thing.

✧ ✧ ✧

One more brick wall and I could build a mansion. My remaining suspects were nowhere to be found, Vince and Orchid weren't answering their phones, and my junk food larder contained only one fun-size Snickers. Talk about a misnomer. The less chocolate, the less fun—it doesn't take a genius to figure that out. Unwrapping my tiny ration, I lay on my couch and stared at the ceiling. An army of dead bugs huddled in the center of my light fixture. Across the room, Labrys whimpered in her sleep, oblivious and uncaring.

I pressed the redial button, and Orchid's phone rang in my ear. But there was no answer. No answers and no one to talk to—that was me. For all I knew, Anne had been transferred to some maximum-security prison five states away, and Neale had taken up with a beautiful, young thing with a fetish for heartless, workaholic cops. At least Neale and I hadn't moved in together, not like me and Anne—or Bridget and her ex.

Bridget.

There was somebody I could call—somebody I *should* call. She deserved to know that I'd cleared all her players. In fact, I'd be remiss if I didn't phone. Swinging my legs to the floor and sitting up straight, I dialed her number.

And got a busy signal. I should have interpreted it as a cautionary omen, but I didn't. Instead, I decided to drive back to Bridget's and give her the good news in person.

✧ ✧ ✧

By the time I got there, I'd lost some of my enthusiasm. Would I look silly? It had barely been two hours since we'd bid each other adieu, yet there I was standing on her doorstep, my hand mere inches from her doorbell. I recalled our awkward silence and stepped back. As the branches of a pine tree rustled against her condo, a cold gust whipped my jacket open. I wasn't dressed for outdoor dithering. Retreat or advance? Which was it going to be?

I needed to ask more questions about Lexie and Tyler. There was no doubt about that. And Bridget had offered me a sympathetic ear. Furthermore, she had revealed a rift between her mentor and herself. She'd sacrificed the appearance of their united front: she'd betrayed her beloved coach. Why? No reason—unless she had done it for me.

My own motivations received a less thorough scrutiny, and thus the doorbell tolled for Bridget.

Her raised eyebrows snapped me back to reality. It was half past ten on a weeknight, and I was dropping by unannounced. She was already in her pajamas—flannel pants and a long-sleeved T-shirt worn thin with age—and her dark curls were shiny and wet from a recent shampoo. I sputtered something about how I just happened to be driving by, and Bridget's eyebrows rose even higher. "I have some good news," I said.

At that, she stepped aside and ushered me in. My glasses steamed over as I followed her up the stairs. At the landing, I took them off, and everything blurred. I've always felt oddly incomplete without my glasses. Usually, I can't talk on the phone or even think without them. Not that I always do a bang-up job with them on. They were half-clear when I returned them to my face, so I could see Bridget's feet as she helped me with my jacket. "How about another Killian's?" she said.

I remained next to the chortling aquarium as she popped open two beers. When she handed me one, my glasses were nearly back to normal. If only I could say the same for myself.

"Take a load off," Bridget said as she headed to the couch, "and tell me this good news."

I glanced around the room. On the TV, two basketball players were frozen mid-play. The shorter one had just flown past her defender in the lane. Across from the TV was an easy chair with some notebooks on its seat. "You were working, weren't you? I should go."

"Don't be silly. I was about to call it a night anyway."

I kept my eyes on the screen.

"The player with the ball," Bridget said, "she's predictable. Likes to go left."

"What else can you tell?" There. After I shared my news, we'd have something to chat about while we finished our drinks. I took a huge gulp.

Suddenly, the hoopsters vanished and a *Seinfeld* rerun flashed on the screen. George Costanza's mother brayed until Bridget managed to find the off-button. Then, excruciating silence. Finally, Bridget extended her beer toward mine. "To good news."

We clinked bottles, and I sat on one end of the couch. She sat in the center, literally on the edge of her seat. Her elbows rested on her knees, and her head twisted toward me. Except for her beer and pajamas, she was in her usual coaching stance. I took another drink and told her that she no longer needed to worry about me troubling her players or Varenka's parents, that even though I couldn't go into the details, I'd verified all their alibis.

As I talked, all I could think about was Anne behind bars, alone and afraid. "That leaves me with two suspects," I said, "Lexie and Tyler." Much to my chagrin, my voice cracked. "Everybody worships Tyler, and Lexie has managed to deflect suspicion away from herself and onto Anne."

"Mara?" Bridget's voice was gentle.

I squeezed my hands around my beer and blinked back tears. "Neither of them was home tonight," I said. "I looked for Tyler at the arena and Lexie at the office of *The Daily Iowan,* but they weren't there either."

She touched my arm, and I started crying. "What if I can't figure out who did it?" I sputtered through the rest. Anne could be convicted and imprisoned—Anne, who had tried to help

Varenka, who had worked her whole life against violence.

"Shh," Bridget took my beer, wrapped an arm around me, and pulled me toward her.

The waterworks were really going now. "I'm sorry," I said.

She stroked my hair and guided my head to her shoulder. The day's events spiraled through my mind: Varenka sobbing and blaming herself, Orchid panicking and desperate, Anne in jail, Neale calling it quits—and me, unable to do anything about any of it. I dabbed at my nose and eyes with my Kleenex and tried to catch my breath. Bridget's shoulder was soft, and I became aware of her own breathing, her chest slowly rising and falling under my head. I could hear her heart beat. Even though I'd been crying, I fancied that I could smell a trace of her shampoo, earthy and musky. And even though I could have used another Kleenex, I didn't want to leave her arms.

But what to do with my own arms? Tentatively, I reached a hand and rested it lightly on her thigh. My heart started thumping, and as she placed her free hand on mine, a current surged through my entire body. She kissed my forehead, and I lifted my face to hers. In that moment, our lips nearly touching, I wanted nothing so much as to kiss her. But she pulled away and handed me the box of Kleenex.

What had I been thinking? My swollen nose and bloodshot eyes must have been a real turn-on—not to mention my messed-up life. I'd been getting hot and bothered while she'd been playing good Samaritan. I blew my nose, wracking my brain for an exit line.

"Mara." Bridget's hand was on my back again.

I couldn't bear to look at her, but somehow I couldn't force myself off the couch.

Bridget kept saying my name until I looked at her. "I don't want you to misunderstand," she said.

I looked away again, bracing myself for the whole just-friends speech. My day wasn't simply in the toilet. It was in the deep, dark recesses of the sewer.

"I like you a lot ..."

My face burned with embarrassment as I waited for the big "but."

"I'm going to be completely honest with you," Bridget said, "I find you fascinating."

Why, oh why, couldn't she be merciful and get this over quickly?

"I've had a crush on you for a long time."

What?

"Since that time you interviewed me about Title IX. You tried so hard. No way was I taking your bait, but you kept rephrasing your questions."

That interview was a long time ago—had it been before I'd met Neale?—while Bridget had probably still been with the tenure-seeking feminist.

"You were so damn cute and persistent."

How had I not noticed Bridget's crush?

"I'd like to see if we could have something together, but it hasn't been that long since Felicity left me, and you—just today, well, you—"

"Got dumped." I finished the sentence for her.

"Mara." She brushed her fingertips along my jawline and smiled. "Rebounding is for basketball."

TWENTY-FIVE

"You have more love-interests than suspects," Vince said.

I didn't bother arguing. I was just glad he was home when I'd returned from Bridget's. Of course, it didn't hurt that he'd apologized profusely for abandoning me and that he'd brought me a peace offering in the form of a triple-chocolate torte. We dug into it as I explained my investigative dilemmas.

"If I were you," Vince said, "I'd ask Lexie to write a story about how the women's team is trying to raise money for Anne's defense."

I licked some frosting off my fork and thought about it. Lexie would be all over a human-interest piece like that, and Anne would get a lot more donations.

Vince launched into his Hayley Mills imitation. "It's a scathingly brilliant idea," he said. "Weren't you planning to show up at her place super early tomorrow?"

I nodded.

"The story could be your excuse. Then you could subtly ease into interrogation mode."

Subtlety isn't my strong suit, but I had to admit, Vince's plan was pretty decent. "I wish I knew what to ask her."

"What about your other suspect—the guy who used to play behind DeVoster?" Vince pushed away his empty plate. "Didn't you say she was watching him at the memorial service?"

"She didn't want to talk about him, though."

"Lois Lane was just guarding her story. She'll talk if you offer her some scoop."

"I don't have any." I did, of course, but it was about the women's team. And I wasn't going to share that information with anyone, not even Vince.

"Make something up," he said. "Tell her that what's-his-name is taking steroids."

"Tyler Bennet."

"No, wait. I know." Vince grabbed his fork. "Bennet and DeVoster were having a torrid affair, and things went south."

"Right." I rolled my eyes. "Two guys who hardly spoke to each other."

"In public," Vince protested.

"Never mind," I said, "I'll think of something."

"That's the spirit, Mar-Bar. You'll have Anne out of the slammer before you can say habeas corpus."

"I hope so."

He leaned across the table and helped himself to the frosting on my plate.

"You want to come with me tomorrow?" He hates getting up early, but I figured he'd make an exception, given my status as a recent dumpee.

"I've got to be at the shelter extremely early tomorrow. And

I want to be well-rested. The head inspector is to die for."

The shelter's annual inspection. I'd forgotten. I picked up our plates and took them to the sink.

"Ask Bridget," he said. "It'll be a bonding experience. Savor the rosebuds while ye may."

"Vince," I said, "it hasn't even been twenty-four hours since I was dumped." But I wondered how much time would need to pass before Bridget no longer considered me on the rebound.

✧ ✧ ✧

Vince nearly walloped me as he swiveled in the passenger seat, flicked on my car's interior light, and peered into the rearview mirror. "After losing so much sleep, I'm going to look positively drab. That inspector won't give me a second glance." He stroked his goatee. "Have you noticed any silver in my beard?"

"Stop it," I snapped. "I need to see if there's a car behind me."

"Trust me." Vince turned off the light. "There's not. It's 4 A.M. We're the only fools who aren't in bed."

"You're awake enough to complain." I reached for my travel mug and sipped my coffee. I needed the brew in my system ASAP, but it was too hot to gulp.

"It's so early—Lexie Roth isn't going to be able to remember her own name," Vince said, "let alone answer your questions."

"We'll be sure to catch her."

"In a bad mood," Vince muttered. "You'd think an ambitious reporter would live in town where the action is. How much farther?"

"Just a couple miles." We'd driven past the south edge of Iowa City about five minutes earlier and were immersed in total darkness. No streetlights, no stars.

"How are we going to see it?

"It's past a curve."

"Mar-Bar, this road has more curves than J-Lo."

I was having second, third, and fourth thoughts about why I'd brought Vince along, but thankfully, he remained silent until we reached Lexie's. Gravel crunched under my tires, and my headlights flashed on the bare trees that lined her long and windy driveway. Finally, the beams revealed a tiny house nestled amid some pines.

"All that driveway for this?" Vince said. "How utterly anticlimactic."

As I turned off the ignition, my car rattled and sputtered. It's grown noisier in its golden years. I left the lights on so we could make our way to the door.

"Here's hoping the battery is good," Vince said.

As we neared the front door, the wooden porch creaked, and a sharp wind hissed through the pines. I was glad to have Vince by my side. If Lexie were indeed a killer, I didn't want to be alone with her out in the boonies. I pushed the doorbell and studied the boxes and piles of recycling that filled Lexie's porch. A gust opened a magazine and whirred through its pages, but I heard nothing from inside.

"I hope she doesn't mistake us for burglars and greet us with a shotgun," Vince said.

"Do burglars knock?" I rang the bell again and pounded on the door.

"She might not be thinking clearly in the middle of the night," Vince said. "Few people do. Take you, for instance, and this plan—"

"Shh. I hear steps."

Vince leaned toward the house. "I don't hear a single thing

except my teeth chattering."

I pummeled the door. "Lexie," I called. "It's Mara Gilgannon."

"You need to go Marlon Brando." Vince tilted his head back and bellowed, "Stella, Stell-aah!" Then he shouted Lexie's name a few times and gave up.

The magazine pages kept rippling. What if Lexie had spent the night somewhere else, and we'd gotten up early for nothing? "Lexie," I yelled, "we've got a scoop about DeVoster."

The porch flooded with light, and the door flew open. There she stood, wearing black-and-gold sweats. Smack-dab in the middle of Lexie's chest was a glow-in-the-dark Nike basketball.

She followed my gaze and tried to shut the door, but Vince and I pushed our way in.

"This is harassment," she said. "I'm calling the cops."

"Tell them to hurry. They'll be eager to see your loungewear."

The wind slammed the door shut, and we all jumped.

Lexie's eyes were puffy, and a lacy pillowcase had left its imprint across one of her cheeks. Her hair rivaled Medusa's. "What do you want?" Lexie glanced at Vince. "Who's this?"

I ignored her questions. "Where did you get those sweats?"

Lexie tried to smooth her hair out of her face. "I don't have to answer you."

"True. The sooner we leave, the sooner we can phone the police and tell them about your telltale clothes."

"I'll get rid of them," Lexie said.

"It matters not." Vince whipped out his phone. "My trusty cell doubles as a camera. I'll take a few candids before calling the men in blue."

"Who knows?" I said. "Maybe we'll send a few photos to the papers. And you can have a taste of your own medicine."

Lexie lunged for the phone, and I lunged for her.

"Careful," Vince said. "This cost a pretty—"

"Leave her alone," another male voice said. "I gave her the sweats."

Tyler Bennet tightened his robe, loped down the dimly lit hallway, and eased himself onto a futon couch.

Color me flummoxed. My remaining suspects were bedfellows?

Lexie rushed to Tyler's side, her eyes on me. "You've got to promise not to tell anyone."

"I'm not promising anything. It's your fault Anne Golding is in jail."

She reached for Tyler's hand. "I was just trying to stir things up for DeVoster. I didn't mean to—"

"You misrepresented her," I said, "and now she's facing a murder charge."

"Ladies," Vince said, "surely we can discuss this in a civil manner?"

"I think the ship pretty much sailed on civil when you woke us up in the middle of the night." Tyler cracked his knuckles and stared at Vince.

I scanned the living room, trying to formulate a new plan. Behind Lexie and Tyler was a Degas print of ballerinas. Lexie had the body and posture of someone who'd once studied ballet. No slouching for her come hell or high water.

Well, I could be poised too. I flipped on a floor lamp and gestured for Vince to join me on the love seat across from the futon. The message was clear: We weren't going anywhere until we got some answers.

Tyler kept staring at Vince. Finally, two plus two equaled four. "Hey," he said. "You're the pizza guy."

Vince gave a tiny bow.

Tyler cracked his knuckles again. "Were you thinking your friend needed protection while she questioned me?"

I couldn't tell whether Tyler was angry because we'd deemed him dangerous or because we'd deemed Vince adequate protection.

A tailless gray cat crept into the room and studied us with her one good eye. Then she dashed to her scratching post and began blissfully clawing at its carpet. When she stopped, the room fell silent until she started slurping at her front leg. As she began attending to a less seemly place, Tyler spoke up. "Neither one of us killed DeVoster. We were together that night. Right here."

Lexie interrupted him. "We didn't tell you because we want to keep our relationship quiet." Her brow furrowed. "For obvious reasons."

I've always appreciated irony, and this irony was particularly fine. Lexie Roth, eternally scrambling for a scoop on the Hawkeyes, was herself such a scoop. I could see the headline: DEVOSTER'S FEMINIST NEMESIS BOFFING HIS BACKUP.

"After all I've written about DeVoster and men's athletics," she said, "Tyler would have a rough time if his coaches and team knew he was with me."

Not to mention that Lexie's crowd would be far from impressed if they learned that she'd been getting it on with one of DeVoster's teammates.

"How long have you been together?" Vince asked.

"Pretty near six months." The lamplight shone on Tyler's red hair as he smiled at Lexie.

One more closeted relationship and I'd scream. "So you're each other's alibi," I said. "That's convenient. How do we know you were here instead of with DeVoster?"

Lexie tilted her head defiantly. "The cops believe us."

"Do they?" I said. "Or are they too gutless to go after Eldon Bly's new starter?"

Tyler extracted his hand from Lexie's and glowered at me.

"You both hated him." Even as I peppered Tyler and Lexie with accusations, my heart sank. If the cops believed these two, I had no idea how to help Anne.

The cat strutted toward them and rubbed herself against their legs.

I decided to try a gentler approach. "Please," I said, "you two must know something that can help Anne."

"Sorry," Tyler mumbled.

Lexie reached down to stroke her cat, but it darted away.

"You said that Varenka White wasn't the first woman DeVoster raped. What did you mean by that?"

"Nothing." She started picking at a cuticle, and Tyler shot her a puzzled look.

"Lying," Vince mouthed.

"Come on," I said. "You must have meant something."

"I was just guessing. Really." Her eyes flicked from me to Tyler.

He stood and jerked his head toward the door. "You've bothered us long enough."

As Vince and I made our way in the cold darkness, I tallied my losses. I had no suspects, no leads, and—as it turned out—no reliable transportation. My battery was dead.

TWENTY-SIX

Sheepish didn't begin to describe my feelings as we headed back to the house for a jump, but much to my surprise, Lexie was quite gracious. "Tyler, why don't you and Mara's friend go find the cables, and we girls can stay here where it's warm."

We girls. Lexie Roth had never struck me as a fan of traditional gender roles.

She shut the door behind the guys and leaned against it. "Tyler doesn't know what I'm going to tell you," she whispered, "and he can't find out." Her forehead creased, and her eyes filled with pleading. "You can't tell anyone. If you do, I'll deny it."

I felt trapped with her towering over me in the cramped entryway, but I didn't want to waste time suggesting that we sit.

"I never meant for Anne to get in trouble," she said.

Outside, her garage door moaned open.

"Just tell me," I said. "It doesn't take forever to jump a car."

She gathered her hair in one hand and pulled it over the basketball on her sweatshirt. "I had a friend at the Women's Center, another volunteer. We used to work on the mailings together." Lexie paused. I was afraid that she'd changed her mind about telling me, but she took a deep breath and continued. "Last spring, we were working on a mailing—just the two of us—and she started crying. I asked what was wrong. She wouldn't tell me at first, but then she said that she'd been at a party after the men made it into the tournament. DeVoster got her really drunk and they started messing around."

Just like Varenka White, I thought.

"When she told him to stop, he wouldn't." Lexie's eyes blazed with anger.

"Who was it?"

"She trusted me."

An engine roared to life.

"I won't tell anyone," I said. "Please. Tell me."

Lexie looked past me at the door.

"I'll just ask Anne who you did the mailings with."

"Ryesha Anderson."

Anderson. "Is she related to Roshaun?"

"His little sister. That's why Tyler can't know. He'd tell Roshaun—I know he would."

"Was she a cheerleader?"

Lexie nodded.

I thought about my visit with Roshaun's mother and about the photo of her lovely daughter. My intuition had been right—I had seen her somewhere else. She was in the group shot in Varenka's room, all smiles, braids, and pom-poms. Ryesha Anderson probably knew all the basketball players—women and men.

"She wouldn't come forward because of her brother. She didn't want him doing anything that would make him lose his position as manager. He needed the scholarship, she said. So when DeVoster was bragging about how he had her—" Lexie shook her head in disgust. "She made Roshaun think it was consensual. She teased him about being overprotective and told him to stay out of her business."

"Did he believe her?"

"I never heard about any big blowups between him and DeVoster."

I thought about Roshaun's mother saying that all the managers disliked DeVoster because he treated them like servants. But what if Roshaun's antipathy ran deeper? What if he'd learned the truth about Ryesha? For that matter, what if Tyler had?

"Roshaun doesn't fit the witness's description," Lexie said.

"Where can I find Ryesha?" I asked. "I need to know if she told anyone else." Please, I thought, let it be someone tall and white, someone with access to the incriminating sweats. But not Tyler. Someone the cops would be willing to go after.

"You won't—"

I interrupted her. "I won't tip my hand. She'll never know we spoke."

Lexie picked at a cuticle. "You'll have to ask Roshaun where she is. She didn't come back this year."

"Because of what happened?" I asked.

Lexie nodded. "She said it was a race thing. She didn't like being the only black cheerleader. The campus was too white—that kind of thing."

A believable story, one that let her keep her shame to herself. DeVoster must have counted on her shame and silence. "You didn't stay in touch?"

"We talked a few times, but not since right after Varenka ..." Lexie trailed off. "I called Ryesha to get her to come forward. She told me to leave her alone."

Vince's laughter floated toward us as Lexie rushed through her story. "I phoned a couple days later to say I was sorry—that I wouldn't pressure her again—but her line had been disconnected and her new number was unlisted. I tried to get it from Roshaun, but he wouldn't talk to me because of my coverage of the men's team." Lexie paused at the sound of a car hood banging shut. "I wanted to help her," Lexie said. "She was so happy her first semester—on the dean's list, pledging a sorority—but DeVoster took all of that away."

The more I believed in Lexie's good intentions, the less I believed in her and Tyler's alibi. Even if Tyler didn't know about Ryesha, he knew about Varenka. He and Lexie both had a personal score to settle with DeVoster—a friend to avenge. I could imagine the secretive couple plotting together, but what I couldn't imagine was a way to prove their guilt.

TWENTY-SEVEN

Roshaun's roommate was in desperate need of coffee, manners, and an expanded vocabulary. Eyes half shut, he met my polite inquiry about Roshaun with two grunts: "Not here." Then he tried to shut the door in my face.

"Please," I said. "Do you know where he is?"

The roomie scratched his shaved head. His pasty face—some two feet above mine—was dotted with acne that flamed red like his robe. "Mom's," he finally managed.

"When will he be back?"

A shrug and another attempt to shut the door.

"Are you on the basketball team?"

He looked at me as if I were a moron.

I took that as a yes. "How well do you know Tyler Bennet?"

"Still dark."

"He has a dark side?" I asked.

"Need sleep," the roomie growled.

My watch read 5:10. "It is early," I acknowledged, "but this is important. Did he ever say anything to you about—"

"We're done." He shut the door and turned the deadbolt.

"I'm still here, and I'm not leaving until you tell me what you know about Tyler Bennet."

"Leave now." The door muffled his voice.

"I want to ask you about Roshaun's sister too."

At that, the door opened a few inches, and a pale-blue eye peered at me over a chain lock. "I'll call the cops," he said, "and tell Coach. This is harassment."

Harassment. He'd finally waxed multisyllabic, but I thought it best to leave. The last thing Orchid needed was another phone call from Eldon Bly.

✧ ✧ ✧

When I got back to my car, there was good news and bad news. The good news was Labrys thumping her tail in the backseat, happy to see me. The bad news—a ticket. I yanked it off my window and tossed it on the passenger seat next to my phone. As Labrys poked her head in between the two front seats to investigate, I flipped on my interior light and searched through my backpack. Underneath a bag of doughnuts was the list of phone numbers Shelly had given me, and on the third page was the listing for Roshaun's mother, Francine Anderson. I punched in her number, trying to think of a subtle way to inquire about the tall white people in her daughter's life, but I got a machine. When its garbled static morphed into a feeble beep, I asked her and Roshaun to call me ASAP, and I reviewed my morning. Before Vince and I left Lexie's, I'd persuaded her to write a feature about the fund-raiser for Anne's defense, but in the time since I'd dropped Vince at home, all I had to show for my efforts were the doughnuts and a so-called coffee from the Kum & Go. I sipped the bitter brew and started my car.

Labrys barked at a shaggy mutt straining against its leash on the sidewalk next to us. The canine's less-energetic human companion huddled against the cold, clutching a sack of poop. The reflector stripe across his chest flashed under a streetlight as he vanished into the darkness. I steered out of my costly parking spot, pondering my next step. Whatever it was, I needed to be more alert. I'd missed a lot of clues about Lexie and Tyler's relationship. Each of them had been quick to dismiss the other as a suspect. Lexie had been watching Tyler at the memorial service, not because she was planning to write about him, but because she couldn't keep her eyes off him. For all I knew, she'd been at his apartment when I'd first talked to him, and that's why the reputedly polite hoopster refused to let me in.

On Clinton Street, I drove by a brightly lit sign that advertised a vegetarian harvest dinner at Old Brick Church and Community Center. I recalled Tyler's sudden conversion to vegetarianism, his retreat from Roshaun and the team. Chalk up both to the vegan Lexie and her rural love shack. What other connections had I failed to make? What other details had I overlooked? "What am I missing?" I asked Labrys. But she simply panted in my ear.

Glancing at Old Capitol's gold dome, I turned left on Iowa Avenue and cruised past Darth Herky, Herkules Herky, and Patriot Herky. As Orchid would say, too much male energy. At the moment, I would have been happy with any energy. Where was Perky Herky when you needed him?

I rested my eyes during a red light. What next? *Who* next? I needed someone who could tell me about Ryesha. I needed to know if she'd told any of her friends about DeVoster raping her. If any of them might have guessed. If any of them were tall, white, and vengeful. A horn behind me alerted me to the green light, and I headed toward Varenka and Shelly's. Hopefully one of them would know something about Ryesha. If they didn't, the only good news I'd have for Anne and Orchid would be Lexie's forthcoming story about the fund-raiser—that and my own efforts to keep Labrys company.

Who was I kidding? I'd brought the dog along to keep me company. She wasn't much of a talker, so I turned on the radio.

"Who's telling the truth about the economy? Next on KICI, but first your local news."

I recognized the voice of the announcer, Gary Altimore, an intense guy who always brought miniature quiches to our office parties. As he detailed our unseasonably cold weather, I had one hand on the wheel and one in my backpack fishing around for a doughnut. The one I extracted was covered with white frosting. It was also stale. I'd gotten up too early for fresh doughnuts. That was a first. I sighed and offered the offending pastry to Labrys.

"A recent development in the Dave DeVoster murder."

I turned up the volume.

"Last evening Darren DeVoster, father of the slain basketball star, held a press conference hours after Anne Golding, director of the University of Iowa's Women's Center, was arrested and charged with his son's murder."

Bile rose in my throat, but I forced myself to listen. With a voice more sonorous than Gary's, the senior DeVoster thanked the police for their efficient work and offered his sincere hopes that the courts would be just as diligent in bringing the perpetrator to justice.

Anne, a perpetrator! I wrenched my steering wheel to the

right and zoomed down Dodge Street. Labrys whined softly in the backseat.

"On behalf of my wife and family and on behalf of Dave's basketball family, I'd like to issue a statement about the cassette tape that the police received."

Gary stopped the press conference replay and continued with his own summary. "Darren DeVoster claims that someone created the cassette in an attempt to blacken his son's reputation."

"As if he needed help," I said.

Labrys barked.

Gary continued: "The cassette in question features Dave DeVoster saying 'I won't take no for an answer, not from some—'" Gary paused and spelled the *c* word. "During the question-and-answer session of the press conference, several reporters asked what Darren DeVoster made of the fact that the police had verified the voice on his son's cassette. DeVoster Senior had this to say."

Here, I was once again treated to Darren DeVoster's voice. "Tapes can be spliced and manipulated. The woman who murdered my son has close friends in radio."

What? Was he implying I made that tape? Or Orchid? If we had, wouldn't we have wiped off Anne's fingerprints? Darren DeVoster wanted to have his cake and eat it too. He wanted to avenge his son's death, but he didn't want the police to use any evidence that made his son look bad.

"According to a police department source," Gary said, "experts are testing the tape for signs of splicing."

I fumed and pressed harder on the gas.

The intersection? The pickup crossing it? I didn't see them until it was too late.

I swerved hard. Hit my brakes. Squeezed my eyes shut.

A quick bump, metal on metal.

And I was on the other side of the intersection.

The street was lined with parked cars, so I double-parked under a streetlight. My heart racing and my palms clammy, I peered into the backseat.

Labrys gazed at me balefully. Then she barked and licked my face. Thank God—she didn't seem hurt. I didn't either. But my heart was pounding so fast that I could barely breathe.

Headlights flashed behind me and went off. Seconds later, there was a loud wham on the hood of my car. The front of my car dipped and rose as if handling a bumpy road. There was someone strong out there—someone strong and mad.

Fortunately, my doors were locked, and I kept them that way.

"You stupid bitch, you ran a red light." A man pounded on my side window inches from my face.

I leaned away, hoping the window would hold. He was fogging it up with his breath.

"You smashed my bumper." He pounded the window again. "Open up."

The nearby houses were all dark. I reached for my phone, ready to call 911. But did I really want an encounter with the police? Would the officer who would show up arrest me for phony cassette–making?

The Neanderthal outside began maligning my entire gender.

I opened my window the tiniest crack and waited for some silence. "Look," I said. "I admit the accident was my fault, and I'll pay for your bumper. I'll give you all my information. You can take my license plate number. But let's leave the police and the insurance companies out of it."

He remained silent.

"Please," I said, "I don't want my premiums to go up." That was the truth—the partial truth, but still the truth.

He responded with a colorful rant about insurance companies, which I interpreted as agreement. Keeping my face averted, I scribbled my information. I didn't want him to get a good look at me in case he was a DeVoster fan who'd seen my newspaper photo with Lexie. My hand shook when I slid the piece of paper through the open crack in my window.

He grabbed it and tromped away.

I didn't move until his pickup truck vanished into the darkness. Then I became dimly aware that my car was still running, my radio still on.

"Feel like horsing around?" Gary's bright and energetic tone told me that a cheesy human-interest story was in the offing. "You can win the opportunity to play a game of H-O-R-S-E with your favorite men's or women's Hawkeye basketball player." He explained that there would be ten lucky winners, and he listed a bunch of places where you could buy $5 raffle tickets. "All proceeds will go to the crisis center and its food pantry," Gary said. "H-O-R-S-E with the Hawkeyes and help the hungry."

After that alliterative frenzy, I pulled onto the street.

"Yesterday," Gary said, "I had the opportunity to talk with Hawkeyes Tyler Bennet and Jessie March." As the two hoopsters discussed the pantry and the growing numbers of people who needed it, I considered the possibility that they'd worked together to end DeVoster's life. Neither had a rock-solid alibi. Tyler had only his girlfriend, and Jessie had only her teammates—Kate and Win. Granted, Kate despised Jessie, but she still might have lied on the rookie's behalf for the sake of the team. And, of course, both Jessie and Tyler had been involved with Varenka. Jessie had been one of the few people to cast blame on Tyler, but maybe that had been intended to throw me off. Maybe, maybe, maybe. I needed more than wild guesses.

Gary asked Tyler and Jessie how many players would participate in the fund-raiser.

"All the guys," Tyler said. "It'll be fun to play H-O-R-S-E with our fans. We enjoy getting involved with the community."

"In this game of H-O-R-S-E," Gary said, "everyone wins."

Including Eldon Bly. What a transparent attempt to polish his program's tarnished reputation. I wondered how Bridget felt about her players being used as PR pawns. The interview with Jessie and Tyler had clearly been designed to reveal a common bond between the two teams. One great big happy family.

I parked in front of Varenka and Shelly's apartment and tried to recover a question that had been forming at the edges of my consciousness. But it was gone. Across the street, a worn basketball net fluttered in the wind, taunting me.

TWENTY-EIGHT

Like the door to her apartment, Varenka's eyes were barely open. "What do you want now?" she asked in a slow scratchy whisper. "What's happened?" Alarm crept into her voice.

She'd been through so much, and there I was, waking her up and scaring her. As I assured her nothing was wrong and went through a litany of apologies, Varenka loosened her grip on the door and opened it a bit wider. Her fingernails were painted a soft pink. A sign, perhaps, that she was taking good care of herself, that she would be okay. "This won't take long," I said. "I just need to ask you a few questions about Ryesha Anderson."

Varenka gazed at me blankly.

"Roshaun's younger sister. She was a cheerleader."

"Why do you want to know about her?"

I'd been prepared for this question. "I'm contacting all the cheerleaders to see what they know about DeVoster."

Varenka nodded and gestured me in. We both remained standing next to the dining room table. On its surface, a stack of books towered behind a nearly empty bag of Doritos. She apologized for the mess, and I assured her it was no big deal. "About Ryesha?" I asked.

"I didn't know her very well."

"She's in a group photo in your room," I said. "Were any of the people in that photo close to her?"

Varenka went to her bedroom and returned with the picture. Grasping the frame with both hands, she studied it and sighed. "She probably spent some time with Tyler Bennet. He and Roshaun used to be kind of tight."

My heart quickened. What if Lexie was wrong and Tyler already knew what DeVoster had done to his friend's sister?

"I think she mostly hung out with other cheerleaders."

I held out my hand, and Varenka gave me the picture. Most of the cheerleaders in it were white, but none of them were tall.

"Shelly could answer your questions better than me," Varenka said, "but she's not here right now."

"Where is she?"

Varenka's brow furrowed. "What time is it?"

I glanced at my watch and told her that it was 5:30-ish.

Her frown deepened. "She's probably at the arena. I think she was going to rebound for Win, or maybe Jess. If you want to talk to her today, you better hurry. She has a flight to catch this morning. To Michigan, I think. She's going to her great-aunt's funeral."

"What time does her plane leave?"

"Early was all she told me." Varenka paused and looked up as if she were trying to remember the exact departure time.

"You know," she said, "it might have been a regular aunt who died. I can't remember exactly."

✧ ✧ ✧

I braced myself for another wild goose chase as I pulled off Hawkins Drive into the parking lot across from Carver-Hawkeye. It was only 6 A.M., so I could have parked in the nearly empty lot next to the arena, but I wasn't taking any more chances with the parking police. I steered my Omni into a well-lit spot and took a long drink of cold coffee. Labrys barked and whined until I let her out. Big mistake. She raced away from me—away from the arena—toward the makeshift shrine that surrounded Marilyn MonHerky. I was glad that the dog was still spry after my fender-bender, but I was less than thrilled to see her doing her business on a black-and-gold bouquet. By the time I caught up with her, she was wagging her tail as if expecting praise for the desecration. Dead leaves skittered across the sidewalk, and I imagined the killer stalking me.

"Come on, girl," I said softly, hoping she'd follow me back to the car. Instead, she grabbed a small stuffed Herky with her mouth and dropped it at my feet.

Okay, I could work with this. I picked up the soggy bird and flung it toward the parking lot. Labrys dashed after it, and I took a few steps forward before she returned. I'm no softball star, but little by little, throw after throw, we made it back to the car.

The dog wasn't about to forfeit her freedom, however. I tossed the bird on the back seat, but Labrys simply cocked her head. Ruing the fact that I hadn't brought any doggy treats or a leash, I grabbed my cell phone and slammed the door. At least

I wouldn't have to enter the stadium alone. Huge deserted buildings creep me out.

So much so that I delayed our entrance by examining the big gouge on the driver's side of my front bumper. No way would I be able to afford fixing it and the pickup. In fact, I should have taken my chances with the police and let my insurance company pay for his damage. My premiums would have risen, but I'd have something to donate to Anne's defense. Hindsight can be downright discouraging.

As Labrys and I waited to cross Hawkins Drive, a Cambus droned past us toward *The Hawk,* a monstrous metallic sculpture of our mascot swooping down on some hapless prey. Its wings were silhouetted against the football team's practice bubble. Labrys sniffed at a tree to my right: the Chris Street Memorial, a tree planted in honor of a basketball player who'd been killed in a car accident some ten years ago.

When the traffic finally cleared, Labrys and I crossed against the light. The sky was turning a murky white behind the cage-like metal bars that crowned Carver-Hawkeye Arena. They made me think of Anne in jail, so I picked up my pace, hissing at Labrys when she paused to check out Elvis Herky.

The doors to the right of the bird were an exit only, so we headed toward the South Entrance. Its doors were all locked. Through their glass, I could see that the arena lights were on, but there was a concourse and forty-some rows of seats between me and the basketball court. If Shelly and Win—or Jessie?—were down there on the court like Varenka thought, they wouldn't hear me tug and pound on the door. The wind whipped through my hair and stung my cheeks as Labrys and I retraced our steps. We were just past the exit doors when a car crept through the parking lot. "Come on," I said. "Let's see how they get in." Labrys abandoned a gold hydrant, and we negotiated a cluster of bare trees and bushes, hustling past the West Entrance.

I froze.

Tyler Bennet sauntered toward the ticket office door. His red hair was unmistakable even in the semidarkness, and, if he turned around, he'd be able to identify mine too. I didn't want him to know I was there, and I didn't relish the idea of being in the nearly empty stadium with him—not when I still suspected him of killing DeVoster. I held my breath, praying that Labrys wouldn't bark. At the door Tyler paused, and my heart beat a manic conga. He glanced to his left, but not all the way around, and entered. I exhaled and started shivering. Labrys licked my hand, bounded in front of me, stopped, and waited. Time to forge ahead.

Unfortunately, the door that had opened for Tyler remained firmly locked for me—even after I yanked on it three or four times.

Now what?

Labrys barked and ran toward a set of concrete stairs. I had nothing to lose except my footing, so I began following her down them. Under sporadically placed lights, there were piles of leaves and cigarette butts. At the end of the first flight, I looked up and saw headlights flash on Highway 6. A taxi turned onto Newton Road, zipping past its row of apartments. I was descending toward the very back of the arena. Two more flights wound around a humming generator before Labrys and I arrived at a loading dock. She scampered back and forth between garbage cans, nearly knocking over a couple of folding chairs. A smokers' haunt, I imagined, where weary maintenance folks took their breaks. A few university vans, all empty, were parked in the lot.

I turned toward the building and gazed at the door. If it wasn't unlocked, I'd have to cool my heels until Roshaun or his mother called me back. And I wouldn't get to talk to Shelly until she returned from her aunt's funeral. Whenever that might be.

I pulled my hand out of my jacket pocket and placed it on the doorknob. Its cold metal turned easily. When I peeked inside, I saw the tunnel that led past the locker rooms to the arena floor. On my left was a Caterpillar surrounded by crates, flats, dollies, and traffic cones. On my right was a tiny office. The fiftyish guy at the desk simply gave me a bored glance before returning to his paperwork. I took advantage of his apathy and let Labrys in.

As she checked out the Caterpillar, I peered through the bars of the equipment room. Shelly wasn't there amid the towers of towels, so we moved on. The tunnel's walls were Hawkeye gold, and its ceiling was festooned with Big Ten banners. The bright colors set me on edge. Something was off. An I-shaped window in the weight room door revealed a silver-haired guy spotting a tiny woman. She benched a laden barbell as if its weights were made of cotton candy. A gymnast and her trainer, I figured. Labrys wagged her tail at them, prancing alongside me, her nails clicking on the concrete. *Click, click, click.* That was it. It was too quiet. No one was dribbling. No one was shooting.

When Labrys and I neared the proverbial light at the end of the tunnel, there was no one on our end of the court. And when we stepped into the stadium proper, the court was empty. As I gazed up at the empty seats, row upon row, rising to Brobdignagian heights, I felt small. And insignificant. Looming above me were blank scoreboards and unreadable banners, an American flag that looked no bigger than a sheet of notebook paper.

Something squeaked.

I whirled around, but no one was there. I studied the press

section and then moved my eyes back up to the concourse, tracing the railing at its perimeter. On the opposite side of the court stood a tall figure with a basketball at one hip. "Shelly?" I called.

The figure waved and started down the steps. What if it wasn't her? What if it was Tyler or his coach or someone else who wouldn't appreciate my presence? I wanted to bolt, but I held my ground. "Shelly?" I called again.

The figure paused halfway down the stairs. "Mara?"

It was Shelly. I could make out her ponytail atop her broad shoulders.

There was that squeak again. If there were someone else in the stadium—someone dangerous—Labrys wouldn't protect me, not when there was spilled pop to lick off the bleachers.

Shelly slowly dribbled the ball across the court. Except for her tennis shoes, she was in street clothes—black low-rise jeans and a tight burgundy top that didn't quite meet the top of her jeans. These days, neither rain nor sleet nor snow can keep young women from baring their navels. Not that I dislike female navels, but surely they should be covered when the temperature dips below freezing. I wondered if Shelly would change before her aunt's funeral, and I snapped to my senses. "I'm sorry about your aunt."

"Thanks. It'll be real different not having her around." She gave me a puzzled look.

"Varenka told me," I said.

Labrys moved to a new area of the bleachers and began slurping again.

"She said you were going to rebound for someone before catching a plane to the funeral."

Shelly nodded and dropped her eyes to the court's wooden surface. It was two or three inches higher than the concrete around it. I could use those inches when talking with her, so I stepped onto the hardwood.

"What are you doing here?" she asked.

"I have some questions about Roshaun's sister, Ryesha." I'd need my finesse game if I wanted to tease out Shelly's knowledge without revealing my own.

"What questions?" Shelly held the basketball behind her back.

I decided to give her the same lie I gave Varenka. "I'm contacting all the cheerleaders to see what they know about DeVoster."

Again, the squeak.

"I wouldn't have bothered you here," I said, "but I couldn't reach Roshaun and I wanted to catch you before you left town."

Shelly moved the ball back in front of her and bounced it hard with one hand, then the other. "Ryesha and I aren't friends. I didn't start dating Roshaun until after she left."

Crap. "Who was she close to?"

"Nobody, really."

Double crap. "Has Roshaun ever said anything about why she left?"

Shelly's gray eyes drilled into mine. "He thought it was a race thing. Ryesha was the only black cheerleader, the only black person in most of her classes."

So, I thought, Ryesha had given her brother part of the truth, and he had mistaken it for the whole. "Do you know when he's going to be back in town?"

"He's got class this morning." She checked her watch and looked past me toward the tunnel.

"Who are you waiting for?"

Shelly's brow furrowed. "Jessie."

Labrys bounded over and sniffed the ball. Shelly raised it above her head and stepped off the court. "Let's keep the dog off the hardwood," she said, nodding me toward the concrete and tossing me the ball. Labrys dashed after it, but not before I could throw it back. Canine keep-away.

When the ball smacked into my hands the second time, it occurred to me that I was playing basketball—sort of—near a Division I court. Giddy from too much coffee and too little sleep, I asked Shelly to hold Labrys's collar, and I dribbled toward the nearest hoop for a layup.

Labrys barked as I chased after my miss.

"If you find her a big patch of yummy spilled pop," I said, "she'll stay off the court. Then you can shoot with me until Jessie gets here."

As if to prove me right, the dog began licking the floor.

"Let's play H-O-R-S-E," I said.

Shelly released Labrys and folded her arms over her chest.

"Come on." I took a shot from near the free-throw line and made it. "One game." When would I have this opportunity again? Even Anne in her jail cell wouldn't begrudge me this chance to pretend to be a Hawkeye.

Shelly sighed and strolled back onto the court. "I'll rebound."

Once more I heard the squeak, but I wasn't so nervous now that I'd found Shelly. I dribbled the ball. "It'll be more fun if we both shoot."

"Sorry." Shelly paused near the three-point line.

Then I remembered what Jessie told me about Shelly. When she started managing the Hawks, she had vowed never to shoot again—a drama queen kind of vow, if you asked me. I dribbled out past the three-point line and squared up to the basket. As the ball left my hands, arcing toward the rim, I remembered something else. The story Roshaun's mother told me about the last time her son and Shelly visited. They'd been awakened by a phone call in the middle of the night, she'd said. About the time of DeVoster's murder. She hadn't said that—I'd made the connection myself. Maybe that's why I missed her lie, the one about the next morning when she watched Roshaun and Shelly playing H-O-R-S-E in her driveway.

TWENTY-NINE

My shot dropped through the net and bounced a couple times before Shelly retrieved it and sent me a bounce pass. Reliable, responsible Shelly. She was tall and white with access to the telltale sweats. She had a motive. And now she had no alibi. Had she killed DeVoster? Or had it been Roshaun? One thing I knew for sure—his mother had lied for them. And I could guess why. Not simply because she loved them, but because she also loved her daughter, Ryesha, and she knew what DeVoster had done to her.

I dribbled the ball furiously. Theory, mere guesswork. It would take more than that to get Anne out of jail.

"You going to shoot or not?" Shelly scowled and tugged at her ponytail. Her hands were the size of softball gloves.

The squeak pierced the quiet. I tightened my grip on the ball and glanced around.

"It's the ad signs." Shelly pointed at a scoreboard. "They squeak when the ads change."

The sign next to the slot for the visiting team's score looked like a venetian blind opening and closing as a real estate ad metamorphosed into a Wendy's promo—burger, fries, and Coke.

"I don't think they ever stop," Shelly said, "not even when the place is empty."

Sweating badly, I wanted to remove my jacket, but I couldn't bring myself to set the ball on the floor. I hugged it to my chest and pondered my situation. No one was watching Shelly and me. I was on my lonesome with a woman twice my size who might have committed murder. "When is Jessie supposed to get here?" I asked.

Shelly glanced at her watch. "Ten minutes ago."

I tried to spot Labrys in the bleachers, but all I could see was her tail. I hoped she'd come when I called her so we could get the hell out of there.

"If she doesn't get here soon," Shelly said, "I'm going to take care of a few things in the office before I have to leave for the airport."

I found it hard to believe that dedicated Shelly would bail on a player—even a late one—and I wondered if she'd really been planning to meet Jessie. But it seemed like a strange thing to lie about. I dribbled the ball and took another shot. It nicked the edge of the backboard and bounced into the stands.

"You've lost your touch," Shelly said.

I was losing something—maybe my mind—because I was trying to think of a way to get Shelly to talk about the night she or Roshaun—or both of them—killed DeVoster. I couldn't bear the thought of Anne sitting in jail while Shelly flew the friendly skies.

She made no move to get the ball. "I think I'll head to the

office now. Keep shooting if you want."

"I'll come with you. I left a notebook up there."

Shelly frowned. "I haven't seen one."

She didn't want me to come with her. That made me all the more eager. "I really need it. I've looked everywhere."

Shelly squared her shoulders and headed off the court.

I shook off my jacket, following her and calling to Labrys, who—bless her little doggy heart—trailed after me.

As we passed the weight room, I noticed that the gymnast had been joined by some wrestlers and Tyler Bennet. I tried to catch his eye, but he was concentrating on his biceps. No one saw me with Shelly.

What did it matter? She didn't know I suspected her. I was safe, perfectly safe. I kept telling myself that as we neared the elevator. When its doors slid open, Labrys hesitated before following us in. I wasn't too enthused about the elevator myself. Its black walls sported gold panels—total Hawkeye claustrophobia. I kept my eyes on the emergency phone as we made our ascent to the third floor.

The doors opened on a dark hallway, but Shelly knew where the lights were. Their fluorescent hum added to the steady whoosh of the stadium's ventilation. The whole third floor sounded like the inside of a seashell. Labrys examined a potted tree while Shelly unlocked the door to the women's basketball offices. Once inside, I glanced down the hallway that housed Bridget's office. It was dark.

"You gonna look for your notebook?" Shelly nodded toward the corner desk where I'd interviewed most of the players.

I glanced at the bulletin board above it and made a show of shuffling through a stack of papers. Something seemed off. "No luck yet," I mumbled.

"I work there almost every day. I told you, I haven't seen it."

Labrys poked her nose at Shelly's hand, but she ignored the plea for attention.

"It's really great how you organized that fund-raiser for Anne Golding."

Shelly gave me a small smile and looked away.

"You know her well?" I asked.

"She helped our team after Varenka …" Shelly absently stroked Labrys's head. "It was the least I could do."

That was for sure. Anne was taking the rap for Shelly and her boyfriend. "Do you think she did it?" I asked.

"Of course not." Shelly stood and checked her watch.

I squatted and pretended to look underneath the desk.

"Maybe it's in the locker room," she said. "I do homework down there sometimes. I might have accidentally grabbed it with some of my stuff. I'll go look."

"What about your work here?" I asked, still squatting.

"It's not going anywhere."

I gazed at an army of dust bunnies and told myself that it would be a good idea to follow her to the locker room. I'd have more time to ask questions. And it's not like I'd be alone with her. The locker room was kitty-corner across from the busy weight room, and I'd have Labrys. As I grabbed the desk to hoist myself up, the bulletin board once again caught my eye. There was no poster of the cathedral in Barcelona, no exchange student, no photo of Shelly and her co-manager in their Santa hats, no team in the Bahamas. No trace of Shelly at all.

✧ ✧ ✧

When we entered the locker room, Shelly hurried past the trophy case and into the players' lounge. I hung back, clutching my jacket as she strode around the U-shaped couch. At the end closest to me was a monstrous suitcase, monogrammed SS. Shelly Swanson. It was taller than the back of the couch and broader than Labrys from nose to flank. The dog sniffed at a matching carry-on that was stuffed to the gills. I wondered why Shelly had brought her luggage into the lounge.

"If it's here," she said, "it'll probably be back by the computers."

I'd almost forgotten we were supposed to be looking for my notebook. "Thanks for checking," I said. "I know this is a difficult time for you." It would be even more difficult if I could get her to incriminate herself. "Is Roshaun going to the funeral with you?"

Shelly nodded, her eyes fixed on the computers.

Labrys began biting the carry-on.

"Does he think Anne Golding is guilty?"

Shelly scowled as she opened and shut a drawer underneath the computers.

Maybe I should try a lighter approach. "It looks like you packed enough for both of you." In fact, it looked like she'd packed enough for their entire teams. Then it hit me. Maybe she was packing up for good. Maybe that's why her bulletin board was empty and her suitcases bulging. Maybe she'd brought them into the locker room so she could gather her basketball things before she left.

"I'm a heavy packer," she said.

If Shelly was fleeing, I'd never have another chance to discover the truth about DeVoster. What would happen to Anne then? "How long will you be gone?" I asked.

She opened a cupboard above the computers and didn't answer me.

"Roshaun's interview with the Kobe Bryant author is Monday," I said, "so I guess you'll be back by then."

Labrys chomped the handle of the carry-on and dragged it toward me. I was about to chide her when I noticed a piece of paper sticking out of the bag's side pocket. Shelly's itinerary? If only I could get a look at it.

"Sorry," Shelly said. "I don't know where else your notebook could be." She eyed me, so there was no way I could check the paper.

"Do you think I could trouble you for one other thing?" I said. "I'm dying of thirst."

"No prob." Shelly came around the other side of the couch and pulled a bottle of water out of the cupboard next to the big-screen TV.

That wouldn't do. I needed her out of the room. "Sorry to be a pain, but do you have anything with sugar? I haven't had breakfast."

Shelly raised her eyebrows.

Although she was used to handling the players' requests, maybe I was a different story. "Please?"

"We don't have anything with sugar," she said, "but there might be some Gatorade."

As she disappeared into the locker room proper, I reached for the paper. It was lodged behind a billfold, so I grabbed that too. I thrust both into my jacket's inside pocket, and when Shelly returned with a bottle of bright-red Gatorade, I stood between her and Labrys. The dog kept nipping at the bag, and I didn't want Shelly to notice her missing things.

She loosened the lid and handed the bottle to me. My only other encounter with Gatorade was via those commercials that feature various hues of the beverage oozing out of athletes' pores. I tried not to think of the blood on DeVoster's face, and I took a sip. It was no vanilla latte, but I thanked Shelly and took another drink. Then I asked to use the restroom.

Shelly snuck a look at her watch. "There's one in the locker room. Far left corner."

Edging past her, I hoped she wouldn't ask why I was taking my coat, but I needn't have worried. She seemed oblivious—even to the dog's noisy obsession with the damn carry-on.

I raced past a row of tall wooden lockers, each adorned with a player's name and photo. When I reached the bathroom stall, I threw open the door and locked it behind me. I set my Gatorade on the floor and hoped that the fluorescent light blinking above me wouldn't die before I could check the paper. I pulled it out of my jacket pocket and, hands shaking, unfolded it.

It was an itinerary. Shelly had purchased a one-way ticket to Barcelona. She was fleeing the country.

I studied the United Airlines logo as if it held the key to her secrets. Her flight left the Cedar Rapids airport at 8 A.M. My watch said 6:35. I took a deep breath and forced myself to think through the timing. It took about half an hour to get to the airport from Iowa City. The plane would start boarding around 7:30. Shelly would need to leave soon.

So I needed to do something quick. Get her to confess or at least make her miss her flight. Jamming the itinerary into my jacket pocket, I pulled out Shelly's billfold and unsnapped it. As the dark leather fell open in my hand, I saw her driver's license, her student ID, a debit card, and a Visa.

As long as I had Shelly's plastic, she wasn't going anywhere.

I opened the checkbook cover below the cards and discovered some wallet-sized photographs encased in plastic. Roshaun. A middle-aged couple that looked like her parents. A young woman with lovely flowing hair.

Wait a minute. It was the exchange student from Barcelona. Shelly wasn't simply running away. She was going to visit her old friend.

I flipped through the rest of the photos: Varenka, Kate, Win, group shots of the team, and what looked like grandparents. Shelly was leaving these people for good—almost everyone she'd known and loved in her twentysome years. My throat tightened, but before I could get too choked up, Labrys's nails tapped against the floor and stopped outside my stall. I crouched down and looked beneath it. Only paws. But in case Shelly stood off to the side, I spun the roll of toilet paper and flushed the toilet. As it roared, I tucked the billfold back into my jacket pocket and summoned my acting abilities. I needed to convince Shelly that I had nothing to hide, that I had no agenda other than going home ASAP and getting some sleep.

My hand was on the lock when I heard a creak. A building sound or Shelly's sneakers? I tried looking through the crack between the door and the rest of the stall, but I saw only a sliver of Labrys and some shelves. What I needed was a better view. The toilet didn't have a lid, so I'd have to stand on the rim. If only I'd listened when Anne tried to talk me into doing yoga, I could have gracefully ascended the porcelain and balanced there, strong, stable, and centered. But, alas, I'd be lucky if I escaped with dry feet. I enhanced my odds by donning my jacket and thus freeing both hands. Placing one foot on the toilet seat, I grabbed onto the toilet paper dispenser and heaved my other foot onto the rim. With a wobble, I stood and peered over the top of the stall.

Shelly stared right back, her eyes narrowed, her arms cradling her carry-on. "You took my billfold."

"Why would I do that?" I said. "Don't be silly."

"You're the one who's standing on the toilet." She seemed puzzled—as if she had no idea I was scared shitless of her.

Then it struck me. She didn't know that I'd linked her with DeVoster's murder. Maybe she hadn't noticed her missing itinerary either. I could still act my way out of this. "It's so embarrassing," I whispered. "How can I even look you in the eye?" With that bit of melodrama, I jumped off the toilet and removed Shelly's billfold from my jacket. I extracted her IDs and credit card, shoved them in the back pocket of my Levi's, and climbed back up on the toilet.

Shelly hadn't budged.

"I can't help stealing things," I said, "and then I feel so ashamed. I want to lock myself away."

Her brow furrowed.

Perhaps my performance was less than Oscar caliber. "Please," I said, "just leave me alone. I'm so humiliated."

"Okay," Shelly said. "Just give me my billfold."

I tossed it far away from the stall, and Labrys charged after it. Shelly set her bag on the floor and followed a few steps behind. She was a smart girl, so it would take a miracle for her not to check the contents of her billfold. A miracle or a big distraction. I let out a wail. "I'm so sorry," I said. "I can't help myself. I've taken things ever since I was five. It all started with my grandma's talcum powder. And it kept getting worse. I stole something from every single member of my Brownie troop."

Shelly had no interest in my fictionalized kleptomania. She removed her billfold from Labrys's mouth and soon discovered the missing items. "You still have my credit card and my driver's license." She headed back toward me with Labrys on her heels.

"I can't help it," I said. "I've tried therapy and medication, but nothing helps. I live to steal."

"Why didn't you take my money?"

That was a fine question. "Cash doesn't interest me," I lied.

"I want my things back," Shelly said. "If you don't give them to me, you're going to be sorry."

It was an empty threat. She was too large to crawl underneath the stall, and if she tried, I could hit her with the Gatorade bottle. Although I was trapped, I was safe, and time was on my side. "What's up with the one-way ticket to Spain?"

Shelly slid her hand into the side pocket of her carry-on. She crouched next to it, her eyes fixed on me.

Maybe I shouldn't have tipped my hand, but it was too late now. "You're fleeing the country because you killed DeVoster, aren't you?"

Shelly's temple throbbed, and her face flushed.

The fluorescent light flickered wildly. If it went off, I wouldn't be able to read her face. "I know that you and Roshaun weren't at his mother's the night DeVoster was murdered. I know about Ryesha."

"Roshaun didn't touch—" Shelly struggled for words. "He didn't do anything." She leaned over her bag and removed something small from a zippered pocket. "If you don't come out and give me my cards, I'll spray you."

Pepper spray.

Time to call the police. I pulled out my cell. It was dead.

Labrys slobbered over the luggage, completely clueless.

"I mean it." Shelly's index finger curled above the canister.

I jumped off the toilet again and whirled toward the back wall. If she sprayed me, no way was I taking it right in the eyes. I closed them for good measure and pressed into the wall. Its concrete smelled of fresh paint and disinfectant.

"I'll spray your dog."

Why hadn't I ever asked Neale about pepper spray? I didn't think it would cause Labrys permanent damage, but I didn't want Anne's dog hurt at all. And I was afraid of how Labrys would react. What if the spray turned her crazy and she attacked Shelly? "You do that," I said, "and I'll flush your Visa down the toilet."

Shelly was quiet as she considered my bluff.

If only I could risk a peek at her face. I didn't like sparring with a disembodied voice. I flattened my palms against the wall, trying to steady myself.

"If you don't come out now and give me all my stuff, I'm going to spray your dog, and I'm going to spray you through the crack in the door."

Opening one eye just a sliver, I tossed the cards in the toilet. If Shelly sprayed me and I writhed on the floor in pain, she wasn't getting any plastic. "How about if I just slide the cards out and you leave me and the dog alone?"

"No," Shelly said. "I want you out."

I didn't have to ask why. She was going to have to do something to keep me from going to the police. Although truth be told, I had nothing but theories to offer them. Not even a confession.

"I promise I won't hurt you or your dog," she said. "If you come out with the cards, I won't use the spray. I'll lock the dog in the supply closet—"

I cut her off. "Labrys doesn't like closets. She won't go near them." A lie. But I wanted to rattle Shelly.

"I've got a roast beef sandwich in my bag. She'll follow that anywhere."

So that was why Labrys was so taken with the carry-on. I wanted to cry at the thought of her in the closet and me all on my own against Shelly.

"I'll put you in a locker," she continued. "Since you're short, you won't be too uncomfortable. Don't worry, they're ventilated. When the girls show up for practice this afternoon, they'll let you out."

At 3 or 3:30? I'd be trapped for hours—driven half mad by claustrophobia and a full bladder—and Shelly would be well on her way to Spain.

"The Spanish police will send you back," I said.

"Spain isn't my final destination. I'm going to a place where that can't happen."

She sounded confident, but I knew she wasn't. She'd asked me about living abroad, about homesickness. "You're going to leave your entire life behind?" I asked.

"Roshaun is coming with me."

Where was he anyway? Would he come barging in if Shelly didn't meet him soon? "So you're going to leave your families behind? You wouldn't have to if you explained things to the police—if you told them about Ryesha."

"They wouldn't believe us," she said. "But even if they did, we'd still have to deal with DeVoster's fans and his rich and powerful family."

That silenced me. Shelly and Roshaun could be in real danger if they stayed. Maybe they'd be better off leaving. And if I could get her to tell me what happened, maybe that—coupled with their suspicious flight—would be enough to get Anne out of trouble. "Here's the thing," I said. "Your cards are in the toilet—literally—so there's no way you're getting them unless I give them to you. If you tell me what happened, they're yours. You can lock Labrys and me up and make your escape."

"I'll send a letter that explains everything once I get to—. Once I get to where I'm going. I don't want Anne Golding to pay for my mistake."

That was probably true. Shelly had organized a fund-raiser for Anne, but I couldn't take any chances. "Tell me now," I said. "Or you're not going anywhere."

"I'll send other proof too," she said. "Everyone will see that Anne had nothing to do with it."

Now who was bluffing? The malfunctioning light hummed, and Shelly's cards floated in the toilet like miniature rafts. "You don't have much time," I said, "if you want to catch your flight."

Labrys sniffed loudly—presumably at Shelly's luggage. I was too worried about the pepper spray to risk a peek.

"I didn't mean to kill him," she whispered. "It was an accident."

I thought about the bruising on his neck and back, his smashed-in skull, all the blood.

"You don't believe me." Shelly's voice quavered. "But I was only planning to confront him. I was trying to help the team."

It sounded like she'd moved away from the stall, so I squinted through the door. She sat on a stool, biting her lip, close to tears. Labrys abandoned her quest for roast beef and padded toward Shelly.

Suddenly, I had an idea. "You were trying to help the team by committing murder?" I asked. "Didn't you realize that Varenka and her parents would be prime suspects?"

"I told you," Shelly said, "I didn't mean to kill him." She bit her lip harder and clenched both her fists. "I thought I could trick him into confessing on tape."

My stomach lurched. That was what I'd done to my Aunt Glad's killer. And when Shelly had been an intern at KICI, I'd told her all about it. Bigmouth-me, I loved to tell my own story so much, I never thought about why Shelly wanted to listen. It was my fault that she'd killed DeVoster, that her life was ruined, that Anne was in jail. Tears burned my eyes, and Labrys bounded toward me and started pawing at the stall. I took a deep breath and tried to relax my throat. "I'm okay, Labrys," I said softly. "I'm fine." I needed the dog to focus on Shelly, but Labrys could see through my lie. Her paws remained firmly planted inches from the stall. "Why didn't you just tape him then?" I asked. "Why'd you kill him?"

Shelly stared into space, and Labrys edged toward her.

"I tried to get him to admit what he did to Varenka and Ryesha, but he said they wanted it. He said—" Shelly stopped and hung her head. "He said terrible things, and he kept laughing at me, but none of what he said was a 100-percent clear confession, so I lied and told him that Ryesha was going to come forward." Shelly raised her eyes. They remained fixed and vacant as her story spilled out. "He went ballistic—started coming at me—so I sprayed him. He shrieked and grabbed his eyes. He crumpled to his knees, but then he got up and lunged at me again. I was scared, so I pushed him. Hard as I could." Shelly paused and squared her shoulders. "His neck hit the beak and snapped. It was a horrible sound." She clasped her fingers together in her lap. "On the way down, his back crashed into the bird's knee and his head smashed against the elbow—the one raised in the air. When he landed on the cement platform, his head hit the corner. His blood splattered on the bird's dress." Shelly shivered.

I wondered how many times the scene had replayed in her head. But now was not the time for sympathy or compassion.

Shelly demanded her cards again, her tears long gone. If anything, unburdening her secret seemed to have strengthened her resolve.

"Why did you think he'd confess to you?" I asked. "Why was it your job to incriminate him?"

Shelly tried to meet my eyes, but she couldn't. "I take care of the team," she said. "It's my job."

I didn't like goading her, but there was no other way. "Why didn't Roshaun step to the plate? It was his sister DeVoster raped."

"I wanted to do it," Shelly snapped. "I made him let me."

"Why?" I said. "Was it for the glory? After four years of fetching drinks and towels, you deserved some, didn't you? Shelly's time to be the star."

She shook her head, her lip trembling.

"Why then? So you could kill DeVoster and make it look like an accident?"

"No," Shelly cried. "Weren't you listening? I wanted him to live so I could ruin his life just like he ruined my—my roommate's life—and Ryesha's."

Shelly's hesitation made me wonder if she was being completely honest. Why hadn't she simply said Varenka's name?

"I wanted everyone to know what really happened at his parties."

I recalled Shelly's reaction when I'd asked her about the party where Varenka was raped. No way had Shelly been there. She didn't like big parties. She didn't even like hearing about them. I'd attributed her vehemence to anger on her friend's behalf, but maybe there was more to it. A lot more.

"Did DeVoster ever do anything to you?" I asked.

Shelly's lip trembled.

Labrys whined and edged toward her.

Shelly's eyes brimmed with tears. When she finally spoke, I could barely hear her. "I never told anybody until it was too late. If I'd told Varenka, she never would have ..." Shelly started crying in earnest, her shoulders shaking.

I had about two seconds to absorb Shelly's revelation before Labrys leaped at her, tongue out, eager to offer solace, knocking Shelly right off her stool and onto the floor. I burst out of the stall, leaped over the fallen stool, and sped out of the locker room.

Labrys wouldn't keep a big girl like Shelly down long. I sprinted to the weight room and threw open the door. "Help," I yelled, "I need help in the women's basketball locker room."

The female gymnast and some of the wrestlers paused mid-lift.

"Please," I said. "The woman who killed Dave DeVoster is about to get away."

That got Tyler Bennet's attention. He dropped his weight to the mat and ran after me. Everyone else followed suit, thundering toward the locker room. When Shelly burst through the door—her luggage and Labrys trailing behind her—she was greeted by a rock-hard wall of jocks.

THIRTY

By the time I left the police station, the last thing I wanted was to answer more questions. But as the song says, you can't always get what you want. The cement area in front of the station was filled with journalists. A shaggy cameraman perched atop a huge cement planter and tried to film me as I no-commented my way through the crowd. Someone leaped from behind the Law-Enforcement Herky statue and thrust a mike in my face. I dodged it only to run smack into Lexie Roth. "What did Shelly Swanson tell you before she was arrested?" Lexie had one hand poised above a notebook. With the other, she lowered her muffler and brushed a spiral of hair out of her face. "Come on," she hissed. "I helped you."

I wanted to repay her, but I didn't want to encourage the reporters that were jockeying for position between us. And I didn't want to destroy any more of Shelly's privacy than I already had.

"Where's your dog?" Lexie asked.

"I don't have one."

"The one that was with you," Lexie said. "I want a photo."

I'd dropped Labrys at home before going to the station to give my statement, but if I told Lexie that, a herd of photographers would follow her to my door. "Maybe tomorrow." I strode past, ignoring an avalanche of questions. Truth be told, I had plenty of my own. I knew that the cops had released Anne—I'd asked and asked until they told me—but I didn't know how she was doing. And I had no idea what happened to Shelly after her arrest. No idea how Bridget and her players were taking the news.

My watch said 3:36. Practice time. And I was sure the Hawks would be practicing—no matter what was happening with their manager—because they had a game the next day. The show must go on. We thespians have nothing on Div. I athletes.

The parking lot behind the police station was jammed with news vans. My Omni was lodged in between two of them, encrusted with frost. It took me a couple minutes to pry the door open and start the engine. My defroster wheezed, and I discovered that I didn't have a scraper.

Someone rapped on my window.

I couldn't see who it was because of the frost, but I assumed it was a reporter and locked my doors.

"Mar-Bar! Open up. We're perishing out here."

I opened my window a crack. Behind Vince were Orchid and Anne, all grins. I jumped out of the car.

When I extricated myself from the inevitable group hug, I gazed at Anne, every inch of her. "Are you okay?" I asked.

She nodded. The circles under her eyes looked like ripe

plums. "What about you?"

I shrugged. It was all in a day's work, rescuing my ex from the long arm of the law.

Orchid rested a mittened hand on my shoulder and thanked me. She was about to say something else when Vince cut her off.

"Did I train Labrys right or what?" He started bouncing up and down—from the cold or his own misguided pride, I couldn't tell. "She's going to be famous." He swept his arm around the parking lot at the news vans. "All these stations are going to want footage of the heroic canine and her amazing trainer." He was so enraptured with his future fame that he didn't notice the rest of us exchanging amused glances.

Over his shoulder, I saw some reporters coming our way. "Let's get out of here."

"We'd like to take you two out for dinner later," Orchid said, "to celebrate Anne's freedom and your sleuthing." She nodded toward me.

"Alas," Vince said, "I have a prior engagement with the delightful man who inspected the animal adoption center today." He gave me another hug. "But tomorrow I want all the details about how you caught that murderous manager."

"She's not a murderer," I said. "It was self-defense." But I wondered if the cops would see it that way. Despite Anne's freedom, I didn't feel like celebrating—not with Shelly in so much pain and trouble. I turned to Orchid and asked for a rain check on the dinner. She and Anne both looked relieved.

And I was fine with that. I really was. For once, their desire to be alone didn't hurt me.

✧ ✧ ✧

It was nearly 6:30 when I entered Carver-Hawkeye for the second time that day. From the top of the stadium, I could see Bridget consulting with the other two assistants. Coach Carol was back—the only one on the floor with silver hair. The players I'd come to know best—Varenka, Kate, Jessie, and Win—were scrimmaging against the gray team. Shelly's arrest had no doubt triggered more guilt for Varenka, but she seemed unhampered and focused, driving past a guy with cornrows. I thought about Roshaun and his mother. According to the evening news, they'd been arrested as accessories. Dave DeVoster had shattered a lot of lives.

As I started down the stairs, Coach Carol blew her whistle, and everybody huddled together before heading to the locker room. I called Bridget's name. She whirled toward me, pausing for a moment—her face too far away for me to read—and motioned me to wait. I didn't mind. I'd had more than enough of the locker room.

I slipped into a row and thought about Shelly standing at the top of the arena, basketball resting on her hip. She was probably taking in the stadium one last time before heading to Barcelona, or wherever, and trying to start a new life. Maybe there was a part of her that was glad I'd stopped her, happy that I'd kept her near her family and team. At least that's what I told myself.

✧ ✧ ✧

When Bridget reemerged from the locker room, I wanted to dash down the stairs and hug her, but there were two managers on the court, removing tape. Besides, for all I knew, she was furious with me for uncovering her head manager's secret. So I stayed put as she took the stairs two at a time, arms pumping and whistle swaying across her chest. Her navy sweatshirt deepened the blue of her eyes, but they told me nothing.

"How's Shelly?" I asked.

Bridget glanced toward the managers on the court.

I wondered if they were always so quiet.

"Let's talk somewhere else," she said.

I walked up a few steps and stopped. I understood her need to keep our conversation private, but I'd been waiting for answers all afternoon.

The ad sign made its eerie squeak.

Bridget hesitated. Then she climbed toward me until she stood on the stair right above mine. "I talked with her parents and her lawyer, Cecile Lodge. She doesn't think the prosecutor will press charges."

I was speechless. I'd imagined a lot of best-case scenarios, but not that one.

"There's a videotape," Bridget said. "Roshaun hid behind a tree and filmed the whole thing."

An audio and a video. No wonder Shelly had confronted him in such a brightly lit area. "So the tape shows that it was self-defense?" I asked.

"Not only that." Bridget leaned against the gold railing in the middle of the stairs and folded her arms across her chest. "It makes DeVoster look exactly like the rapist he was."

I thought about Darren DeVoster's reaction to the tiny part of the cassette that Shelly and Roshaun had already sent to the media.

"Lodge thinks that once DeVoster's family knows what's on the tape, they'll beg the prosecutor to drop the charges."

The ad sign squeaked again.

"How did Shelly and Roshaun find out about Ryesha?"

Bridget checked the court. The managers were gone. She

glanced toward the top of the arena and then at her shoelaces. "Lodge said that Shelly wanted the coaches to know the full story, but ..."

"I already know that DeVoster raped Shelly," I said quietly.

Bridget sighed.

"I'm not going to talk to the press about her," I said. "I didn't this afternoon even when I was mobbed." I wasn't sure what I wanted most: to know what happened or to know that Bridget trusted me.

"It happened last April." Bridget's voice went flat. Maybe that was her way of distancing herself from a painful story. "By June she realized she was pregnant."

I sat on the arm of a chair. A rape and an unwanted pregnancy: That's the situation Shelly had been dealing with while she interned at the station—her "tough situation." No wonder she hadn't been her usual responsible self.

"She miscarried in July," Bridget said.

The same month she blew off that interview, I thought, the same month Neale and I saw her drunk downtown.

"She went to Roshaun for comfort, but she didn't tell him about DeVoster—not until after Varenka ..." Bridget trailed off and took a deep breath.

"Shelly told me that she blamed herself for what happened."

Bridget nodded. "She was overwhelmed with guilt that night, so she went to Roshaun's—they were dating by this time—and she told him everything, including a phone call she'd made to DeVoster after she figured out she was pregnant. He denied responsibility, of course. Called her all sorts of vile names and told her—this is a quote—'she was two drinks easier than most bitches.'" Bridget paused. "This last part got Roshaun thinking about his sister. How her grades dropped after her night with DeVoster. How she quit her sorority and never went back to college after her first year. So he called her."

I could only imagine his rage when she finally told him what happened. A lot of it must have been directed at himself—for not figuring things out sooner, for not protecting his little sister.

"He wanted to kill DeVoster," Bridget said, "but Shelly talked him out of it. She said the law would have to punish DeVoster now that he'd raped someone like Varenka."

Someone white, I thought. A popular athlete. But Shelly had been wrong.

"You know the rest." Bridget stood. "Lodge thinks they'll be released soon. Maybe tomorrow."

It made me sad to think of them in jail for even a single night. I met Bridget's eyes. They were tired but still unreadable. "What about you?" I asked. "How are you doing?"

Bridget gave me a sad smile. "I've been wondering the same thing about you." She held out her hand to help me up. We stood inches apart, our fingers clasped together.

EPILOGUE

Win and Varenka received a thunderous standing ovation as they headed to the bench. Because of their double-doubles, the Hawkeyes were a minute away from beating their top intrastate rival, the nationally ranked Iowa State Cyclones. Over the past month, the two seniors had led us to a 5–0 record.

"We'll be ranked in the top ten after this," Orchid said. "I'm sure of it." She grabbed a fistful of Anne's organic popcorn.

Win and Varenka got high fives from everybody on the bench, including Assistant Coach Sue, whose pregnancy was really showing. Orchid had been right about the triplet thing.

Varenka slid her kneepads down to her shoes and took a seat at the end of the bench next to Shelly. It was the manager's first home game back with the team.

Anne leaned across Orchid, her hand cupped at her mouth. "Just think," she said. "If it wasn't for you, Shelly would be miles and miles away from all of this, working at a ski resort in Andorra."

Andorra, it turns out, is the country where Shelly had been planning to flee. I'd never heard of it before, but Vince (who hadn't heard of it either, but lives to Google) informed me that it's an itsy-bitsy nation on the border of Spain and France. It has the largest ski resort in the Pyrenees, a huge thermal spa, zero unemployment, and—most crucial to Vince—duty-free shopping. "What are we doing here?" he'd said. He'd already begun trying to persuade Richard into traveling there with him by saying, "You can bet the leader of Andorra isn't a homophobic C-minus student from Texas."

The crowd roared as Jessie stole the ball and ran the entire court for an easy layup. When the noise died down, I heard a woman in back of us gushing about Shelly. "She's the one—the one who got him on tape before she killed him."

Before Shelly and Roshaun were arrested, they'd wisely mailed a copy of their videotape to Lexie Roth. Her stories had been picked up by the AP, and the few days that Shelly and Roshaun spent in jail became a cause célèbre for rape victim advocates across the country. Yet because *The Daily Iowan* protects the confidentiality of rape victims, Shelly herself was not named as one. Nor was Ryesha or Varenka or any of the other four women who'd come forward after reading Lexie's article.

Shelly received an occasional piece of hate mail from a DeVoster die-hard, but all things considered, she'd been relatively unscathed by the publicity. For Bridget and the other coaches, however, it was a concern. Would people guess DeVoster had raped someone on the team? Would parents of potential recruits decide that the University of Iowa wasn't a safe place for their daughters? According to Orchid, Bridget should remind the concerned parents that there is no safe place for women, but I'm guessing she won't take this advice.

Kate blocked a shot, and Orchid thumped me on the arm. "I heard that she and Varenka are an item."

That would be nice if it were true. "Where'd you hear that?"

A sub snagged a rebound and got fouled. As the players headed to the line, the pep band's trumpets blasted a fanfare, and everybody shouted, "Go, Hawks."

Orchid waited for a patch of quiet. "Latisha's most recent ex showed them an apartment the other day. They're moving in together."

"That doesn't mean they're a couple."

Orchid shrugged and reached for some more popcorn. "Latisha swears by her ex's gaydar. And you know what else, my friend Dani, the one who teaches American Studies? She said that Kate is writing her final paper on Boston marriages."

"Do you know what DVDs she and Varenka have been renting?" I asked.

Orchid waited for me to enlighten her. The sad thing about sarcasm is that it often goes unnoticed.

The sub's first free throw was too hard, but the second one slowly rolled around the rim before dropping through the net. The entire bench leaped to its feet. On the other side of the court, Herky flapped his wings, driving the crowd into a frenzy.

"I love it when all our players get to score," Anne said.

A hapless Cyclone fumbled the inbound pass. Jessie grabbed the loose ball and tossed it inside to a sub, who—despite the help defense and a wide-open teammate—took an off-balance jumper and missed the rim.

"Don't rush your shots," Bridget yelled. "Let the game come to you."

Sometimes I felt like that eager shooter. I wanted to make things happen with Bridget. I wanted us to head toward coupledom at lesbian warp speed, but she was always slowing the tempo, ever the savvy point guard who wanted to make just the right move at just the right time. Not that I was complaining too much. I enjoyed Bridget's moves.

After a few more wild shots on both sides of the floor, the crowd rose to its feet and cheered, anticipating the final buzzer. But I remained quiet, even after it sounded, watching Bridget hug Coach Carol and pump a fist in the air. The pep band started its traditional victory tune, "In Heaven There Is No Beer," and the crowd began clapping along. As Bridget strode toward the Cyclone coaches to shake hands, she looked up at me and winked. I joined the celebration.

Acknowledgments

I'd like to thank the following people who helped me to create *Murder by Mascot*:

Richard Fumosa at Alyson Books for his enthusiasm and thoughtful editing; the members of the best writers group ever— Eileen Bartos, Mo Jones, Kate Kasten, Jane Olson, Tonja Robinswood, Mary Helen Stefaniak, Kris Vervaecke, and Ann Zerkel; Chad Loes, Emily Gersema, and Kelli Grey for answering my questions about police procedure, college newspapers, and Carver-Hawkeye Arena; and my consultants on all things canine—Cathy Cutler, Kirby Salisbury, Kate Aspengren, Kathy Janz, and Nancy Reinke.

Most of all, I'd like to thank my partner, B.D. Thiel, who makes it possible and fun for me to follow my muse.